Let Sleeping Dogs

DIE

A Skye Donovan Photographic Mystery

Published 2009 by Medallion Press, Inc.

The MEDALLION PRESS LOGO
is a registered trademark of Medallion Press, Inc.

Copyright © 2009 by Liz Wolfe
Cover Illustration by Adam Mock

Printed in the United States of America
Typeset in Adobe Garamond Pro

ISBN# 978-193475565-5
10 9 8 7 6 5 4 3 2 1
First Edition

CHAPTER ONE

"Connie, I can't shoot photographs for an eighteen-month calendar with no art director. That's just insane." It was more than insane, but I couldn't come up with a word that meant more than insane at the moment.

"Don't be silly, Skye. You'll do fine."

"No. I won't do fine. I've never even photographed animals before, and these layouts call for lots of animals." I flipped through the layouts. "There are at least a dozen dogs and probably as many cats. There's a parrot and little birds and a really scary lizard-looking thing."

"Iguana," Connie said.

"What?"

"The lizard is an iguana and they aren't scary at all."

"Well, of course they aren't scary to you! You'll be in the Caribbean lying on some beach getting skin cancer and wrecking your liver with Bahama Mamas while

I'll be taking my life in my own hands trying to take a picture of the beast."

"Skye, I'm getting married."

"Connie, you can't get married. You aren't even engaged." Connie Nishimoto had become a good friend last year when I took it upon myself to replace my boss on a fashion shoot that she was art directing. She'd liked my photography and we'd liked working together so she started asking for me when she booked a shoot. I didn't understand how she could do this to me as a friend or as an art director. Possibly I was being a little unreasonable, but it was only because of the panic that had set in. We'd only been friends for less than a year, but we were close. I'd know if she had gotten engaged.

"Well, I am now. Tyreese asked me to marry him yesterday."

"Who the hell is Tyreese?" I asked.

"Oh, Skye, he's wonderful. He's everything I've ever wanted in a man and could never find. I can't wait to become his wife."

"That's a lousy excuse." I gritted my teeth. "People get married all the time. And they *schedule* it around the rest of their lives. Don't the bridal magazines recommend at least a year to plan a wedding?"

"I don't have time to plan a wedding for a year. We want to get married now. Oh, Skye, it was love at first sight. I met Tyreese at a beach party in the Cayman

Islands, then we went to Jamaica. It's been so romantic. We want to celebrate our love where it began, so we're going back to the Cayman Islands for the wedding."

"There's no such thing as love at first sight, Connie. It doesn't happen. Not even in the Cayman Islands." I knew it didn't happen because I'd thought it was love at first sight when I met my ex-husband, Craig, at the tender age of nineteen. After twenty-two years of marriage, turns out he was gay. Don't talk to me about love at first sight.

"You're just being a bitch because you're afraid. Don't worry. You'll do a wonderful job on this shoot."

"Aren't you going to get fired for not showing up? Isn't your boss going to have your ass in a sling for dereliction of duty?" I sounded a little hysterical, even to myself.

"I *am* the boss, Skye. Remember? I opened my own agency? Then I hired you to do this shoot because I *knew* you could handle anything whether I was there or not." Connie's voice had taken on that overly patient tone that mothers use with toddlers.

"You are so full of . . . hold on, my other line is ringing." I punched the *hold* button and then the flashing button on the new phone system and hoped I hadn't accidentally cut her off.

"Hello?"

"Hey, darlin', how you doing?" Bobbi Jo's soft Texas

drawl had a calming effect on me, which was probably a good thing right then.

"Hey, Bobbi Jo. I'm kind of busy right now. What's up?" I didn't want to just cut her off in case she was calling to tell me she was in labor. Bobbi Jo had discovered she was pregnant shortly after her husband died. It had been a surprise to everyone. Actually, Edward's death had been a surprise even though he'd had a terminal illness. Before he could pass from natural causes, Bobbi Jo's stalker had murdered him. The pregnancy had been a really big surprise, too, since Bobbi Jo and Edward had tried to have a baby for years with no success. His poor health had prevented them from having marital bliss for several years, but it turned out that Edward had one good night left in him at the very end and Bobbi Jo was now close to delivering her first child at the age of thirty-nine.

"Oh, I just wanted to talk for a bit. Did I tell you I got the nursery all done up? Oh, my gawd, Skye, it's just so sweet. Makes me want to cry every time I look at it. Actually, I really do cry every time I look at it. A lot of other times, too."

"Listen, I'm on a long distance call right now. Let me call you back." I felt immeasurably guilty about brushing off my best friend when she was in the throes of gestational irrationality, but I had business to attend to. I had to talk some sense into Connie.

"Oh, sure, darlin'. Hey, you want to come over for

dinner? I haven't seen you for over a week. Lily said she was making some kind of chicken dish, and she always makes enough to feed an army. See you around seven, okay? And bring Sheridan if she's available."

"I'll be there. I don't know what Sheridan is doing, but I'll check with her."

Bobbi Jo had managed to swing from tears to planning a small dinner party in the span of a few seconds. Bless her heart. I scrawled *seven* on my notepad and punched the button to reconnect with Connie, only to be rewarded with giggles and suggestive murmurings.

"Connie? Are you there?"

"I'm here, Skye." Connie giggled softly and whispered something that I couldn't quite make out but I was pretty sure I heard the words *beach towel*, *champagne*, and *midnight*. I could imagine what they had planned, and a part of me completely understood why Connie wasn't ready to come home. But marriage? That was just ridiculous. And I still needed her for the photo shoot.

"Listen, I can't do this shoot without you. You need to get your butt on a plane back here. Now."

"That's ridiculous, Skye. You know exactly what I want. And you have my layouts. Just shoot to the layouts, and maybe get me a few candid shots, and I'll be there in a couple of weeks to look at the film."

Dial tone.

She gave me freaking dial tone. I stared at the

phone. Shoot to her layouts? Sure. Fine. No problem. But who was going to tell the dogs and cats that
they had to pose according to her layouts? Working to
layouts with human models was one thing, but shooting
animals was something else entirely. At least I assumed
it would be. I'd never photographed animals before, but
it stood to reason that their understanding of directions
would be limited. I had no idea how it would go and I
really wanted my art director to be there. Besides, she
hadn't stayed on the line long enough for me to tell her
that we weren't shooting in the studio, but on location
at K-9 Stars.

My art director was in lust with some Rastafarian in
the Caribbean and evidently determined to stay there to
celebrate her nuptials. Normally, Connie was the most
down-to-earth, sensible person in the world. I could
only wonder about what she'd been smoking to put her
in this frame of mind. I also wondered who this Tyreese
guy was. For all I knew, he could be some beach bum
who was marrying Connie just so he could move back
with her and live off her. He could be involved with
white slavery and just romancing her to later sell her to
some sleazy person who would ship her off to a foreign
country and I'd never hear from her again.

"What?" I screeched when someone dared to knock
on my door.

The door opened and an enormous white animal

bounded across the room and pushed his snout into my crotch. From that behavior I was pretty sure it was a dog. Although it could have been a sheep. The thing stood almost three feet tall and was covered in white dreadlocks, some of which were splayed over my chino-covered thighs while the animal made my acquaintance doggie-fashion. I scooted back in my chair, but the padded vinyl back prevented a full retreat.

"Captain!"

The dog removed his snout and turned to the man standing in my office doorway. Evidently, the dog was pleased because his long, dreadlocked tail wagged back and forth, sending dust and fuzzy dog hair flying everywhere. I waved my hand to clear the air and sneezed.

"May I help you?"

"Frank Johnson," the man said. He removed his white cowboy hat and nodded to me. "You the gal that's taking pictures for that pet calendar?"

Gal? I clamped my lips together to prevent any unseemly words from popping out and held out my hand. Frank appeared to be in his midfifties, tall and lean, with a shock of silver hair. He wore jeans and a blue western shirt with brown boots that were polished to a gleam.

"You're the owner of K-9 Stars."

"That I am." Frank snapped his fingers and the dreadlocked dog bolted to his side and sat.

"And who is this?"

"O Captain, My Captain. That's his AKC name. I just call him Captain. He's a Komondor, a Hungarian sheepdog."

"So, you're a fan of Walt Whitman."

"Who?" Frank's brows lifted.

"Walt Whitman. He wrote the poem 'O Captain! My Captain!'"

"You don't say. I never knew where it came from. Just sounded like a good name for my buddy here." Frank laughed and sat in one of the leather chairs in front of my desk. Captain jumped up on the other one and I tried not to imagine what his nails might be doing to the leather.

"Now, Captain, did the nice lady say you could sit on that chair?" Frank asked his dog in a tone that made me wonder if he expected a verbal answer. Captain jumped down and curled up at Frank's feet. I wondered if I should have said it was all right for the dog to sit on the chair, but suffering Benjamin Steinhart's wrath for having scratches on the new leather chair didn't seem worth it. Besides, the dog looked perfectly comfortable on the floor. Benjamin Steinhart owned the photo studio where I worked. He'd given me a job as a photographer's assistant last year even though I didn't have any experience. I think he was impressed by my willingness to do just about any kind of grunt work he wanted done in order to be in the studio. Benjamin was a superbly talented photographer who was beginning to make a name for himself in art circles. He'd had the photo studio for commercial work for years and now hired photographers to do the work for his clients while he explored his artistic side. He was also a demanding and picky person.

"I suppose Captain is one of the dogs I'll be shooting?"

"No, no. Captain's my companion dog. He goes everywhere with me. The other dogs are the talent."

"I see. Did you have any questions about the photo shoot?"

"Well, I wanted to get a few things clear. I've had problems with photographers who haven't worked with my talent before."

"I want this to be a pleasurable experience. For everyone involved. What do I need to know?" I tried to sound enthusiastic rather than apprehensive. Photographing animals was going to be difficult enough without a lot of restrictions imposed by Frank.

"I've only got one person to handle the dogs right now, so we'll need to shoot in half-day sessions." Frank shook his head. "I wish I could be more accommodating, but Peter has another job so he can't be available all day long."

"I see. I suppose we can accommodate that." It meant at least eight half-day sessions instead of four full days, but that was only a guess. Having never done this kind of job before, I didn't really know how long it would take. I'd set aside two weeks just in case I ran into problems. "As long as the stylist is available, it shouldn't be a problem."

"That's good. I'll have the handler give you a schedule of when the talent takes their breaks. And there's no make-up allowed. Some of the dogs have had allergic reactions, so I just can't take the chance." He laughed and winked at me. "They're my bread and butter, after all. I have to keep them healthy."

"That won't be a problem. We want the dogs to just look like dogs." Makeup on a dog? I couldn't imagine how you'd put blush or mascara on a dog, but Frank appeared to be serious about it.

"Are you using any of Miss Kitty's talent?" Frank asked.

"Yes, we are. She's providing all the cats and kittens for the photos."

"Well, I don't mind if you shoot them on the same day, but Miss Kitty will be having a fit about it. She's real particular about those cats. Thinks the dogs upset 'em." He shook his head. "Total nonsense, if you ask me. My dogs are very well behaved. It's her cats that are so finicky."

"Thanks for that information. I'll make sure to schedule the cats for a different day. Except for the shots that involve cats and dogs together." I thought of Miss Kitty Romano as the Cat Lady. She looked like the stereotypical elderly woman who lived with a bevy of cats. Short and plump, she wore her gray hair in a bun, and her fashion choices ran to floral cotton dresses and sensible shoes. At our first meeting, I'd learned she was also a pretty sharp businesswoman.

"I'm surprised she agreed to that," Frank said.

"It wasn't easy to talk her into it, but she seems to be fond of your handler."

"Peter." Frank nodded. "I remember she took to him. Seems to think he's a cat person, although he works with dogs. Go figure."

I nodded and smiled. "She said that as long as she was present and Peter was handling the dogs, she'd give it a try. I'm trying to accommodate everyone's needs on the shoot."

"Best to avoid conflict when you can, I always say." Frank stood, put his hat on, and slapped the side of his leg twice. His dog, Captain, rose from his position at Frank's boots. "Nice to meet you, young lady." He turned and left, the dog following at his left side.

Benjamin Steinhart would have a fit if he saw the dog walking on his cedar floors. I'd only been working as a photographer for Steinhart less than a year and I'd never have gotten such a plum job as the calendar for the Pet Place if Connie hadn't insisted. Fortunately, she had insisted, and since she threw a lot of work his way, Steinhart hadn't argued with her. He usually gave me the really crappy jobs and called it *paying my dues*. I knew he did that because the photographers who had been there longer would refuse to do those jobs. They might even quit and start their own studio if they were stuck with too many low-end jobs. Steinhart knew that, too. He was making a name for himself with the art photography, but he still needed the revenue from the photo studio and he wasn't going to risk losing one of his more experienced photographers if he could give a crap job to me. That was just a fact of life at the bottom of the totem pole, which was only a little better than life at the bottom of the food chain.

But at least this time, I'd snagged the plum assignment, thanks to Connie. It wasn't the most artistic shoot, but it was great for my reputation. I'd get a credit on every page of the calendar. Millions of people would see my name—well, tens of thousands, anyway. I gathered the layouts Connie had done for the calendar shoot and some contact sheets I needed to look at later tonight, and stuffed them into my tote, then I shut down my computer and sent my phone to voice mail. It was already five thirty and I wanted to go home to change before I went to Bobbi Jo's for what was sure to be a delicious dinner.

❀

"Are you sure you don't want to come with me?" I asked Sheridan.

"I wish I could. But this paper is due soon and I've barely started on it." My daughter set a stack of textbooks on the coffee table and lined up six recently sharpened, bright yellow pencils next to them. She opened a spiral-bound notebook and plucked the little paper scraps from the wire, rolled them into a ball, and tossed them into the trash can next to the table. I watched her move each item until everything was lined up to her idea of perfection and wondered if that slight obsessive-compulsive-disorder activity was inherited from her father. My ex-husband, Craig, had exhibited the same kind of behavior the entire time we'd been married. Sheridan only did it when she was under a lot of stress. A control issue, no doubt. And I worried about her when I thought she was stressed. I tried not to. After all, she would be nineteen soon and she considered herself an adult. I tried very hard to let her believe it even though I still thought of her as my little girl. I probably always would.

"Maybe you should lighten your load a bit," I suggested. "You're taking a lot of classes, plus your singing lessons, and the theater group." I walked to the sofa and turned on a lamp so she wouldn't go blind from reading in the dark.

"Great idea, Mom." Sheridan looked up at me and grinned. "And don't forget my social life. Hey, maybe I could give up my social life entirely. And you're probably right about the singing and the theater." She threw an arm over her eyes and collapsed back against the sofa. "Why, I don't know how I've managed this far." Her voice had taken on an affected drawl. "How can I ever thank you for pointing out my folly?"

I picked up a cushion from the sofa and threw it at her, scattering her carefully aligned pencils.

"Go." She waved a hand toward the door and started to realign her pencils. "Enjoy dinner with Bobbi Jo and Lily. Give them both a kiss for me."

"Don't forget to eat." I leaned down to kiss the top of her dark brown hair. It smelled like sunshine and lemons. Part Sheridan and part twenty-dollar-a-bottle shampoo. I ignored her eye roll and hurried out.

My loft was located in a rehabbed warehouse so the only elevator was a creaky old mechanism designed to haul things like heavy equipment up and down the four floors. Usually, I just took the stairs from my loft on the fourth floor if I was going down, but I often took the scary elevator when I was going up. The first level had recently been turned into a garage for the tenants. As far as I was concerned, the parking garage made my loft apartment just about perfect. I'd rented the place shortly after Craig and I had divorced and put quite a bit of time and effort into turning the former photo studio space into a two-bedroom apartment with a darkroom. I loved the high ceilings and wood floors. The big windows let in a lot of light and offered a beautiful view of the mountains in the distance as well as part of the river.

Bobbi Jo had tried to talk me out of it, arguing that it was so different from the large, suburban home I'd occupied with Craig. But that was exactly why I wanted it. I liked the idea of something completely different. It felt like a fresh start and a new outlook on life. Bobbi Jo had wanted me to stay with her in the mini-mansion she lived in. Her husband, Edward, had left her a very rich woman. But also a very lonely woman.

I stopped by the market to pick up a bottle of wine for dinner. Bobbi Jo couldn't drink, but I knew Lily would appreciate it. Lily, Bobbi Jo, and I had been friends for what seemed like an eternity. Lily had been in a poly-amory relationship for years. Married to one man, lover to another. The men were fine with it and became good friends. She left both of them last year and the men were still best friends. Lily said she needed some time to work on herself. Bobbi Jo wanted a doula to help her through the pregnancy, and Lily was happy to move in temporarily and fit the bill. It was the perfect solution since it gave Lily a place to live, provided a doula for Bobbi Jo, and exonerated any guilt I might have felt about moving into my loft.

I pulled my Escape into Bobbi Jo's driveway and stopped in front of her triple garage. The motion-sensor lights came on and the front door opened. Bobbi Jo wore a pair of dark green leggings and soft suede boots with a pale yellow sweater and stood in the classic third trimester pose with one hand bracing her lower back. I was amazed at how big she was. Well, not all of her. Just her belly.

"You look great," I said. I remembered how unattractive I'd felt at the end of my pregnancy, and I figured Bobbi Jo felt the same way. There are times when a woman just needs a little flattery. Besides, Bobbi Jo was still beautiful even if her tall, willowy figure had been lost to the pregnancy. She still had the short, dark red curls and brilliant green eyes that caused both men and women to stop and stare.

"I look like a mountain." Bobbi Jo wrapped her arms around me as best she could, angling her belly to the side.

"Well, I wasn't going to say anything."

Bobbi Jo laughed and pulled me into the house. "You didn't bring Sheridan? I haven't seen her in ages."

"She wanted to come but she has a paper due and, as usual, the deadline is now at critical mass."

"Hey, Skye," Lily called from the great room. "Oh, good, you brought wine." She took the bottle from me and walked to the bar in the corner of the room.

"Oh, gawd, I'd give anything for a glass. But it's not good for the baby." Bobbi Jo patted her belly and laughed. "And it makes me puke." She picked up a crystal goblet filled with what appeared to be grape juice. "Only a few more weeks, though."

"Are you ready?" I asked. "Do you have everything you need?"

"Are you kidding?" Lily asked. "Every baby store in town is reporting a booming business because of her."

"Now, that's just not true, darlin'." Bobbi Jo laughed and shook her head. "Okay, maybe it is true, but this is my first baby. Probably my last one, too, so I want her or him to have everything."

Lily handed me a glass of wine. "And now that Jasmine's pregnant, she thinks she needs everything that Bobbi Jo has."

Jasmine was Lily's daughter. I'd helped her plan and execute her very unusual wedding the previous year, and I remembered that she'd wanted to have a baby right away. "If the babies are six months apart, then that's perfect for hand-me-downs."

"Oh, you're right, Skye." Bobbi Jo turned to Lily. "Tell Jasmine that I'll be giving her all my stuff as soon as the baby outgrows it."

"I can't believe this will be my third grandchild," Lily said. "When did I get to be so old?" Lily didn't seem old to me even though she had ten or fifteen years on me. She was plump and her hair was streaked with gray, but I'd never known a woman with more energy. Lily had come of age during the Sixties and completely embraced the prevalent philosophy of the time. She wore clothing that would look outrageous on most middle-aged women but suited her to a tee. Lily owned a new age shop called *The Goddess Chalice*, practiced paganism, and had been in a poly-amory relationship until last year. I was pretty sure she'd done things that I wouldn't have considered doing in my wildest dreams. There was nothing old about the woman, no matter how many grandchildren she had.

Between the three of us—a mother, a grandmother, and a soon-to-be mother—we kept the baby talk going until Lily announced she'd better see to dinner and headed for Bobbi Jo's spacious, state-of-the-art kitchen. Bobbi Jo watched her leave, then turned to me.

"I'm going to do drugs, and you're going to help me."

"Drugs?" I hoped Bobbi Jo was referring to her delivery, but it's always best to clarify with her. "What kind of drugs?"

"Shhhh! Lily will kill me if she finds out."

"Bobbi Jo." I lowered my voice when Bobbi Jo pressed her finger to her lips. "Lily is your doula. She's your labor coach. She's going to know if they give you drugs."

"That's where you come in."

Uh-oh. That was exactly what I was afraid of. I really didn't want to hear her plan.

"You just need to distract her while I get the drugs. Once I have them, there's nothing she can do about it."

"Bobbi Jo, why don't you just tell Lily you want something to make you more comfortable during the labor? A lot of women have epidurals now."

"She'll freak. I mentioned the other day that I might want to have an epidural and she completely lost it. She went on and on about how women are made for this and how I'll be missing out on the most incredible experience I'll ever have in my entire life if I take the epidural. Then there was something about some woman who gave birth in some field and just picked the baby up and went right on picking cotton. Or vegetables. Something like that." Bobbi Jo shook her head. "That is just sick. No one should tell a pregnant woman stories like that."

"Calm down." I reached over and patted my friend's hand. "Lily is from a time when natural childbirth was usually a lot better than the drugs they gave women. She really believes she's giving you good advice."

"I know. That's the problem. She's never going to go along with this, and I know myself. I'm not that strong a woman. I cry when I get a hangnail. I'm going to need those drugs." She leveled a gaze at me. "And you're going to help me get them."

"You make it sound like we're going to rob a pharmacy."

Bobbi Jo's eyes got wide and filled with tears; her lower lip trembled.

"Now, stop," I said. "This is all going to be fine. I'll be there when you have the baby, and I'll make sure you get whatever you want." Wasn't this precisely why Bobbi Jo had made Lily her doula? Wasn't the doula supposed to be in charge of making sure the mother got everything she wanted during the birth? Why was this suddenly my job? Then I immediately felt guilty for thinking that way. I should want to help my best friend. And I did want to help. It was just that I was incredibly busy with my job.

"You girls want to get to the table?" Lily called from the dining room. "It's almost ready."

I stood and held out an arm for Bobbi Jo to use to leverage her bulk off the sofa. "Do you want some more juice?"

"I'm sick to death of juice. And milk." Bobbi Jo's voice held an edge of hysteria. "I want a martini. I want scotch on the rocks. I want to do shots of tequila off the six-pack abs of a twenty-year-old male stripper." Her face puckered and tears flooded her eyes again, then flowed down her cheeks.

"It's going to be all right, sweetie." I snatched a tissue from the box on the end table and dabbed at her eyes. She took the tissue from me, wiped her tears, then blew her nose.

"Should we eat in the kitchen since it's only the three of us?" Lily stood in the opening to the dining room holding a stack of plates and bowls.

"I want to eat in the dining room." Bobbi Jo shook her head and looked like she might cry again. "I love the dining room. Edward and I bought the table and hutch when we went to Monterey two years ago." Her lip trembled again, but at least she was smiling this time.

A variety of emotions flickered across Lily's face. Exasperation, sympathy, maybe a little fear. "Then the dining room it is." Lily turned around and almost ran to set the dinnerware on the table, then pulled napkins and silverware from the hutch.

I walked Bobbi Jo to the dining room and settled her in an upholstered chair at the head of the walnut table that would easily seat twelve. Bobbi Jo folded the napkins into intricate fan shapes while I arranged the plates, bowls, and silverware.

"I learned to do this watching one of those decorating shows," Bobbi Jo said. She handed me the napkins, and I placed one in the center of each dinner plate. The table was so pretty with Bobbi Jo's designer stoneware and handmade glasses, I decided to light the candles. It must have been the right thing to do because Bobbi Jo smiled and this time her lip didn't tremble.

Lily returned from the kitchen with a salad bowl and two bowls of dressing, a vinaigrette and a creamy, light green concoction. She hustled out and came back with a basket filled with sliced French bread and a butter dish. Her final delivery was a casserole dish she placed on an iron trivet. We sat and she dished up the entrée. A boneless, skinless chicken breast, stuffed with herbed ricotta and topped with marinara sauce. My mouth watered just looking at my plate. This was way better than the leftover chicken chow mein I would have had at home.

"So, tell me about your next shoot." Bobbi Jo helped herself to salad and topped it with the creamy green stuff. "It's pets, right?"

"The calendar for the Pet Place. Eighteen photos of dogs and cats, plus a parrot and an iguana. But Connie called me today from the Bahamas and she's met someone there and she's getting married. So I have to do the shoot without her."

"Oh, my gawd! Connie's getting married? Who is he?" Bobbi Jo asked.

"His name is Tyreese. That's all I know. I tell you, she sounds like she's lost her mind. I mean, Connie has always been so sensible. But she was giggling and silly on the phone."

"That's what love can do to a girl," Lily said.

"Maybe. Still, I'd feel a lot better if she came back for the photo shoot. I'm really nervous about it."

"Oh, darlin', it'll be all right," Bobbi Jo said. "You know what she likes. You'll do a great job."

Just thinking about it made me want some of Bobbi Jo's drugs.

"It sounds like a great time with all those animals," Lily said. "I was always good with animals. I volunteered for years with the Humane Society, so if you need any help, just holler."

"You can't do the animals," Bobbi Jo said. "You're doing me, remember? I could go into labor anytime."

"I know." Lily patted Bobbi Jo's hand. "But, remember, the doctor said you haven't even started to efface yet. It's probably going to be a few more weeks."

"Your due date is three weeks from now, right?" I asked.

"Three long, endless weeks," Bobbi Jo agreed. "And I could be late. It's very common for first pregnancies to go a little longer. *Gawd!* How will I stand it? I'm already big as a barn."

"No, you aren't. It just seems that way to you. After you have the baby, you'll shrink back down to your regular size in no time."

"I don't know," Lily said. "Some women carry an extra twenty—"

I kicked her shin under the table, eliciting a muffled yelp and a mean look from her. "Of course she will," I insisted. "Bobbi Jo's healthy and in good shape. She's never had a weight problem."

"Not until now." Bobbi Jo frowned and rubbed her bulging belly.

"Have you decided on a name yet?" I thought maybe we needed to change the topic of conversation to something that would make Bobbi Jo think about the positive aspects of pregnancy. Like the baby.

"I'm still thinking about it. Of course, if it's a boy, Edward James Melrose Jr. But if it's a girl, I just can't decide. I thought about Edwina, but that sounds kind of old-fashioned. Maybe Edwynyth or Edalyn."

"Is Edwynyth a name?" I asked.

"It is if I say it is." Bobbi Jo attacked her salad. "I want to name the baby after Edward. That's what I would have done if he was alive."

I wasn't about to argue with a woman that close to her due date. "Did you finish the nursery?"

"Oh, you have *got* to go up and look at it. I did it all in greens because that's so earthy, you know, and earth colors are just the thing right now. And I had a chest of drawers painted to match the bedding. It's so adorable." Bobbi Jo forked salad into her mouth and chewed for a moment. "I still haven't found the right nanny, though. I called one of those nanny agencies, but I didn't care for anyone they sent over. But Lily said she'd stay with me until I do."

"I said I'd stay for two months. That's plenty of time

24

to find a nanny." Lily rolled her eyes at me and I figured she'd had just about enough of being the doula for Bobbi Jo. "Besides, my apartment will be ready by then and I'm looking forward to living there."

"You've already got an apartment?" Bobbi Jo's lower lip trembled. "Don't you like living here with me?"

"Calm down, Bobbi Jo." Lily patted Bobbi Jo's hand. "I told you before that I'd planned to move into the apartment over my shop."

"I've never seen the apartment," I said. "What's it like?"

"Well, right now, it's a mess. I don't think you could really call it an apartment. Mostly it's two huge rooms with a sink."

"Sounds like it needs professional help," Bobbi Jo said.

"It does. I've hired a friend of Jasmine's to help me turn it into a livable space. We're still working on the plans."

"I can't wait to see it," I said.

"Well, I can," Bobbi Jo grumbled.

"I'd love you to see it, Skye. You should come over soon. Maybe you could give me some help with the initial plans. I really like what you did with your loft."

"Oh, *gawd*, I'm stuffed." Bobbi Jo pushed her plate away. It was still full of food. "I swear, I can't eat more than three bites of food before I'm full, then half an hour later, I'm starving again."

"It's the baby." I nodded at her tummy. "You're carrying high, like I did. I bet you're out of breath if you walk more than ten feet, too. The baby is crowding your stomach and your lungs."

"They say that carrying high is a sign of a girl," Lily said.

"It was true for me. What about you? Did you carry Jasmine differently than Bo?" I asked.

"Goodness, that's been so long ago, I'm not sure I remember. Maybe I should see if I have any pictures of me when I was pregnant with them." She lifted her wineglass and laughed. "These days, it's not an issue because they can tell you the gender of the baby with an ultrasound less than halfway through the pregnancy."

"I can't believe you didn't want to know," I said. "And you had the amniocentesis; they would have known for sure if it's a boy or a girl."

"I guess I'm just old-fashioned about it." Bobbi Jo shrugged and toyed with her salad. "Edward and I used to talk about having a baby. Before we gave up. Anyway, he always said that was a big part of the excitement."

"I think it's sweet," I told her. "And it's definitely exciting."

"You want to see the nursery?" Bobbi Jo struggled to rise from the dining chair. I didn't feel like I had any choice but to follow her as she waddled down the hall to the stairs. I turned back and made frantic motions to Lily indicating that I wasn't finished with my meal.

Bobbi Jo had turned the bedroom next to the master suite into a nursery. But next door wasn't close enough for her so she'd had a doorway installed between the two rooms. On the other side of the nursery was Lily's bedroom, and Bobbi Jo had installed a doorway between those rooms, as well. This baby wasn't going to get a minute to her or himself.

"What do you think?" she asked.

Bobbi Jo had done a great job with the decorating. A multitude of soft greens and beiges blended with pale shades of orange that gave the room a serene atmosphere. The antique reproduction crib was dressed in sheets and a comforter covered with delicate drawings of nursery rhymes. A fluffy, frilly pillow was placed at one end and I made a mental note to remind Bobbi Jo to take the pillow out. It was beautiful, but I guessed Bobbi Jo didn't know that you never put a newborn in a crib with a pillow. One chest of drawers had been painted a delicate green, and an artist had duplicated some of the pictures on the bedding. The second chest had the same artwork on a light orange base. But Lily had been right when she said Bobbi Jo had bought every baby item she could lay her hands on.

"Why two chests of drawers?"

"I needed both of them. I read that babies need to

be changed up to a dozen times a day in the beginning. That's a lot of onesies."

"I think they meant diaper changes, Bobbi Jo. Not necessarily outfits."

Bobbi Jo waved a perfectly manicured hand. "I know, but still it can't hurt to have extras. And I'll just end up giving them all to Jasmine anyway."

"Good point." It wasn't like the room wasn't big enough for the two chests, a crib, bassinet, changing table, diaper holder, swing, gliding rocker, upholstered chair with matching footstool, and twin bed with canopy.

"The room is beautiful. You did a great job."

"I painted it four times," Bobbi Jo admitted. "It was so hard finding just the right shade of green. Anyway, I painted it once with Lily; the other three times, I hired a painter because Lily said she wasn't going to waste her time. You know, Skye, I love Lily and all, but sometimes she can be a little testy."

I smothered a laugh because Lily had told me on several occasions that Bobbi Jo was having a rather high-maintenance pregnancy. Probably they were not the best match for a gestating woman and a doula, but at the bottom of it all, they loved each other and that would get them through it.

"Ohhhhhh." Bobbi Jo groaned and sank down onto the upholstered chair.

"Are you all right?" It wasn't unusual for women to

deliver three weeks early. And even if the doctor had said she wasn't effaced yet, I knew it could happen in a matter of hours in some cases.

"I think so." Bobbi Jo grunted again.

"Are you in pain? Where? What does it feel like?"

Bobbi Jo wrapped her arms over her expanded belly and grunted again.

"Bobbi Jo! Answer me!"

"I don't know. It hurts, but it's weird."

"That's it; we're going to the hospital." I held an arm out to help her up. "Lily!"

Lily appeared in the doorway in a matter of seconds. "What? Is she in labor?"

"I don't know. But I think we'd better get her to the hospital."

Bobbi Jo gasped and looked up, her green eyes wide with surprise. "I'm wet," she wailed.

CHAPTER TWO

"Bobbi Jo is fine and she's not in labor," the doctor said. "It was just a false alarm."

"I should have known," Lily said. "We're so sorry to have bothered you, Dr. Simmons."

"No bother at all. I'd rather you bring her in than to wait too long. I don't like to take any chances with older women. Especially when it's the first child."

"But I thought her water broke," I said. Bobbi Jo's pants had been visibly wet, so I knew she hadn't imagined it.

"The test showed that it wasn't amniotic fluid." Dr. Simmons shook his head. "The baby was pushing against her bladder. She just urinated." The doctor sounded so matter-of-fact that I had to bite my lip to keep from laughing. "She's getting dressed now. Should be out in a few minutes." He turned to leave, and Lily and I looked at each other. She laughed first.

"Bobbi Jo's going to be humiliated. We can't say anything about it." But I laughed, too. "And did you hear him refer to her as an older woman? I hope he never says that in front of her."

"Oh, dear. Just thinking about Bobbi Jo wetting herself." Lily's ample bosom heaved with the laughter she failed to suppress.

"Stop laughing. She's going to be out any minute. Besides, we've all had a little accident or two at the end of pregnancy."

"Oh, I know." Lily waved her hand. "It's just that every time I try to tell her anything, she brushes me off. She's sure that her pregnancy is different from anything any other woman in the world has experienced. You should have been there for the hemorrhoid discussion. There weren't going to be any hemorrhoids in her precious—"

"There you are." I elbowed Lily when I saw Bobbi Jo emerge from the examination room.

"Oh, *gawd*. I am totally embarrassed."

"Don't worry about it," I said. "Every pregnant woman has embarrassing moments."

"I don't even know what happened. I mean, I understand about the Braxton-Hicks contractions. As soon as they mentioned them, I remembered reading about them, but I was wet." Bobbi Jo's hand reached around to feel her bottom. "I'm still wet. When the water breaks, you only have a short time to deliver the baby. I read that. So, what happened?"

Lily and I looked at each other. One of us had to say something, and I was really glad it ended up being Lily.

"One word, Bobbi Jo," Lily said. "Depends."

Bobbi Jo's eyebrows arched in a look of confusion, then her eyes widened and a hand flew up to stifle a gasp.

"Oh, my *gawd!* I peed my pants?"

"It's not that big a deal. The baby was pressing against your bladder. It happens a lot," I offered.

"I peed my pants!" Bobbi Jo wailed. "And now everybody knows about it 'cause I just *had* to come to the hospital. Oh, *gawd*, I hate being pregnant. I can't wait until this is all over."

"Lily and I insisted on bringing you to the hospital. And besides, Dr. Simmons said we did the right thing."

"Now, Bobbi Jo, this is just a normal part of pregnancy," Lily said, giving her a stern motherly look. "You're almost at the end. This is no time to turn into a wuss. You're a woman, for Goddess's sake. Now, act like one."

Bobbi Jo stopped grumbling, although she didn't look all that happy about it. Minutes after getting into the car, she fell asleep. I remembered Hillary Clinton's comment that it takes a village to raise a child. What would it take to get Bobbi Jo through childbirth? At least a village. Maybe more than one. And Lily and I were the head villagers.

A mocha latte with two extra shots of espresso can almost make up for five hours of sleep when eight are really required. I sipped on the latte as I made the half-hour drive from Portland to Hillsdale. I pulled into the long driveway to Frank Johnson's house and drove past a long, low structure in the back to the large building we'd be using for the photo shoot. I could hear dogs barking as my car moved over the paved driveway. It sounded like I'd accidentally driven by Animal Control.

Steinhart wouldn't allow the dogs into his studio, and it was easier to do the shoot right where the dogs lived anyway. That was my theory, and I'd almost convinced myself I was right. It wasn't that I'd never done a location shoot before, but this wasn't exactly models wearing the latest fashions standing on the beach. I shoved the transmission into park and guzzled the last of my coffee drink. I hadn't seen the building until now, and I had to start shooting tomorrow. I hoped that it wouldn't take a lot of work to create a temporary photo studio.

Peter Machio was supposed to meet me here. Peter would be the handler for the dogs and I'd heard he and Frank were partners but Frank had only referred to Peter as his associate, which seemed a little strange. I could only wonder about what had happened to cause Peter to slip from partner to associate, because I was too chicken to ask. I walked to the door and started to knock before I realized the door was open a crack.

"Hello? Anybody here?" I called.

"Hey, come on in."

Peter was as polished and attractive as the first, second, and third times I'd met him. Dressed in a white shirt, khaki pants, and three-hundred-dollar sneakers, he was the poster boy for Northwest Cool. He spread his arms and turned in a circle.

"So, what do you think? Will this do for the shoot?" He trotted over to a raised platform and slapped his hand on it. "I built this for you. I figured it would be better to have the dogs elevated." He laughed. "Easier on your knees, anyway."

"And I very much appreciate that." I walked around the raised platform he'd built. It was sturdy and the floor of the three-foot-high platform had been done in a smooth plywood, which would make it easy to do the set changes. It was the perfect height for my camera. If we had the dogs on the floor, I would have been down on my knees almost all day. The only thing that would make it better would be a mechanism to raise and lower the huge rolls of seamless I'd use if I were shooting in Steinhart's studio. But, unable to use those, I'd have to come up with some alternatives. I had almost a whole day to come up with an idea that would work and a way to implement it. No pressure at all.

"This is great." I walked around the eight-by-eight-foot platform he'd built. One side had a ramp, which I supposed would be for getting the dogs onto the platform, and the whole thing was on wheels. "I can even move it around."

"I'm glad you're pleased. I figured you might like to move it to take advantage of the skylights. I don't know how you like to work, so if there's anything else you need, anything I can do to help, just let me know."

"Thanks a lot. This building is huge. What's it used for?"

"We used to train our show dogs here. Before Frank decided he'd rather be a talent agent."

"I see. Did you show dogs very often?"

"I still do. Presently, I'm training four dogs for showing. I've shown dogs at a lot of the smaller shows and a few of the bigger ones. Frank was never very interested in that end of the business. It takes a lot of time and patience to train a show dog."

"I'll bet."

"We'll be shooting in half-day sessions, right?"

"That's my understanding. Frank said you were the only handler at the moment."

Peter nodded. "I need some time to do my real

estate business and work with the show dogs, but I can be pretty flexible about which hours. Just let me know what the schedule will be."

"Great. I thought we'd probably do the photography in the mornings, but it's good to know you can be flexible. And if you need me to change the times, I can do that, too."

"Thanks." Peter grinned. "Sounds like everything will work out fine. Which shots will we be doing tomorrow?"

I moved to the table where my stylist, Lionel, had spread out the layouts and looked at them. I had no idea how many shots I could get done in a half-day session, but I selected two of the layouts and placed them side by side on top.

"Let's start with these two shots. If we have time, we'll try to squeeze another one in."

"That sounds good," Peter said. He looked closely at the layouts. "Frank said you hadn't asked for a go-see with any of the dogs. Did you want to see them now?"

I was used to go-sees with human models. Generally, the models would be interviewed by the art director, and Connie had often asked me to sit in on go-sees. I hadn't even thought about a go-see for the dogs, and now seemed rather late in the process.

"I don't think that I really need to. You're familiar with the dogs' sizes and colors, so why don't we just go over the layouts?"

"Sure. This one looks like you need one of the larger dogs and either a small dog or a puppy. I have Ruff, who's a lab mix with a nice golden coat, and we could use one of the lab puppies or I have LeRoi, who's a Beagle."

"The lab's coloring would look good with the blue background. Could you bring both the puppy and the beagle?"

"Sure, no problem." Peter pointed to the next layout. "This one needs small dogs, right?"

"Yes. Something about this big?" I moved my hands around to indicate the general height and length I thought would work. "Connie talked about the cute little dogs that women seem to love so much."

"I've got the perfect dogs. Fifi is a small Pekinese and Snoozie is a Shih Tzu. Together they're so cute, it makes you want to cry."

"That should work. Both of those breeds require a good amount of grooming, don't they? We're highlighting no-tear shampoo and conditioner and some combs and brushes."

"Great. Fifi and Snoozie definitely require a lot of grooming."

"Sounds like we're all set, then," I said.

"I'll have the dogs ready to go. They've all been groomed but I like to give them a good brushing before they're photographed. If you need me just call my cell phone and I'll come running. Otherwise, I'll plan on having the first dogs here tomorrow at nine."

As Peter left, my stylist, Lionel Tyler, came in. He carried a large box over to the raised platform and set it down.

"This is it, huh?" he asked, looking around the building. Lionel was in college and supplementing his grants and student loans with stylist work. He looked like most of the other college students I'd seen lately. Messy hair covered most of his eyes, and he wore baggy pants with a drab shapeless sweater, a canvas messenger bag slung across his chest, and a paper cup of coffee in one hand.

"We're roughing it," I said. "All the ease of a location shoot with none of the charm. I need to find some way to duplicate some seamless."

"Good luck with that."

"You're supposed to have some kind of brilliant idea about how we can accomplish that." I'd worked with Lionel several times and we'd developed a relationship that included a lot of teasing.

"I'm going to need a lot more coffee for a brilliant idea." Lionel unloaded the box, placing a variety of items on the platform. "How big are the dogs that I need party hats for?"

I dug the head sheets out of my briefcase and handed them to him. "I haven't decided which dogs we're using for that shot yet. But you can probably get an idea of what you'll need from these." Lionel shuffled through the photographs that showed each dog in several poses along with their individual stats—height, weight, coloration, breed, and what stunts and tricks they were specifically trained to perform. They weren't much different from the head sheets or comp cards for human models and for some reason, I found that a little disturbing.

Lionel thumbed through the layouts and pulled out the party shot. "Man, there's half a dozen dogs in this shot and they're all different sizes. I'll have to make party hats to fit each of them. Damn, there's cats, too."

"Don't you like cats?"

"They're all right, I guess. But you can't train a cat like you can train a dog."

"Cat people say that's because cats are more intelligent," I said.

"I'm sure they do, but I don't see it." Lionel studied the layouts. "Aren't cats and dogs enemies or something?"

"Not necessarily. I guess it depends on how they've been raised. We only have a few shots with both cats and dogs together."

"That ought to be fun." Lionel grinned.

"I just hope it's possible. The Cat Lady can be really picky about how her clients work."

"Don't the Pet Place people realize we're talking about animals here?" Lionel pointed to one of the layouts. "I mean, I don't get why you'd want to dress them up like people. I like dogs, and some cats are okay but, really—they're animals."

"Not everyone would agree with you. A lot of people are bonded to their pets. They have as much affection for them as they would for a human companion."

"Yeah, well, that still doesn't explain dressing them up like people."

"Tell you what. You help me with the lighting and I'll help you with making the party hats."

"You would? Cool. I've never had a photographer offer to help me with anything."

I still got a little thrill hearing someone refer to me as a photographer. I mean, that's my job and everything, but it still doesn't feel real sometimes. I grinned at Lionel. "You don't know what's involved in the lighting yet."

For the next five hours, I ran Lionel all over the building while I took readings with my light meter. Unfortunately that meant I had to run all over the place, too. The building had some skylights and big windows and I was hoping to get some shots with natural lighting. Of course, we were in Portland, Oregon, which meant the light could change several times a day. Especially in March. The readings I took would only be good if we had the same weather during the shoot. I've seen rain, snow, sleet, hail, and bright sunshine within the span of an hour or two in March. Probably my readings would be useless but I had to do it, just in case I got lucky. By the time we finished, Lionel was giving me dirty looks and mumbling under his breath.

"Okay, we're done." I packed the light meter into my case.

"Really? Are you sure there's not a few square inches somewhere that you need a light reading on?"

"Very funny," I said.

"What time are we shooting tomorrow?"

"Nine. Which means I'd like you to be here by eight thirty. No, make it eight. I'm going to need help with some stuff."

"My social life goes to hell during a shoot. Especially one of yours. You're a perfectionist." Lionel waved and walked out.

I finished packing up my stuff and locked the door behind me. It was already six, I still had to stop at a department store, and I was tired to the bone. My evening plans included a frozen dinner, fuzzy slippers, and a good book. That seemed to sum up all too many evenings lately. Two months earlier my evening would have most likely included some time with Detective Scott Madison of the Portland Police Bureau. If not actual face time, then at least a long phone conversation where he would tell me how attractive he found me and maybe what he was planning on doing to me the next time we were together. I really missed those conversations.

Scott and I had been dating since last fall. It was mostly good, but between me being recently divorced after twenty-two years of marriage and his job demands, there had been some rough spots. A couple of months ago everything had come to a head and we'd decided we needed a break. The break was going on a bit longer than I'd thought it would. We'd talked a couple of times, but Scott had always been hurried and preoccupied. He blamed it on his caseload, but of course, I had my doubts. Scott thought I involved myself in his investigations, but I thought I was just showing an interest in his work. And it *was* interesting. Scott worked in the robbery and homicide division as a detective. I enjoyed hearing about the crimes he investigated. That's all it was, really. Of course, we'd met when he was investigating the death of Bobbi Jo's husband and I was marginally involved with that, but only because Bobbi Jo was a suspect. How could I just sit back and do nothing when one of my best friends was suspected of murdering her own husband? I couldn't. Evidently, that had left Scott with the belief I wanted to be involved in his work.

And then there was the living together or getting married issue. Scott had suggested we should get married. When I told him I wasn't sure I was ready for that, he suggested we live together. He just couldn't see that I needed more time. I can't even say why I felt that way, but I did. I'd been married for twenty-two years and only divorced for less than one. I was thoroughly enjoying the freedom of being a single woman and I wasn't sure I could give it up just yet. It wasn't that I didn't love Scott. I loved him very much. And I absolutely could see us getting married later. Just not right now. Plus I wasn't sure how Sheridan would feel about him moving in. She liked Scott a lot, but enough to live with him? Not that I'd asked her. I was thinking Scott and I could just table that discussion until Sheridan graduated college and moved out on her own. Scott hadn't been pleased with that proposal at all. So we had mutually agreed to take a break. I missed him more than I'd thought I would.

The stop at the department store was brief and I was in the elevator to my loft in short order. I set my case on the table next to the front door and headed for the kitchen. I still needed to look at some contact sheets and transparencies, so I put on a pot of coffee and cast a longing glance at a bottle of merlot I'd purchased last weekend. I heard music coming from Sheridan's room and sighed. Maybe tonight we could just sit and talk for a while.

At eighteen, Sheridan seemed to have taken a quantum leap into adulthood. Or at least into her own life. A year ago, I'd been privy to her life. At least I liked to think so. Now she was in college, she had friends I'd never met, and I was constantly being surprised by her. I wasn't at all sure I liked it. Okay, I didn't like it. I hated it. I wanted her to be six years old again. I wanted to arrange her playdates. I wanted to choose her wardrobe. I wanted to be the person she looked to for everything. I wanted to know every single detail of her life.

And I'd tried. Evidently she didn't feel the same way because all my efforts had been blocked.

I poured myself a cup of coffee and took the contact sheets and transparencies to my light table. Half an hour later, I'd chosen twenty black and whites to have enlarged for the newspaper ads I'd shot for the Organic Northwest Stores. I shoved the color transparencies aside and took my coffee cup to the kitchen for a refill. Before I could do that, the buzzer sounded from the building entryway. I pressed the *talk* button.

"Yes?"

"Hi, Sheridan?"

"No, this is Skye."

"Oh, right. Her roommate. I'm Zack."

"Zack?" I asked. *Her roommate?*

"Right. Sheridan's expecting me."

"Oh, sure. Come on up." I pressed the *open* button and waited. He must have taken the stairs instead of the slow freight elevator because he was leaning on the doorbell in no time. I opened the door and the breath left my body.

"Hey, Skye. I'm Zack." He extended his hand and I automatically took it in mine.

He wasn't what I was expecting. For one thing, he was older than Sheridan. A lot older. He had to be in his late twenties. What the hell did he want with an eighteen-year-old college girl? The obvious answer occurred to me and I lost my breath again. Not only was he considerably older than my daughter, he was tattooed. I mean, he was really tattooed. In spite of the cool weather, he was wearing a sleeveless T-shirt. His exposed arms were covered with tats. Dragons, Celtic knots, some intricate lettering I couldn't quite make out without being too obvious. His head was just shy of being shaved. Granted it was a handsome head and he had intelligent-looking brown eyes and an open smile. Still, he was there for my baby girl.

"I'll get Sheridan." I waved a hand toward the living area. "Make yourself at home." I walked to Sheridan's door and knocked. No answer. I knocked louder. The door jerked open.

"What?" she demanded.

I arched an eyebrow and she backed down.

"Zack is here for you."

"Oh, cool." She looked past me and waved. "I'll be right out." She looked back at me. "Don't say anything to him. In fact, you should go to your room."

"Oh, it's all right, sweetie. He seems to think I'm your *roommate*, but I'll clear that up while you finish getting ready."

"Oh, no. Mom, please. I can explain. Just don't say anything, okay?" She closed the door and I turned back to Zack.

"Sheridan will be out in a minute. Can I get you something to drink?"

"A beer would be good."

Beer?

"Should you be having a beer if you're going out?" I asked.

"Why not?" He looked genuinely confused. I wasn't shy about educating him.

"Surely you don't drink and drive?"

He laughed. "Oh, I see your point, but it's not a problem. Sheridan's driving."

"I see. So, how did you get here?"

"Walked. I just live a few blocks from here."

Great. An older man I didn't know. Covered in tattoos. Probably an alcoholic. Dating my daughter. And he lived within walking distance.

"Hey, Zack, let's go." Sheridan gave me her brightest smile. "See you later, M . . . Skye."

I waved helplessly as they scooted out the door.

There were half a dozen empty plastic cages with wire doors lined up against one wall when I arrived at the arena building adjacent to Frank Johnson's house and the K-9 Stars kennel, but no sign of Peter yet. It was still early, though. I wouldn't start shooting for another two hours. I lugged my camera cases, lights, poles, umbrella reflectors, and assorted equipment from the truck into the building.

"Hey, Skye," Lionel called.

"Hey, you're early. I appreciate that. Can you give me a hand?" I picked up a spool of clothesline and carried it over to the platform.

"What are you doing?" Lionel asked.

"We're going to string this clothesline up and then use bedsheets as seamless."

"Man, that's brilliant. I never would have thought of it."

"Thanks," I said.

We were both staring up at the twenty-foot ceiling wondering exactly how we could get it done when Peter joined us.

"What are we looking at?" he asked.

"Actually we're looking for a way to string this clothesline so we can hang bedsheets on it," I said.

"Okay. I didn't expect you to bring your laundry but let me see what I can come up with."

I looked over at him ready to protest before I saw the twinkle in his brown eyes. "I'll try to keep the clothes-pins out of the shots."

"I think I have an idea that will work. I just need to get a ladder and some tools from the garage. Be back in a few minutes." He trotted to the door and disappeared. I stood grinning after him. I'm a sucker for handy men.

"Imagine that," Lionel said. "Everyone's got brilliant ideas today."

"Except you?" I teased.

"Mine just haven't risen to the surface yet."

I helped Lionel unpack his boxes of props. I'd told him to bring anything he thought might be useful in addition to the ones called for in the layouts. Since I was winging it without Connie's direction, I wanted as many options as possible. We filled a table with an assortment of items that ended up looking like a yard sale. I directed him to a corner with an electrical outlet. "You can plug in the iron over there."

"What am I ironing?" he asked. "We aren't doing clothes." He looked at the kennels. "This sure isn't a fashion shoot."

"Sheets have wrinkles when they come out of the package. If they're going to look like seamless, they'll have to be ironed. I'll need the blue ones first."

"Right." He carried the iron and ironing board that I'd brought over to the corner and set it up.

I didn't envy him. Ironing sheets would be a bitch. Not that I'd ever done it. Well, once, but just to impress my former mother-in-law. Peter finally returned and set up the ladder behind the platform. Soon he had the clothesline strung and ready for the sheets.

"You're probably going to be ready for the dogs soon. I'll get the ones you wanted and a couple more. They can rest in their kennels until you're ready for them." Peter trotted off again.

Lionel climbed the ladder with the blue sheet and I handed him clothespins. He got the sheet hung, and together we spread it over the platform, securing it with pushpins.

"Yoo-hoo!"

I turned toward the door but only saw the silhouette of a person outlined by the bright sunshine streaming through the open doorway. The figure stepped inside and I could tell it was a woman. She continued to walk across the floor until she reached me and stuck out a hand.

"Irene Knutson," she said, grasping my hand. She was a strapping, Nordic-looking woman. "I'm the mayor of Hillsdale."

"Skye Donovan." I tried to match her grip and not grimace. I thought I felt some of the smaller bones in my hand snap and couldn't help looking down. Her nicely manicured hand engulfed mine. I sneaked a glance at her face, which was decidedly feminine.

"I just stopped by to see Mr. Johnson, but he didn't answer. I thought he might be here."

"No. I haven't seen him today. We're shooting a

calendar for the Pet Place."

"Oh, I know. Frank told me. Well, if he's not here, then I'll just call him later." She turned back to the door, then stopped. "If you see him, tell him I stopped by to talk about the next city council meeting."

"Sure." I kind of stared at her as she left. She had to be six feet tall. Even without the heels. Most of that height seemed to be taken up by her legs. And she was gorgeous. Long blond hair, light blue eyes, a dazzling smile. I stared until she closed the door behind her.

"Who's the beautiful giant?" Lionel asked.

"The mayor of Hillsdale. She was looking for Frank."

"I saw a guy kind of close to the house when I got here. But I couldn't say if it was him. He had his back to me and it was pretty far away." Lionel shrugged. "The guy could have just been walking by."

"If it was Frank, he must not have heard her or he left. She said he wasn't home."

"What's a babe like that want with an old man anyway?" Lionel asked.

"City business, I guess. Get the platform set up for the April shot. Peter will be back with the dogs soon."

I moved the lights and umbrella reflectors around until I thought the light was perfect, while Lionel placed a six-inch-high picket fence on the platform. When he had the fence secured, he climbed up the ladder to hang two child-sized umbrellas with fishing line, and placed bright yellow rain boots behind the fence. The final touch was bags and boxes of doggie cookies and chew sticks—the Pet Place brand, of course. They were giving the calendars away for a reason.

Peter came in with six dogs on leashes, all of them barking. He shushed them and directed each one to his or her own plastic kennel. Rather than closing the kennel doors, he simply gave them a command to stay. Each dog walked into a kennel, turned in a circle a few times, and settled down. I was impressed.

"Sorry about the barking. They do that when they see someone they don't know well. They'll be quiet for the rest of the day, but they'll probably do it again tomorrow morning." Peter grinned apologetically.

"No problem. They really respond to you," I said.

"I've worked with them a long time," Peter said. "Which ones do you want first?"

"We're shooting the April page." I looked at my layout. "I'll need Ruff and LeRoi and the puppy." I compared the layout to the set Lionel had created, wishing again that Connie was here. Normally, she'd be the one to make sure the set matched her layout, or she'd change her mind at the last minute and change the shot. I could make sure the set matched the layout, but I couldn't make the last-minute changes that she'd make.

Peter guided Ruff and LeRoi up the platform, holding the puppy against his chest with his other arm.

"What do you think? LeRoi or the puppy?"

I grinned at the puppy. He was adorable and looked like a miniature version of the big lab mix, Ruff. "He's so cute. Is Ruff the father?"

"No. This little guy is a purebred Labrador retriever."

"They look like they could be father and son. Let's try the shot with the puppy, then maybe with LeRoi."

Peter removed LeRoi from the platform and placed the puppy next to Ruff. Lionel put their feet into the tiny yellow galoshes. Ruff stood still while Lionel pulled on the fishing line until the umbrellas were positioned correctly. Peter kept the puppy occupied. Even when Lionel placed the umbrella handles behind their shoulders, it only took a small sound from Peter to keep Ruff in place. Peter seemed to know what he was doing. He'd get the puppy into position, then quickly move away so I could snap off a few shots. Then he'd go back and move the puppy into position again. I shot a roll of film from the camera on the tripod, then picked up my digital camera.

"Peter, can you get Ruff to relax just a little? I don't want them cavorting around, but a little movement? Something more natural than a pose?"

"Sure." He snapped his fingers to get the dogs' attention. "Okay." Immediately Ruff laid down. The puppy stepped out of his yellow boots and started pulling on one of Ruff's boots. When he couldn't get the boot off Ruff's paw, he moved on to the larger dog's ear.

I quickly snapped some digital shots, moving around to get different angles. After a few minutes of trying to play with Ruff, the puppy yawned and settled down for a nap, his fuzzy head draped over Ruff's boot-clad paw.

"That's good," I said. "I don't think we need to try it with LeRoi. I really liked what I saw through the lens. You can take them down now."

Peter clipped leashes on the two dogs and guided them off the platform. "I'll take them out for a quick walk and give them some water while you set up the next shot."

"Lionel, set up for the August layout, so we can use the same background," I instructed.

"Hey, Skye, I need to go back to the house to get some water dishes for the dogs," Peter said.

"I can get them for you. I should go say hello to Frank anyway." I knew it would take Lionel another half hour to set up the shot and all I had to do was change the film in the camera, which would take about half a minute.

"That'd be great. Tell him I need the two big dishes. He'll know which ones. If he's not there, just go on in. The dishes are in the pantry."

I nodded and jogged to the door. Frank's house was about a hundred yards from the arena building we were shooting in. I walked around to the front and knocked on the door. Immediately, Frank's dog, Captain, barked, but Frank didn't come to the door. I knocked again, sending the dog into another round of barking. Still no Frank. His car was in the driveway, so where was he? I pulled my cell phone out and punched in his number. It rang a few times, then went to voice mail. Great. I wasn't about to go in with Captain sounding like he was going to rip apart anyone who invaded his territory. I punched Peter's number into my phone.

"Peter? Frank's not answering, but Captain is barking and I'm not really comfortable going in alone." I sounded like a wimp, but it was better than getting a leg chewed off.

"If Captain's there, Frank has to be there. He never goes anywhere without his dog."

"He's not answering the door. And even if he didn't hear my knock, he has to hear the dog barking."

"I'll be right over."

Peter hung up and I thought he sounded strained. Like maybe he thought something was wrong. Lionel had referred to Frank as an old man and I wondered if he'd fallen or something, although he didn't look old enough to need one of those alert necklaces. Peter arrived and opened the door, calling out to Captain. The dog stopped barking but pranced around the entryway, running down the hall and then back again. That made me think of the old *Lassie* television series where Lassie was trying to tell everyone that Timmy was trapped in a well or a mine shaft, and I worried again.

Peter scratched behind the dreadlock dog's ears and told the dog to heel. Captain meekly followed Peter down the hallway, stopping at one of the doors and whining. I peered around Peter's shoulder when he opened the door, then let out a shriek muffled by the hand I'd pressed over my mouth.

Frank Johnson lay on the bed, his gray body half-covered with the sheet, lifeless eyes staring at the ceiling.

CHAPTER THREE

"Do you think he's dead?" Peter asked.

"Does he usually sleep with his eyes open?" I couldn't believe Peter was asking me if I thought Frank was dead. Could he really not tell the difference between someone who was sleeping and someone who was dead? Aside from the fact that hardly anyone sleeps with their eyes wide open, there was the pasty gray pallor of his skin and the fact that his chest didn't move with breathing.

"Should we check?"

"No, we should call nine-one-one."

"What if he's alive and needs help and we just waste time calling nine-one-one?"

"If he needs that much help, he needs nine-one-one anyway. I'm going to call." I punched the number into my cell phone and waited. Peter stepped into the room and took halting steps toward the bed. He touched two fingers to Frank's neck just as my phone connected.

"Nine-one-one. What is the nature of your emergency?"

"I think we have a dead body." My voice came out high and squeaky.

"Ma'am, you'll need to speak up. I can barely hear you."

"Sorry." I cleared my throat. "I think someone is dead."

"Give me your address."

"I think we should do that later. We need someone *here*. Right away." Then I realized she wanted the address of where I was, not my home address. Well, she could have been a little more clear about that. Didn't she realize that people who called nine-one-one were probably on the verge of hysteria? Fortunately, I knew the address since I'd just driven there that morning.

"Thirteen forty-three River Creek Drive. In Hillsdale. In the house."

"Did you say that's a house?" the woman's voice asked.

"Yes, of course it's a house. It's just that there are other buildings here, too. The body is in the house, not in one of the other buildings."

"Is there a phone in the house?"

"What do you think I'm talking to you on?" I asked. Normally, I'm a pretty calm person, but this situation was more demanding than most and the stupid woman should be intelligent enough to know that if we were talking on a phone, then of course there was one in the house. Oh. She meant a landline.

"I'm sorry. I don't know. This isn't my house."

"Just stay calm, ma'am. I'm sending a police officer over."

"I think we need more than an officer. We need an ambulance or something." I said *ambulance*, but I'd really meant a hearse. Or whatever they use at the coroner's office. I just didn't want to say it.

"Yes, ma'am. I'm sending an ambulance, as well. Can you stay on the phone with me?"

I didn't really see the need to stay on the phone with her, but if that's what she wanted, it was fine by me. It wasn't like I needed to use the phone for anything else. "I'll put you on speaker." I pressed the button for the speakerphone and looked at Peter. He was standing next to the bed Frank lay on and he appeared to be more than a little distraught. I guessed that was pretty normal for the situation. I probably looked distraught myself.

"He's dead?" I whispered.

Peter nodded and slowly walked back to the doorway. Captain lay down beside the bed and whined. Peter snapped his fingers and slapped his palm against his thigh twice. Captain stood, looked at Frank's body, and slowly made his way to Peter.

"They're sending the police and an ambulance." I

held the phone up to indicate who *they* were. Peter nodded and followed me to the living room where we sat,
glancing nervously toward the bedroom until the police
arrived, followed by an ambulance.

After introducing themselves, the two uniformed
officers stood in the doorway of Frank's bedroom while
the EMTs assessed Frank's condition. I tried not to listen to the sounds they made, tried not to keep looking
toward the bedroom door.

"He's definitely dead," one of the EMTs called to the
officers. He motioned the other EMT to follow him out
of the room.

"You sure?" one of the officers asked.

"Oh, yeah, I'm sure. You might want to call someone. There's bruising around his throat consistent with
strangulation." The two EMTs stripped off the latex
gloves they'd donned on their way to Frank's bed.

"Crap," the older officer said. "Stay here. Don't let
anyone in or out of the room."

"Out?" the younger officer asked.

"You know what I mean. You remember what they
told you about being the first on the scene?"

"Yeah, I think so. Secure the scene and call it in.
Right?" The young officer looked nervous. I figured
it was probably his first murder scene. Maybe his first
crime scene. Hillsdale was a small community mostly
made up of people in a higher-than-average income

bracket. I doubted they had much in the way of crime. At least not this kind of crime. They probably had some white-collar criminals. Some people who should be in jail for lying and taking advantage of the unsuspecting. But probably not many murderers.

"Right. All you gotta do is keep the room secure. I'll call it in." The older officer shook his head and walked out to the squad car.

I waited until the officer had made two phone calls. "Excuse me, Officer. Would it be all right if I went back to my shoot?"

"Your what? You're shooting something?"

"No!" I was rattled by the suspicious look on his face. "I mean, I'm doing a photo shoot. Mr. Johnson was supplying the dogs for our—it's for a pet calendar."

"I see. No reason you can't go. I've got your name and contact information if we need to talk to you."

"Great. I'll be in that big building to the left and behind the house if you need me."

"I can't believe this," Peter said as he moved toward the door and then turned with his hand on the doorknob.

"I know." I was feeling a little freaked out. I'd never seen a dead body before. Well, my great-aunt Maude, but she'd been all dressed up and made up and lying in an expensive coffin. This was very different.

"There's nothing we can do here, and I think you could use the distraction." Peter didn't look like he was doing very well, either. He was a little pale and his eyes seemed unfocused. Maybe he was suffering from shock. Probably I should distract him from the situation. I wasn't sure it would help, but I knew I could definitely use some distraction.

"Peter, maybe we should continue with the shoot. It's not that I'm unfeeling about Frank; it's just that we need something to do, you know?"

"What?" Peter looked at me. "Oh, yeah, the photo shoot. And you'll need me to handle the dogs." He looked at the controlled but urgent activity in the bed-room and the living room. "Might as well. I don't think there's anything we can do here." Peter picked up the water dishes we'd come for and I followed him out of the house, then noticed that Captain was following us.

"Uh, Peter? Captain seems to want to come with us."

"Oh, I should have thought about that." Peter stopped and waited for Captain to catch up to him. "He's used to being with Frank all the time. I'm sure he'll have a lot of separation anxiety over this."

"What are you going to do about him?"

"I'll keep him, I guess. Frank used to leave him with me when he traveled to places he couldn't take Captain. It won't be easy for Captain no matter where he is, but it'll probably be better if he stays with me."

"It looked like the cops thought Frank might have

been strangled."

"Yeah, I heard the EMTs say something about that. I'd like to say I'm shocked, but I'm not, really."

"You aren't?" What kind of person isn't shocked when a friend is murdered?

"Frank had a lot of enemies. It's not like I know of anyone who would really want to kill him, but I know a lot of people who won't be the least bit sorry that he's dead. The cops will probably have a long list of suspects."

"I see."

"In fact, I probably head up that list myself."

"You do?" I didn't think he should be telling me this kind of stuff. I liked Peter and I didn't want to have to tell the cops that he might be a suspect.

"Frank cheated me out of my part of the business a few years ago. I guess it was my fault as much as his. I signed papers without really reading them. Because Frank told me to, and I was naïve enough to trust him. I discovered later that he lied about what was in them."

"I can see why that would make you angry."

"Yeah, but I got over it. After I dealt with the fact that it was due to my own stupidity. We were still co-owners of the business even if I didn't get any of the profits from the talent part of it, so we had to learn to get along, and in time, we got back to being friends. Or at least friendly. Although I never really trusted him again."

I didn't say anything because, really, how do you respond to something like that? Especially now that Frank was dead.

"I'm sorry Frank's dead. I can't say I thought he was a good man, but I don't think he ever did anything to deserve to die."

"If you and Frank were co-owners of the business, what happens to it now?" I asked.

"We had a contract that stated if either partner died, the other one inherited the business. I was still Frank's partner legally, so I guess I'm the owner now."

Uh -oh. That sounded like an awful lot of motive to me. I resisted the urge to put my hands over my ears and sing loudly to prevent hearing any more of what Peter had to say.

"Not that there's much left now."

So, maybe he didn't have all that great a motive to kill Frank. Still, I thought it would be better if we dropped the conversation and concentrated on the doggie photos.

"Lionel should have the set ready for the August shot."

"That's Fifi and Snoozie, right?"

"I can't remember their names. It's the Pekinese and the Shih Tzu. And they're supposed to be in bikinis. Will that be a problem?"

"Not at all. Fifi and Snoozie have worked in commercials

and movies for years. They're both used to being handled and posed and dressed up. Did you bring costumes or do I need to get their own wardrobes?"

"They have their own wardrobes?"

Peter laughed. "Hard to believe, isn't it? But, yes, they have rather extensive wardrobes, including swim-suits."

"I think Lionel brought swimsuits with him. If they work we can just use them."

We had reached the arena building and Peter held the door open for me, then went to check on the dogs. Lionel had done a good job with the August set. We had the same backdrop for a blue sky, and the floor of the platform had been draped with a bright beach towel and accessorized with a sand pail and shovel, a few large sea-shells, and several bottles of doggie sunscreen that was manufactured and sold by the Pet Place. I wasn't quite sure how you would go about applying sunscreen to an animal covered with fur, but all I had to do was feature them prominently in the photograph.

"What's with all the cop cars?" Lionel asked.

"Well, something's happened," I hedged. I wasn't sure how Lionel would react to murder.

"Did somebody break into the place?" Lionel shook his head. "You'd think we would have heard some-thing."

"No, it wasn't that. Peter and I found Frank in his

bed. Dead."

"Dead?" Lionel paled. "What happened? Did he die in his sleep?"

"No. It appears it was, um, foul play."

"Foul play? You mean he was killed?"

Lionel looked horrified, and I thought maybe we should just cancel the shoot and go home. But that meant I'd have to go back to the house and tell the officer. I didn't want to go back to the house, and I didn't think they'd let us leave anyway. I knew from dating Scott that the police would want to ask us a lot of questions. We'd probably be here for hours anyway, and I'd rather have something to do than simply sit in a chair thinking about what had happened.

"Look, Lionel, the police are probably going to want to talk to us at some point, so I thought we'd all be better off if we keep busy until then."

"Yeah, sure. I'll go finish the set."

I checked the lighting and took a few test shots while Lionel brushed dog hair from the set and tinkered with placing the products just right. Peter came in with Fifi and Snoozie and Lionel gave him the bikinis. While Peter got the dogs dressed, Lionel filled the water dishes for the other dogs. Finally, we were ready to shoot.

The little dogs were perfect. In spite of being in their teens, they cavorted like puppies. I snapped shot after shot, happy to have something to take my mind off the vision of Frank's dead body. Then Snoozie dropped like a lead weight.

I stopped shooting and waited for her to get up. She didn't. She didn't even twitch. Oh, dear God, I killed the dog. A sweet, little fluffy dog. I screamed and Peter looked over, then jumped up and ran to the platform where Snoozie had cavorted her last cavort. He reached a hand out to stroke the dog, and she jumped up like nothing had happened.

"Sorry, I should have told you. Snoozie has narcolepsy. That's why we call her Snoozie."

"Oh."

"It never lasts very long. Sorry I forgot to tell you. I guess I was distracted."

I shot a few more photos, but my heart just wasn't in it. I'd had too much death for one day, and now I was afraid that Snoozie would drop into a deep sleep again. It was just too much. I cursed Connie and her beach bum fiancé under my breath.

"Okay, that's it for today. Lionel, just put away what you need to; we'll be shooting again tomorrow."

"What time do you want to start?" Peter asked.

"If we can get started by ten—"

"Skye."

I froze at the familiar voice. My heart fluttered and my stomach did that weird little flip that makes you feel like your knees might buckle. I swallowed hard and turned to face Scott Madison. He looked good. Really good. Maybe too good. Scott stood a little over six feet tall with dark curly hair and brilliant blue eyes. He had the kind of muscular build that looked good in any kind of clothes. And even better without any clothes.

"Scott. What are you doing here?" My voice sounded normal, which was surprising. I'd expected it to come out in a squeak.

"Homicide." He nodded in the direction of the main house.

"You're investigating?" I hadn't expected Scott to be the investigating officer because he worked with the Portland Police Bureau. We were in the tiny town of Hillsdale, where they had their own cops.

"Mayor Knutson called the Bureau for assistance. They have a small police force here and no one trained to investigate a crime of this nature."

"I see." Just my luck that they would send Scott instead of one of the many other detectives I didn't have a personal history with.

"What are you doing here?" he asked.

"I'm shooting a calendar for the Pet Place. Mr. Johnson was supplying the doggie talent."

"And you are?" Scott squinted at Peter.

"Peter Machio. I'm Frank's partner." Peter cleared his throat. "Was Frank's partner."

"Oh, I'm sorry for your loss. I'm afraid you'll need

to find another place to stay for the time being. I only have a couple of crime scene investigators, and it's going to take a while to go over everything."

"That's all right. I don't live here."

"You don't live here?" Scott asked.

"No. I live in Portland."

"Oh. I just assumed when you said you were partners . . ."

"I see." Peter shook his head. "I meant *business* partner."

"Right. Right. Sorry for the misunderstanding." Scott turned toward me and rolled his eyes. I bit my lip to keep from laughing. At least he was trying to be sensitive to other lifestyles.

"So, you're using the dogs that are in the kennel over by the house?" Scott asked me.

"Of course. What other dogs would I be using?"

Scott shot me a look that spoke volumes about my flip answer. "The house is off-limits until we finish our investigation. The kennels are connected to the house, so I can't have anyone coming or going until we finish the investigation."

"How long will that take? I've got to finish this shoot."

"Shouldn't take more than two or three days."

"Great. My biggest job ever and I won't be on schedule." I sounded like a bitch, even to myself. I wasn't that concerned about the shoot. I mean, I was concerned, but I wasn't really thinking about it at the moment. I was just tired and a little strung out by the murder.

"What about the dogs in the kennel now?" Peter asked.

"They can stay there," Scott said.

"No, I mean, what about food, water, and exercise for them?"

"Oh, right." Scott frowned in thought.

"Actually, I can put food and water out in the yard for them," Peter said. "All the kennels have a door that opens onto the yard. But I'll need to get into the house to get the dishes."

"Sure, I'll have one of the officers escort you to do that. And I'll tell the crime scene investigators to go over the kennels first. They should be done by tomorrow afternoon at the latest."

"Thank you. I appreciate that." I turned to Peter and Lionel. "I guess to be safe, we should just cancel the shoot tomorrow. We'll start again on Thursday at nine. Lionel, I'll call Miss Kitty and see if we can start with the cats and kittens tomorrow." The men both nodded, and Lionel moved to the table to put away his props.

"Mr. Machio, you said the kennels all open onto the yard?" Scott asked.

"That's right. The dogs are free to go out into the yard any time they want."

"So, someone could have climbed the fence into the yard, then gone through a dog door to get into the kennel and then into the house?"

"That wouldn't have happened."

"Why is that?"

"Would you climb over a fence knowing that more than a dozen dogs would be there?"

Scott scratched his chin. "I guess it would depend on why I wanted to get in."

"The talent dogs probably wouldn't have attacked anyone," Peter said. "They're used to being around a lot of different people. But Frank also boarded dogs that were here for agility training or attack training."

"What's agility training?" Scott asked.

"We set up a course that has tunnels, ramps, weave poles, jumps, and tables that the dog is trained to go through. It's a competition for dogs, but some owners just do it to give their dogs exercise."

"So, it's like an obstacle course?" Scott asked. "And Frank trained dogs in this?"

"Actually, I did all the agility training," Peter said.

"And you mentioned attack training. Did you do that, as well?" Scott made a note in his small notebook.

"Not really. I assisted Frank when he needed someone for the dogs to attack, but Frank did all the training for that."

"I see. I'll probably need you to go through the

kennel with me and tell me which dogs are being trained for what. And I'm going to need to take statements from all three of you." Scott pulled out business cards and handed one to Peter. He took the card and turned away. I figured he was a little jumpy about the interrogation. Lionel walked over and took a card, stuffed it in his shirt pocket, and went back to his prop table.

"I already have your number." I held my hand up when he offered me a card.

"Actually, I thought maybe I could take your statement tonight. Over dinner?"

"No, I can't do that." I sounded a little short, even to myself. It wasn't that I didn't want to see him. I did. A lot. But it had been a rough day. I wasn't sure I was ready to hear what Scott might want to say to me. "But I'm open for breakfast tomorrow." I didn't know what twelve hours was going to do for me, but it seemed better than dinner. Also, breakfast was a more casual meal compared to dinner. Less serious. Less conducive to bad news. I wasn't ready to let Scott go forever, but I didn't want to rush back in, either. Did I?

"Sure. McKennon's at nine?"

"Okay." For some reason I felt as giddy as a sixteen-year-old on her first date. Although I suppose these days, girls on their first dates are more like twelve. Or eight. The very thought made me glad I didn't have a daughter that age. Although an eighteen-year-old was no picnic, either.

"Great. I'll see you then." Scott had lowered his voice for the conversation, then he turned back to Peter and Lionel. "I'll call you two soon to schedule a time for your statements."

They both nodded. Lionel went about putting away the props and products we'd used. Peter got the dogs who'd been out for exercise back into their kennels.

"I guess I'll take these dogs home with me tonight." Peter handed Scott his business card. "Could you have someone call me when it's all right to return them to the kennel? I live in a condo and five dogs are going to be a crowd."

"Sure. Perhaps we could meet here tomorrow morning around eleven? You can tell me about the dogs and get their water and food dishes out of the kennel. I'll try to get the crime scene investigation done as soon as possible so you can return these to their kennels." Scott took the card and slipped it into his pocket, then turned to me.

"I'll see you tomorrow morning." He gave me a really nice smile before he turned and left. The kind of smile that used to make me giggle and blush. In fact, my face felt a little warm right then, and I felt my lips stretch with the beginning of a grin.

I pulled my cell phone out and called Miss Kitty, hoping she could accommodate the schedule change. It turned out she could, so I let Lionel know that we'd start shooting at ten, then I packed up my cameras and loaded them into the car, said my good-byes to Peter and Lionel, and headed home.

I knew Sheridan would be out that night and thought it was just as well. I could use an evening all to myself. I stopped and picked up some Chinese take-out, then got a bottle of decent sauvignon blanc and a pint of fudge brownie ice cream. Just so all the comfort food bases were covered. Salt, grease, sugar, and alcohol.

When I got to my loft building, I wrestled the camera cases and food bags into the elevator and punched the button for my floor. When I reached my front door, I felt a stab of apprehension. The door was open a crack. Was Sheridan home? She'd said she was going out tonight and even if she hadn't, she wouldn't leave the door open. Surely she hadn't left without locking the door. I reminded myself that the building was fairly secure. A key card was required to enter the front lobby or the elevator from the parking garage. Visitors had to be buzzed in by a tenant. Still, it was unnerving to see the door open. I pressed the toe of my shoe to the door, poised to drop my bags and run away, depending on what I found inside.

And what I found inside made me want to run screaming into the night. A short, plump woman sat on my sofa. Wisps of gray curls escaped the pink hairnet that appeared to cover curlers. She wore a chenille robe

73

in a dusty rose trimmed with sea-foam green, and she had Ugg boots on her feet.

"Mom. What are you doing here?"

"I'm waiting for you, isn't that obvious?" She picked up the remote and turned the television off.

"No. I mean, what are you doing here in Portland?" I set my camera cases down, then carried the grocery bag to the kitchen. Mom followed me with a hurt look.

"Aren't you happy to see me?" she asked.

"Well, of course, I'm happy to see you. I just wondered why you didn't call to tell me you were coming." I turned and put my arms around her. Even though our relationship was sometimes strained, and I didn't feel like I understood her most of the time, it felt good to hug her. Mom and Dad had moved to Arizona when Sheridan was still a toddler. They'd visited a couple times each year until Dad had become ill. I'd thought Mom would want to move back to Portland when he passed away nine years ago, but she'd stayed in Arizona. She didn't have any family there, but she seemed to have a close group of friends and that's as good as family. Better sometimes.

"I didn't realize I needed an invitation. If I'm a bother, I can just pack up and go home."

"No." I stopped and took a breath. Mom had a way of turning everything I said around. We talked on the phone every week, but we hadn't had an in-person visit in almost a year. Now I remembered why I'd been putting it off. I put the ice cream in the freezer and the wine in the fridge. "How did you get here from the airport?"

"I took a cab. Real nice driver, too. He helped me carry my bags all the way up here. Tipped him a whole dollar."

Mom could never be accused of overtipping and usually limited her tips to quarters. A whole dollar meant the cabbie had been pleasant and respectful and gone out of his way to be nice to her.

"Was Sheridan home when you got here?" I didn't expect Sheridan to be home until much later, but how else would Mom have gotten into the loft? I doubted she'd picked up lock-picking skills recently.

"No. I talked to your superintendent, and he let me into the apartment."

"That was nice of him. You look like you're ready for bed. Did you have any dinner? I picked up some Chinese and there's plenty for both of us."

Mom settled herself on the sofa again and patted her pink hairnet. "Oh, I ate hours ago and it's already past eight. Early to bed and early to rise, you know."

Yes, I knew. It was something I'd heard all my life. No matter how late I stayed up, I had to be out of bed by six every morning, weekends included. I'd hated it as a teenager but it had resulted in my being an early riser to this day, and now I enjoyed it.

"If you'll just show me where the extra sheets and

blankets are, I'll make up the couch and tuck myself in."
She turned and looked at the sofa. "Looks comfortable
enough. Probably won't bother my arthritis at all."

"No, Mom, you'll take my bed. I'll sleep out here."
I figured I'd rather give up my bedroom than give up the
rest of the loft.

"I don't want to put you out, honey. Just show me
where the blankets are and we can both turn in."

"Mom, I'm not going to let my seventy-eight-year-
old mother with arthritis sleep on a sofa."

"Are you saying you think I'm too old to sleep on a
sofa?"

She looked genuinely hurt that I might think she
was old, which made me feel like I was the worst daughter on the face of the earth. Until I reminded myself that
this was her normal method of interaction with me. I really didn't need this right now. I'd had a hard day and I
just wanted to eat my Chinese food, have a glass of wine,
and get to bed. The only thing I could do was to stoop to
her level of passive-aggressive communication.

"Mom, you know I'll be happier if you're nice and
comfortable in my bed. Don't you want me to be happy?"

"Well, of course, I do. I can't imagine how you'd
think otherwise. If it makes you happy, then I'll go sleep
in your room."

"Thanks, Mom. I really appreciate it." I gave her a
good-night kiss and watched her toddle off to my bed.

Switching to my mother's passive-aggressive ways had come entirely too easy for me, and I wondered if the inclination to do it was just under the surface waiting to erupt. I didn't want to think too hard about that, so I pulled sheets and blankets from the linen closet and made up the sofa. The kung pao chicken had gotten cold, so I stuck the cardboard container in the microwave and pulled out the bottle of wine. Soon I was settled on the sofa with the food and wine, wondering what to wear to breakfast with Scott tomorrow.

Then I realized that if Scott and I were about to resurrect our relationship, there was no way I could keep Scott from meeting my mother while she was here. It wasn't that I didn't love Mom and I knew that after the first few days of her pushing my buttons—and me pushing back occasionally—we'd settle down and have a nice visit. It was just that this was a really bad time. With the photo shoot not going well and Connie not being there to guide me, plus the murder and thinking that Peter might be a suspect, and Bobbi Jo about to have her baby, and Sheridan dating someone totally inappropriate, I wasn't sure I could handle throwing Mom into the mix. Much less trying to explain my relationship with Scott to her. With that thought, I put the kung pao chicken in the refrigerator, stuck the cork back into the wine bottle, and flopped down on the sofa, pulling the blanket over my head.

CHAPTER FOUR

I woke to the sound of clattering dishes and the smell of coffee and bacon. I pulled the pillow over my head and tried to incorporate everything into my dream, but the noise was too distracting and the smells too enticing. Besides, I knew Mom would be standing over the sofa any minute.

"No breakfast for me, Mom. I have a breakfast meeting." I threw the blanket off and stumbled to the kitchen.

"With who?"

I didn't want to tell her. I could only explain having breakfast with Scott by saying he was a friend, which she would interpret as more than a friend, or by telling her he was a detective and I'd discovered a dead body yesterday. I wasn't up for either explanation.

"And after that, I'm shooting cats and kittens all day."

"Skye! I raised you better than that!"

"Shooting photos, Mom. Geez, did you really think I was going to kill cats and kittens?"

"You're still gullible." Mom grinned and shook her head. "I always thought you'd grow out of it, but you haven't."

I could never tell when Mom was teasing me. Besides, it happened so infrequently I was never ready for it. I poured myself a cup of coffee and lurched for the phone when it rang.

"Hello?"

"Hey, Skye. I was just thinking that McKennon's is going to be crowded and noisy. You want to come by my place and I'll cook breakfast for us?"

"Sure. What time? I need to be at the arena by ten."

"I've got a busy day, too, so the earlier the better. How about eight thirty?"

"Okay. I'll see you then." I wasn't sure how I felt about having breakfast at Scott's. It seemed a little too close, too intimate, considering we hadn't been dating for the past few months.

I'd taken a quick shower and done the best I could with my hair and makeup when Mom knocked on my bedroom door.

"You never told me who you're having breakfast with," Mom said.

"Oh, it's just a friend." I pulled a pair of jeans and a shirt from the closet and grabbed a T-shirt from a drawer. "Would you like to go out to dinner tonight? I'll call Sheridan and see if she has plans."

"There's no need to spend money on going out. I'll go to the store and have dinner ready when you get home."

Great. Mom was an excellent cook, but her food ran to lots of carbs and heavy sauces and gravies. I'd be ten pounds heavier by the time she left.

"How long are you staying, Mom?"

"Oh, I don't know. It's not like I have anything else to do. I just figured I'd stay until I thought of something else to do."

That sounded ominous. Like it might turn into weeks. Months. Even years. But I wasn't about to get into the passive-aggressive tug-of-war with her again.

"That's wonderful. We'll have lots of time to catch up on everything." I pulled my socks on and slipped my feet into sneakers. "Sheridan should be up soon. I think she has an early class today."

"I'll go get her up then. It's already seven and she needs a good breakfast before school."

With Mom distracted with getting Sheridan up and fed, I slipped out of the loft and was knocking on Scott's door twenty minutes later.

"Hey, you're early." Scott stood in the doorway

dripping wet, clutching a towel around his hips. I tried not to look, but I'm a weak woman, and the view was nice. Really nice. I couldn't help thinking about the months we'd dated and how I'd been privy to that view often.

"I had to get out of the house. My mother came to visit."

"From Arizona, right?" Scott turned and trotted to the bedroom but didn't bother to close the door.

"Right." I continued to enjoy the view of Scott toweling off and getting dressed in jeans and a V-neck sweater, but I managed to jerk my eyes away just before he caught me. "So, what's for breakfast?"

"How about a bacon, tomato, and spinach omelet smothered with Swiss cheese?"

"Sounds delicious." I slid onto one of the bar stools at the counter that divided his kitchen and living room. "What do you want from me?"

Scott cracked another egg into the bowl and turned to look at me with arched brows and a grin.

"I mean for the statement." That's what I'd meant, but I still heated up at the thought of what else he might want.

"Not much really. It's just a formality because you found the body." Scott whipped the eggs into a froth and poured them into the skillet.

"How's the investigation going?"

Scott shook his head. "I won't even have the autopsy report until later today or maybe tomorrow. Right now it's all preliminary. The only thing the coroner has been able to tell us is that the bruises indicate they were caused by a large hand. Too large to be a woman's, so all I know for sure is that I'm looking for a man. I'm contacting everyone who might have been in touch with him recently. Maybe I'll get lucky and someone will know something that will help. Hopefully, the autopsy will tell us how he was killed and when." He placed fresh spinach on the eggs, then added chopped bacon and tomatoes and heaped shredded cheese on top.

"I'm shooting the cats and kittens today, but I'll need to finish up with the dogs soon. When will we be able to get back into the kennels?"

"Soon, I hope."

"Do you have any suspects?" I asked.

"We always have suspects. In the beginning anyway."

"So, who are they?"

"Why are you so interested?"

"I was there. I found the body." I shrugged. "Well, Peter and I found the body together."

"Peter Machio. What do you think of him?"

"I don't know." Of course, I knew what I thought. Peter was cute, charming, and had a good sense of humor. He seemed to be honest and forthright, and he had a way with dogs. But did I really want to share that with Scott?

"He's a nice-looking man. And we know he's not gay."

I grinned at the look on Scott's face. "You had no way of knowing that *partner* meant *business partner*. I thought that was very sensitive of you."

"Yeah, that's me, all right. All sensitive about everything." Scott flipped the omelet over and added more cheese to the top. "But you haven't told me what you think of him."

"As a person?"

"Sure. And as a possible suspect."

"He's a suspect?"

"He's a person of interest at this point. I understand he and the victim had a misunderstanding that ended their partnership."

"Peter mentioned that, actually. They still owned the business together, but Frank had Peter sign some papers that limited what profits Peter could share in. He said that it was his own fault because he trusted Frank and signed the papers without reading them carefully."

"You think that could be a reason to want him dead?"

"I don't know. Peter was up front about it. I mean, I'm sure he was angry at the time, but he seemed resigned at the very least. He said that he and Frank had gotten past it."

"Maybe," Scott agreed.

Scott dished the omelet onto plates just as the toast popped up. He set the plates on the counter, poured us each a cup of coffee, and came around to take the bar stool next to mine. "Dig in."

We ate in silence for a few moments. I thought about bringing up the statement again, but that would require talking about Frank's dead body while I ate.

"I've missed you," Scott said.

"I've missed you, too."

"So, I think we should try this again."

"What does that mean?"

"I want us to see each other again. You know, dates, dinners." He waggled his brows at me. "Sleepovers."

I laughed. Actually it was more of a giddy giggle. "I'd like that, too, but . . ."

"But what? We're good together, Skye."

I put my fork down. This was the hard part. "I know, but last time, we ended up arguing all the time."

"That was my fault," Scott said. "I was pushing you too hard."

"It's not that I don't ever want to get married again. But I just got divorced last year. I need some time."

"I know. And I'm okay with that. As long as there's a possibility of us making this permanent. Eventually."

I leaned over and kissed him. It felt good. Really good. He must have thought so, too, because his arms went around me and he pulled me closer. When we finally came up for air, he grinned at me.

"So, does this mean I get to meet your mother?"

"Don't push it." But I kissed him again.

I was only ten minutes late to meet Miss Kitty at Frank's arena. I didn't think it was that big a deal. Evidently I was wrong.

"I've been waiting for almost half an hour," Miss Kitty said.

"I'm terribly sorry. I had to give a statement to the police about yesterday."

Miss Kitty sniffed. "I see. I suppose it couldn't be avoided, then. I was simply shocked to hear about Frank." Miss Kitty shook her head setting her fuzzy gray curls bobbing. "I came by yesterday morning to make sure he wouldn't have any dogs present when we would be here with the cats, but he didn't answer the door."

"What time was that?" I asked.

"Oh, I don't know. I suppose a little after nine. I knocked several times, but when he didn't answer, I just assumed he was avoiding me. We didn't get along too well."

"Really? Why was that?"

"Frank killed Tobias. I never was able to forgive him for that."

"Tobias?"

Miss Kitty nodded. "He was my soul mate. We were together for thirteen years. Ever since he was a six-week-old kitten."

"And Frank killed him?" I was a little relieved to hear that she was talking about a cat. Not that I thought it was all right to kill a cat, but it was better than killing a person.

"Oh, he didn't do it with his own hands. He let one of those dogs of his loose. We were both working a photo shoot, and he let that dog loose knowing how much it would upset my cats. Tobias didn't like dogs at all. He was scared and jumped out of my arms. The dog chased him outside and tore him apart. Frank said he had no idea that the dog would do such a thing, but I never believed him."

"Oh, that's very sad. But I'm sure it was an accident."

"The hell it was. Frank had a mean streak. Ask anyone who knew him." She waved her hand as if to end the discussion. "My son, Jerry, will be here to help with the cats and kittens today." She turned to indicate her son, who was kneeling in front of the cat crates. "Jerry, come over and meet the photographer."

When Jerry walked toward us, I saw that he had Down syndrome. I smiled and held out my hand. "Hi, Jerry. I'm Skye. It's great that you can help us today."

"Sure. I like cats." Jerry turned and walked back

to the crates.

"I had Jerry late in life, but he's been a blessing to me."

"I'm sure he has."

I watched Jerry open a crate and take out a mewling kitten. He held the orange-striped ball of fluff in one beefy hand and gently stroked it with the other. The kitten rubbed against his hand and a purr rumbled from his throat.

"He certainly seems to have a way with the cats."

"Oh, Jerry's been around cats since the day he was born. I think he loves them as much as I do. He still mourns the loss of Tobias."

"I'm sure he does." I'd really had enough of the strange conversation with this woman. "Let's get the shoot started. I don't want to keep your cats here any longer than necessary. I'm sure they're anxious to get home."

Lionel brought out the props we would need for the shot and brushed off the sheet we were using in place of the seamless. My first shot was for June. Lionel had set up the kiddie pool, without water of course. He'd fashioned a little beach umbrella and beach towel and somehow constructed a tiny lifeguard stand from a toy. All of that was positioned on top of the sand that had been poured onto the platform to simulate a beach atmosphere. I didn't envy Lionel the cleanup the sand would require.

"Let's get the cats into the swimsuits," I said to Miss

Kitty. I was half-afraid she'd have a fit about dressing up her cats, but she didn't blink an eye.

"Jerry." Miss Kitty looked at the layouts and motioned to her son. "Bring Zachary, Mittens, and Tutu over." She turned to me. "You only need three for this shot, right?"

"Exactly. Would Jerry mind dressing the cats? I'm sure Lionel won't mind, but I figure the cats will be more comfortable with someone they know."

"I'd prefer to use the cats' own wardrobes, if that's all right with you. They have swimsuits that have been made to fit them. They also have shorts outfits and sundresses, if you'd like to try those."

"Wonderful. I'm sure they'll look better than what Lionel made."

"Jerry, get the swimsuits from the wardrobe and dress the cats, then take them to Lionel."

I was more than a little surprised at Miss Kitty's take-charge attitude. She called out orders to Jerry about which swimsuits to put on the cats and he followed her directions to the letter, never once questioning anything.

"Miss Kitty, you said you were open to having a dog in some of the shots, right?" I hoped she hadn't changed her mind.

"Well, if we can limit it to one dog in here at a time, I'm willing to give it a try. And, of course, I'll want Peter to be the dog handler."

"Of course. I'll give Peter a call and see if he can bring one of the dogs over."

"Just make sure it's a dog that respects cats," Miss Kitty said.

Respects cats? For a minute I thought Miss Kitty was making a joke. One look at her face told me otherwise. I nodded and pulled my cell phone from my pocket, moving away from Miss Kitty so she wouldn't overhear the conversation. It was close to noon and I hoped Peter would be available.

"Hi, Peter."

"Hey, Skye. How's the cat shoot going?"

"Don't ask. Dogs are easier," I said.

"Tell me about it." Peter's warm laughter sounded sympathetic.

"I've convinced Miss Kitty to let us try a shot with one of the dogs. Are you busy this afternoon?"

"I have a meeting later, but I'm free for the next few hours."

"Perfect. Miss Kitty was a little reluctant, but she has a great deal of respect for your dog-handling abilities."

"I'll try to live up to her expectations. Which dog do you want to use?"

"You tell me. Which one would be best with cats? Actually Miss Kitty has requested a dog that respects cats."

Peter's laughter was warm and genuine without being derisive, which made me like him even more.

"I don't think Miss Kitty understands the nature of dogs all that well."

"That's one way of putting it," I agreed.

"Originally, I was going to use Horace. He's a coonhound and does well with cats."

"Great."

"Except Horace is in the kennel, and the police still aren't letting me in except to feed and water the dogs. If you want, we could try to use Oreo."

"I'll try anything at this point. What kind of dog is Oreo?"

"She's a mutt. Part Australian shepherd, part something else. She's about sixty pounds and has long fur. Mostly black with some white, if that helps."

I had no idea how big a sixty-pound dog would be so it wasn't a big help with setting up my shot, but the coloring sounded right for what I wanted.

"Why don't you bring her over? As long as she doesn't try to eat a cat, I'm sure I can make the shot work."

"Sure. I'll be there in fifteen minutes."

Lionel and Jerry had the cats dressed and on the set. One in a bikini, one in a pair of shorts, and the third one in a sundress and hat. They looked for all the world like a mother and two children ready for a day at the beach. Except they were cats, of course. I clicked off shots while Lionel and Jerry worked at keeping the cats on the set.

Then the cat in the shorts decided to take a bathroom break and peed on the sand. That seemed to give the cat in the sundress the idea that the sand was just one big litter box, and he took a dump. Lionel cleaned it up without saying a word, but I didn't like the look he gave me. Maybe I could talk Connie into giving him some hazardous-duty pay.

While Lionel cleaned up the mess and shoveled the sand into a bucket so he could set up for the next shot, I called Peter to let him know we were ready for the dog.

I checked the lighting and gave Lionel a hand with setting up the scene for July. By the time we got the fake grass down and set up the flags, Peter arrived with Oreo. The dog walked docilely next to Peter and sat when he stopped. She didn't seem to be distracted by the cats that were in their crates only a few feet away. I took that as a good sign.

"Miss Kitty, we're ready. Which cats are we using?"

"I think Marmalade will be okay with the dog. She's from a home that had dogs, so she's used to them. And perhaps Keiko." She motioned to Jerry, and he obediently took the cats from their crates and brought them to the set.

"This one is Marmalade." Jerry lifted one of the cats a few inches. "This one is Keiko." He nuzzled the Persian in his other arm.

Marmalade sat quietly when Jerry put her down, but Keiko hissed and turned her pinched, angry-looking face toward me. I tried to squelch a strong sense of foreboding, and clicked off a few shots of the cats. Peter led Oreo over and walked her up the steps to the set. Everything seemed fine while Peter got her positioned and unclipped her leash. I snapped the camera as fast as I could, unsure how long the cats would tolerate the dog's presence. I'd gotten about half a dozen shots when Keiko pounced. Literally. The pissy-looking Persian leapt at the dog, hissing and spitting. Jerry picked her up but the cat leapt out of Jerry's arms and landed on Oreo's back.

The dog yelped and whipped her head around to snap at the cat. I didn't blame the dog. I'd snap, too, if I had kitty claws embedded in my back.

"Jerry! Stop that dog!" Miss Kitty squealed. Jerry moved faster than I thought possible. He pushed Peter aside and scooped the angry cat up in one arm, oblivious to the claws the cat raked over his arm. His other hand wrapped around Oreo's collar and yanked the dog off the raised platform.

Jerry put Keiko back in his crate, then returned for Marmalade, who was still on the platform, ears laid back. The cat hissed and swiped at Jerry, but he ignored the sharp claws and picked up the cat, making soothing noises as he stroked the fur. He put Marmalade in his crate, then turned to Peter, who knelt on the floor running his hands over Oreo.

"I'm sorry," Jerry said. "I didn't hurt the dog, did I?"

"She's all right." Peter stood and patted Jerry on his shoulder. "I understand."

"I think we're done for the day," I said. The idea of trying to get dogs and cats in the same shot had lost its appeal. Maybe tomorrow I could resurrect some of my enthusiasm for this job.

Lionel cleaned up the set while I packed my cameras away and Jerry carried cat crates out to Miss Kitty's van. When he came back for the last two crates, he still looked sad and miserable.

"The dog is okay?" he asked me.

"Yes, Jerry, the dog is fine. No need to worry."

"I like dogs. But Mama told me to stop the dog. I always do what Mama tells me to. I have to. She said." He clasped his hands together, pulled them apart, and clasped them again.

"I know. It's important to do what your mother tells you to." I was a little stunned at how swiftly he'd reacted without any hesitation. Would he do anything his mother told him to do? No matter what? I couldn't help wondering if those large hands could have been the ones that strangled the life from Frank.

CHAPTER FIVE

Even though the shoot had only lasted a few hours, I was exhausted, and I still had to stop at the store to get something for dinner. I pulled into the parking lot of the grocery store and tried to think of something that required little effort while still meeting with my mother's approval. Unfortunately, Mom had never seen the need for frozen, canned, or boxed food. She also didn't like restaurants because she thought it was ridiculous to spend so much money for food you could cook yourself.

I'd just tossed a chicken in my cart and was heading to the produce section when my cell phone rang. The caller ID displayed Bobbi Jo's name, and I flicked the phone open.

"Hey, Bobbi Jo."

"Skye, I just called your home phone and talked to your mother. You're all coming over for dinner."

I sighed heavily enough that Bobbi Jo heard me.

"What's wrong, Skye?"

"Nothing. I guess I was hoping Mom would leave before I had to introduce her to my friends."

"Don't be silly, Skye. Your mom sounded charming on the phone. She's even bringing over some bread she made to have with dinner."

"Bread? How the hell did she find enough ingredients in my kitchen to bake bread?" Sheridan ate out with her friends a lot and I'd pretty much lost interest in cooking regular meals when my twenty-two-year marriage ended, so I didn't keep a lot of staples on hand.

"Your mother sounds like she could make a full meal out of practically nothing," Bobbi Jo said. "We talked for a long time and she's got me convinced that I need to learn how to cook something more than chicken and steak on the grill. Anyway, Lily put a stew in the Crock-Pot for us and your mom said it sounded wonderful."

"I love Lily's stew, and even if I didn't, anything is better than having to cook something myself. What time?"

"Any time you want is fine. Tell Sheridan to come, too."

I wheeled my cart back to the meat section and replaced the chicken. "I'll see you in a few hours. I've had a hard day and want to take a nap first so I'm decent company."

I put the cart back in the stall and almost trotted to

the car. I could get a good hour and a half nap and still have time for a shower before we went to Bobbi Jo's. I drove home, trying to stay within five miles of the speed limit and pulled my car into my assigned slot. I was almost giddy with anticipation of that nap when I walked into my loft to find my mother perched on a stool at the counter clutching a loaf of bread partially wrapped in a large napkin.

"It's about time you got here. I'm all ready to go. I can't wait to meet your friends."

"Actually, I was thinking of taking a nap before we leave."

"A nap? Why? Are you ill?" She waved me over and pressed the back of her hand to my forehead.

"No, Mom. I'm just tired. It's been a difficult day."

"Oh, really, Skye. All you were doing is taking pictures of dogs and cats. How hard could that be?" She waved her hand in a dismissive gesture. "You can sleep when you're dead. Let's go meet your friends."

"Bobbi Jo asked me to bring Sheridan, and I don't know what time she'll be getting home. It could be a couple of hours."

"She's already here. That nice boy, Zack, came home with her and they talked for a while, then he had to go."

I hadn't seen Sheridan's Mini Cooper in the garage, but she usually parked in the back in one of the unassigned spots, so I could have our assigned spot that was closer to the elevator. Mom hopped off the stool and brushed crumbs off her emerald green velour jog suit. Mom had two uniforms of dress. In the winter she wore brightly hued velour jog suits, and in the summer she wore brightly printed muumuus and caftans. I was suddenly happy it was only March and still cool enough for the jog suits.

"But she can't go anyway. She's got a date," Mom said.

"With Zack?"

Mom nodded. "Nice young man."

My day was getting worse and worse.

"Nice? You would have had a heart attack if I'd brought home a boyfriend like that. He's older than her and he's covered in tattoos." I didn't mention I suspected a drinking problem. Even I had to admit that asking for one beer probably didn't constitute an issue with alcohol.

"Oh, all young people get tattoos nowadays. It's no big deal. Besides, it's not what's on the outside that counts, it's what's on the inside."

I couldn't argue with that. As much as I wanted to.

"Sheridan," I called.

"Hey, Mom." Sheridan bounced out of her bedroom wearing low-rise jeans and a short sweater that left part of her tummy exposed.

"Aren't you going to be a little chilly?" I pointed to

her exposed flesh.

"What?" Sheridan's eyes followed my pointing finger, then she laughed. "Really, Mom, you're so funny. Sorry I can't make dinner at Bobbi Jo's, but I thought I'd stop by later, if that's okay."

"I'm sure it'll be fine. Are you bringing Zack with you?"

"No, he has to—he has other plans." Sheridan gave me a quick smooch on the cheek, did the same to her grandmother, and tore out of the loft. It was all I could do to not throw her in her room and lock the door. I tamped down my maternal desire to protect my child and sighed.

"Well, if you really want to take a nap, I can keep myself busy," Mom said. "I noticed that your closet is a mess. I'll just go in and put everything in order. I can do your drawers, too."

Dear God. The thought of my mother going through my clothes made little black dots swim before my eyes. Not only did I have my clothes arranged the way I wanted them, there were some items in my drawers that I wasn't at all anxious for my mother to see. I flashed on the see-through black lace number Scott had given me last year and almost hyperventilated. And I was pretty sure the bottom drawer contained the French maid outfit with the cutout nipples that I'd bought to try to entice my ex-husband into having sex. In my defense,

Bobbi Jo had forced me to buy it and that was before I discovered Craig was gay. My face must have reflected my reluctance to have her organize my clothing.

"Oh, you probably couldn't sleep with me doing that. I'll straighten up your kitchen cupboards. Goodness, you have so many cans and boxes and bags. I don't know how you ever find anything. Although you really should eat more fresh food. Sheridan is a growing girl, you know. She needs good nutrition."

"Sheridan is almost nineteen, Mom. I doubt she's got much more growing to do." Physically, anyway. At that point, I accepted defeat. There would be no rest for me that afternoon.

"You know, Mom, I'm really not that tired. Let's just go to Bobbi Jo's. It'll be fun to visit with her." With any luck Lily would have a bottle of wine. But why leave it to chance? I opened a cupboard door and pulled out a bottle of Shiraz and a bottle of Malbec. I could always counteract the wine with a few cups of coffee after dinner. Or Mom could drive home. If I had a few glasses of wine maybe her driving wouldn't bother me.

Mom chattered as I drove to Bobbi Jo's. Mostly I nodded and thought about the next day's shoot. I still had one more shot with cats and dogs and I wasn't looking forward to it. If Connie hadn't been on her honeymoon, I could ask her if she had an alternative idea. I wasn't even sure Miss Kitty would agree to try it again.

She'd been pretty upset. There were still six shots with dogs and seven with cats left to be done. Miss Kitty had agreed to have her cats and kittens there at ten and I was hoping I could get all the cat shots finished.

Lily answered the door and waved us toward the living room. "Bobbi Jo's lying down in the living room. She's been swelling lately and I'm trying to keep her off her feet as much as possible."

"Is she all right?" I asked.

"I'm sure she's fine. She just saw the doctor a couple of days ago. You remember how it is at the end. Your ankles swell to twice their normal size if you stand for any time at all."

I nodded. "Lily, this is my mother, Ruby Lee."

"Hi, Ruby Lee. Oh, I see you brought the bread." Lily took the bread from Mom and wrapped her arms around Mom's shoulders. "I'm so delighted to meet you. Skye and I have been friends for years. Goodness, this bread smells wonderful."

"Oh, it's nothing. I needed something to do while I was all alone at Skye's apartment anyway."

"It'll be perfect for the stew I made. Go on into the living room and say hello to Bobbi Jo. The stew won't be ready for a while."

I guided Mom to the living room where Bobbi Jo was lying on the sofa. She struggled to get up and finally got an elbow under her, pushing her into a half-sitting position.

"How are you feeling, Bobbi Jo?" I asked.

"Oh, about the usual. Oh, you must be Skye's mama. I'm so happy to meet you."

"Now, you just lie back and get some rest," Mom said. "I know what it's like at the end of a pregnancy. Why, I was so big with Skye I thought I was just going to explode. I could hardly get around." Mom settled herself on the ottoman next to the sofa. "And the heartburn! I almost thought it would be worth starving to death to avoid that."

"Oh, my gawd, I know what you mean. I have it every time I eat anything, Mrs. Donovan."

"Oh, just call me Ruby Lee. No sense in being so formal. Now, tell me how the pregnancy has been going."

It looked like Mom and Bobbi Jo were going to get along just fine, and I'd already heard about how the pregnancy was going, so I slipped back into the kitchen to help Lily.

"What can I do to help, Lily?"

"Take Bobbi Jo home with you," she said, then shook her head. "I'm sorry. I know she's uncomfortable, but really. I told her to lie down just so I could get away from her. Skye, she's driving me insane."

"I can only imagine, Lily. You've been a saint through this pregnancy."

"No, you don't understand. You can't because you aren't going through it. I really don't know how much more I can take. I need some kind of respite care for her. They do that for people taking care of relatives with Alzheimer's or cancer or mental illness."

"Calm down, Lily. Listen, I have to shoot the cats tomorrow, but it might be a while before I can finish with the dogs, so I'll come over and give you some relief."

"May the Goddess bless you, Skye. I think she's terrified to be left alone for even a minute. And I need to see Chase about the remodeling on my apartment. Sometimes when I mention the apartment, Bobbi Jo gets all excited about how wonderful it will be and other times, she acts like I'm about to abandon her."

"How is the remodeling coming?" I asked.

"Slowly." Lily laughed. "That's probably because I'm so anxious. You know, it's only two thirty and the stew won't be ready before five. Do you want to go over there with me and have a look at it?"

"I'd love to." I headed to the living room to tell Bobbi Jo and my mother that Lily and I were going out for a bit. They were laughing and chattering like old friends and didn't seem to mind a bit that I was abandoning them.

The drive to Lily's shop and apartment-to-be took less than half an hour and we spent most of it talking about the apartment.

"I'm spending a lot of money on it, but I figured this is my chance to have something exactly the way I want it."

"Oh, I understand. I felt the same way when I rented the loft after I left Craig. It made me feel free somehow."

Lily nodded. "I feel empowered. Like I'm finally taking control of my own life."

"Absolutely," I said.

"It's not that I wasn't happy when I was married to Grant and when we brought Kyle into the relationship. I really love both of them. But I think I ended up forcing my life to fit the relationship."

"That's hard enough with one man. I can't imagine it with two." We both laughed at that.

"And for the past seven months, I've been living with Bobbi Jo. And, again, I'm happy—even if she does drive me nuts—but I just want to be on my own. In my own place, doing what I want, when I want. Holy Goddess, I sound selfish."

"No, you don't. You sound like a woman who knows what she needs and is determined to get it. And you've put in enough time with Bobbi Jo and her pregnancy. I know it hasn't been easy, even if you love her."

"No, it hasn't been easy, but I wouldn't have it any other way."

We parked in front of her shop and went inside to find Jasmine helping a customer choose some incense and candles. We waved at Jasmine and made our way through the crowded store to a door in the back. The door opened into a small foyer with a door on one side and a wide stairway leading up to the apartment.

"Chase, are you up here?" Lily called.

"Over here," he answered. He turned around and I was surprised to see that he was an incredibly good-looking man. He was well over six feet with broad shoulders covered by a snug white T-shirt tucked into worn carpenter jeans.

"Chase, this is my friend, Skye. I wanted her to see what we're doing here."

"Nice to meet you." His biceps bulged and I noticed he even had muscles in his forearms when he shook my hand.

"Looks like you have a lot of work to do." I looked around at the spacious room that was bare except for a workbench, sawhorses, tools, and building supplies.

Chase raked a hand through his sandy hair and grinned, showing even white teeth. I couldn't imagine why he was doing construction work when he had the looks to be a movie star.

"Yep, it's a mess right now, but soon it'll be gorgeous."

Lily showed me the other room and the room that would become her bath but right now contained only an old toilet and a sink that hung on the wall.

"I'm going to have one of those old claw-foot tubs in here and a separate shower. And Chase said it's big enough to have a double vanity if I want one, but what would I do with two sinks?"

"Well, you might not be single forever, Lily." Chase stood in the doorway watching us. "And if you have a man around, it's nice to each have your own sink."

"I never thought of that. Grant and Kyle never seemed to mind sharing a sink." Lily looked at the wall the vanity would go on. "If I don't have the two sinks, I'd have more room for extra storage."

"True. But if I was the man in your life, I'd prefer the two sinks," Chase said.

"Skye, come tell me what you think about the kitchen area." Lily slipped by Chase and he extended a hand to touch her back as she passed.

"I want to keep this whole area open," she said. "I was thinking of a bar to separate the kitchen from the living area. Then I could put a small table and chairs over by the window. I really like the idea of an open floor plan."

"I think it's a great idea," I said. "I kept everything as open as possible in the loft. The only separate areas are our bedrooms and baths."

"And I want one of those sofas with a chaise so I can stretch out on it. And maybe a couple of oversized chairs. Or maybe a love seat." Lily walked around the room then pointed to the ceiling. "Chase is going to drywall the exposed ceiling and insulate it and he's

LIZ WOLFE

putting a skylight right there. I'll be able to lie on the sofa and look at the moon and stars."

"Sounds romantic," Chase said from the area that would become the kitchen. "But not if you're all alone."

"So what do you think, Skye?" Lily asked.

"I think it's wonderful. How are you going to arrange the kitchen?"

Lily took me over to the kitchen area and pointed out where she wanted the appliances and where the bar would separate the two areas. Chase went back to work in the living area, but I noticed he kept looking over at us.

"I'm going to run down and see how Jasmine's doing. Chase, would you show Skye the granite and cabinets we picked out for the kitchen?" Lily went down the stairs and Chase waved me over to the workbench.

"This is the granite." He handed me a small piece of green granite streaked with a reddish brown and a darker green. "And the cabinets will be like these but in a rosewood finish." He handed me a photograph of kitchen cabinets that were simple and sleek looking. I'd always figured Lily for the traditional or antique look, which is what she'd had in the house when she was married.

"These are beautiful," I said. "I think Lily will be very happy with the space you're creating."

"I hope so. She's a special woman and she deserves a place as nice as she is."

"Yes, she's very special." I knew why I thought Lily

106

was special and I had to wonder why she was special to Chase. Lily had mentioned that he was a friend of Jasmine's so it was possible he'd known her for some time.

"Skye? Are you ready to go?" Lily called up from the bottom of the stairs. "It's after four and I told Bobbi Jo and your mother that dinner would be at five."

"Sure, I'll be right down." I turned to Chase. "It was nice to meet you. I can't wait to see how the place turns out."

"Stop by anytime and check it out," he invited.

"Thanks." I joined Lily downstairs and we headed back to Bobbi Jo's house.

"So, what did you think?" Lily asked.

"It's going to be beautiful."

"No, I meant about Chase."

"You mean, did I notice that he's one of the most gorgeous men on the planet? It's kind of hard to not notice."

"He is that, but what did you think about the way he was with me?"

"What do you mean exactly, Lily?"

"I don't know. Maybe it's all in my head, but it seems like he's almost too attentive to me. He's always putting a hand on my back or shoulder and making little jokes that are a bit suggestive." Lily glanced at me. "Am I crazy or what?"

"I don't think you're crazy. I mean, I noticed that he

was attentive to you but it's hard to say what that means. When we were alone he told me you're very special."

"Oh, crap. I don't want this to happen, Skye."

"Well, you're a big girl. If he suggests anything, just tell him you're not interested."

"I'm not really good at that," Lily said.

"At saying no?" I asked.

"Well, I've never been very good at saying no. That's why I end up volunteering all over the place. But I'm especially not good at saying no to a man."

"You mean sexually?" I asked.

"Not that. But anytime a man has been interested in a relationship with me, I just kind of let it happen. I don't want to do that again."

"I see. Well, maybe he's not interested in you in that way. Maybe it's just a friendship thing. How well do you know him? Have he and Jasmine been friends very long?"

"Oh, a couple of years, I guess. I saw him a few times, but this is the first time we've spent more than a few minutes together. I thought maybe I'd just not be at the apartment when he's working on it. Maybe I should have him come over to Bobbi Jo's when we have to talk about anything. Or I could have you come with me if I have to go to the apartment."

"My time's kind of tight right now, but I'll do what I can. And if you want to meet with him at Bobbi Jo's, I think that's a good idea, too."

Lily seemed relieved that she had a plan to avoid too much alone time with Chase, and the rest of the trip was filled with talk of Jasmine and her pregnancy.

Mom and Bobbi Jo were still talking about her pregnancy when we arrived. Lily went to the kitchen to get dinner together and I took a seat in the living room and tried not to listen to the pregnancy discussion.

"I swear, I've never been so uncomfortable in my life," Bobbi Jo said. "And now Lily wants me to lie down all the time because my ankles are swollen."

Mom leaned over and patted Bobbi Jo's knee. "I know, honey, but it looks like you don't have much longer to go."

"Gawd, I hope not. The doctor said first babies can be late, and I'm still several weeks from my due date."

"Oh, I doubt you'll be late. And with any luck, I'll be here to greet the little thing."

I tried not to cringe at the thought of two weeks or more of sleeping on my sofa and having Mom organize my home.

"Oh, that would be so nice. I'd love you to be here."

"Well, anything I can do to help." Mom got up from the ottoman she'd perched on. "I'm going to see if Lily needs any help with dinner."

I listened to Bobbi Jo whine and complain until my

cell phone rang. I looked at the display, which showed a string of numbers I didn't recognize. I almost didn't answer it until I realized it might be Connie. I had a lot to tell my art director.

"Hold on, Bobbi Jo. I think this is Connie, and I need to update her on the shoot."

"Oh, sure, darlin'. And don't forget to tell her about the murder."

Like I could forget it.

"Hello?"

"Hey, Skye. How's the photography going?"

"Connie, it's good to hear from you. We've had a few problems on the shoot."

"Like what?"

I'll admit her voice carried some concern. Maybe it was a good sign that she would dump this wild idea of marrying some guy she'd just met and come home to help me.

"First of all, the owner of the doggie talent was murdered the first day of the shoot."

"Oh, my God! What happened?"

"We don't really know yet other than he was strangled in his bed. The police are investigating. Actually, Scott is the detective."

"Isn't Frank's house in Hillsdale? Why is Scott investigating?"

"Yes, his house is in Hillsdale, but the Portland

Police Bureau loans out their detectives to the small towns that don't have large police forces."

"I'm sorry to hear that. I mean about Frank. Not about Scott."

"Well, other than that, this shoot is a bitch. I was almost in the middle of a dog and cat fight today and every shot is taking forever."

"Oh, I'm sure you're doing a great job. That's why I've decided to stay a few days longer."

"Longer? No, you can't do that!" Had the woman completely lost her mind? I was in trouble here. I needed her to be on the set while I was shooting this mess. I needed her to run interference for me with Miss Kitty. She should be the one worrying about how to turn sheets into seamless and helping Lionel make party hats. Not me.

"I think I can, Skye." Connie laughed. "You're doing a great job and I don't have to have the art boards ready for the client for another month. I have plenty of time. Besides, Tyreese wants more time with me."

"Did you get married?" I swallowed hard, hoping she'd somehow come to her senses and realized that a brief affair with someone totally unsuitable was one thing but tying yourself to that person was another.

"Oh, not yet. He's making plans. Isn't that romantic? He said he wants everything to be just right. We're getting married on the beach, and I'm having my wedding gown made by one of the local women here. It's going to be beautiful."

"Connie, really, what do you know about this man? What does he do for a living? Is he going to move back here with you?" Yikes, I hadn't even considered that until this moment. What if Connie decided to stay in the Bahamas?

"Skye, you're such a worrywart. You need to let go and just let life happen to you. Oh, I've got to run. The men caught a bunch of fish and we're having a traditional dinner on the beach, and the women are teaching me to make some of their traditional dishes."

Dial tone. Again. Connie's habit of hanging up on me midconversation was getting annoying. I closed the phone and dropped it into my pocket. Between Connie's affair with some Jamaican beach bum and Bobbi Jo's cascading hormones, Lily seemed to be my only sane friend.

At that moment, my only sane friend came in to tell us dinner was ready. Bobbi Jo struggled to sit up and I remembered how difficult it was with abdominal muscles stretched to their limit. I stood and held out a hand, but that wasn't enough, so Mom came in and between us we got her off the sofa. Mom put a plump arm around Bobbi Jo's back and walked her into the dining room.

"Ruby Lee, you are the soul of kindness. I hate to be a bother, but it's just so damn hard to get around these days."

"Oh, bless your little heart, Bobbi Jo. You're going

to be fine. Once you hold this little bundle in your arms, you won't even remember any of this."

"Bullshit," Lily mumbled to me. "I remember every single moment of discomfort with both of mine."

I stifled a giggle and jabbed her with an elbow. But I had to agree with her. I remembered the discomfort of being pregnant with Sheridan. And the labor and delivery. Even the soreness later. I wouldn't trade them for the world. But Mom was partially right. Once Bobbi Jo held her baby, she might not forget the discomfort, but she would know that it was all worth it. There simply isn't anything to compare with holding your baby for the first time.

Mom got Bobbi Jo settled at the table and dipped out a serving of stew for her, then placed two slices of bread on her plate while Lily and I helped ourselves to a portion of the food.

"Now, are you having a boy or a girl?" Mom asked.

"Oh, I don't know. They offered to tell me after the second ultrasound, but when Edward and I were trying, we'd agreed that we'd like to be surprised." Tears filled Bobbi Jo's eyes. "I just felt like I had to keep to that, now that Edward's gone."

"Well, of course you did, dear. It's the only thing to do."

"I know, but sometimes I wish I knew. I mean, I've had to come up with two different names, and if I just knew if it was a boy or a girl, I'd only have to think of one."

"Have you settled on a name?" I asked.

Bobbi Jo nodded as she spooned stew into her mouth. "Edalyn Marie." She took a bite of bread. "If it's a girl, of course. If it's a boy, then he'll have Edward's name. Marie was Edward's mother's name."

"That's nice. I think Edalyn is a beautiful name, and it lends itself to several shortened versions. Eda, Edie, Lyn."

"Exactly. That's what I was thinking because I always hated that I was named Bobbi Jo. I wanted a real name that could be shortened. Like Roberta Josephine. Then people could have just called me Bobbi Jo. But my mama named me Bobbi Jo 'cause she said that's what she was going to call me anyway."

I tried desperately to think of a topic that didn't concern Bobbi Jo's pregnancy. She was obsessed about the pregnancy, the delivery, and the baby. I cast a beseeching look across the table at Lily. She nodded and rolled her eyes.

"So, Lily, tell us what you've got planned for your apartment remodel." I didn't care if Bobbi Jo got upset at the thought of Lily leaving. She was going to have to get used to the idea at some point anyway.

Lily slid her eyes over to Bobbi Jo, then seemed relieved that Bobbi Jo didn't burst into tears or accuse her of abandonment. Maybe bringing my mother over was the perfect solution. She hadn't heard any of Bobbi Jo's pregnancy complaints, so she was more sympathetic than Lily or I would be.

"Chase has suggested skylights," Lily said. "It's more money, but I love the idea. Besides, it's either that or we have to make more windows. This way I get all the light without having to have a lot of drapes."

"I love skylights, too," I said. "I had one in the family room when I was with Craig. I especially loved it when it rained. I could just curl up with a good book and a cup of tea and listen to the rain spatter on the skylight."

"Well, Chase says they won't cost any more than windows. He has so many good ideas about the remodel. I'd be lost without him."

"Where did you find him?" Bobbi Jo asked. "You've checked out his credentials, haven't you? Is he a licensed contractor?"

"Oh, he's licensed and everything. Jasmine introduced us. They belong to the same coven," Lily said.

"Coven?" Mom asked. "What's a coven?"

Uh-oh. I wasn't at all sure how Mom would deal with hearing about witchcraft and paganism. I think I held my breath while Lily explained that Jasmine was a member of a Wicca coven, which was a pagan religion that was earth based.

"Sounds interesting," Mom said. "Do you do that,

too?"

"I don't belong to a coven. Actually I don't even consider myself Wiccan. I have my own beliefs and they follow a lot of the Wiccan beliefs but they aren't identical. I'm what they call a solitary witch."

Mom looked like she was going to ask more questions about Lily's beliefs, but Lily decided to change the subject.

"How's your photo shoot going, Skye? You're doing dogs and cats, right?" Lily asked.

"Yes. I am shooting dogs and cats. In fact, I did several shots of cats today and pretty much got one shot of dogs and cats together. It wasn't easy, either."

"Well, of course, it wasn't easy, Skye. Dogs and cats are natural enemies." Mom buttered a slice of bread and shook her head. "I don't even see why anyone would want a picture of them together."

"Actually, a lot of people have both dogs and cats and they get along fine," I said. "Although the ones I was photographing today didn't really like each other all that much."

"Natural enemies." Mom dipped her bread into the stew and arched an eyebrow at me.

"Anyway, I'm just shooting cats tomorrow so it should go easier. Miss Kitty's son is really good with her cats."

"Her son is a cat wrangler?" Mom asked.

Bobbi Jo laughed. "Cat wrangler. That's a good one, Ruby Lee."

"Well, her son has Down syndrome, so he still lives with her. And he's very sensitive, which probably helps with handling cats. His mother just tells him which cat to get and what costume to put on and he has it done in no time. He does everything his mother tells him to do."

"Is that a problem?" Lily asked.

"No. Not really. It's just that he does whatever she tells him to do without any questions. I hate to say it, but it made me wonder if he would have strangled Frank if she told him to."

"Well, why in heaven would his mother tell him to strangle someone, Skye? That doesn't make any sense at all," Mom said.

"It's just that Frank was killed by strangulation. Evidently they know it was a man because the bruises left on his throat were made by a hand too large for a woman. And Miss Kitty blames Frank for the death of one of her cats."

"Well, maybe so, but it was just a cat," Mom said.

"But Miss Kitty doesn't feel that way. She considered this cat to be her soul mate."

"Well, I never heard anything so ridiculous. What's wrong with this woman?"

"From what I could tell, probably a lot."

"Can we not talk about dead cats?" Bobbi Jo asked.

"It's kind of upsetting my stomach."

"You're right. Dead cats aren't good table conversation." Mom leveled a look at me that indicated the conversation was my fault, and I should fix it immediately. Before I could think of anything to say, Bobbi Jo changed the subject.

"Now, where are you sleeping, Ruby Lee? As I recall, that loft of Skye's doesn't have a guest room."

"Well, last night I slept in Skye's room, and she took the sofa, but she can't keep doing that. She has to get up and go to work, so tonight I'm going to insist that I take the sofa so she can get a good night's sleep."

"Oh, don't do that," Bobbi Jo said. "Stay here with me. I've got four bedrooms just going to waste. And besides, Lily has to go to her shop all day so I'm here all alone. And you'd be all alone at Skye's loft. If you stay here we could keep each other company."

"Well, thank you kindly," Mom said. "But I don't have my night things with me."

"Oh, that's not a problem." Bobbi Jo waved her hand. "I've got everything you need. I was watching one of those home shows one time and they did a segment on guest rooms. So I went out and bought everything an unexpected guest would need. Toothbrush, nightgown, slippers, and a bunch of bath stuff with special lotions."

"I don't want to put you out, Bobbi Jo. You've got a lot on your mind right now with the baby coming,"

Mom said.

"Well, that might be so, but I don't have anyone to talk to and it gets so damn lonely around here. Oh, gawd, I'm gonna start crying again. I swear, I don't know what's wrong with me."

Mom was up and patting Bobbi Jo on the shoulder before the first tear fell. "Now, you don't worry about a thing. I'd love to stay and keep you company, as long as it's not an inconvenience to you."

Lily and I watched the exchange between Bobby Jo and my mother in fascination. I figured it had to be a southern thing. Mom had been born and raised in Alabama and Bobbi Jo was from Texas. Before they could stretch it out any longer, the doorbell rang. Lily and I both jumped up.

"I'll get it," Lily said.

"No need. I'm sure it's Sheridan. She said she would stop over after dinner." I raced down the hall to the door before Lily could beat me to it and opened the door to Sheridan's back. She held a helmet under one arm and was waving to a figure on a motorcycle with the other.

CHAPTER SIX

I'd only managed to get about four hours of sleep when the insistent screech of the alarm clock broke through my dreams. I slapped at the alarm and managed to hit the snooze button so nine minutes later I got to enjoy the screeching again. Whoever invented the nine-minute snooze alarm should be drawn and quartered. Nine minutes is just enough time to fall deeply asleep only to be roused again. After the third snooze I was so irritated at the alarm and my inability to shut the thing up, that I turned it off and sat up in bed. Sheridan and I had gotten home before eleven and it was a relief to be able to sleep in my own bed, knowing that Mom was safely tucked into one of Bobbi Jo's luxurious guest rooms. But between thinking about Sheridan's new friend with the tattoos and the motorcycle and wondering about Frank's murder, I hadn't dozed off until well after three. I stumbled into the shower and enjoyed the warm spray of water until it turned tepid and I knew I had about two minutes before I would be treated to icy cold water, which would be even worse than the damn snooze alarm. I dried off, blasted my hair with the hair dryer, and applied makeup all the while thinking about the investigation into Frank's murder.

When Scott and I had talked, he hadn't seemed the least bit convinced that Peter no longer held any animosity against Frank. I figured Peter had to be somewhat bitter still. I mean, who wouldn't be? He'd lost his share of a good business because of Frank's underhandedness. But he was still working with Frank. And Peter had mentioned that he would own the entire business now that Frank was dead. Was that enough reason to kill the man? But Peter had seemed sincere when he told me he and Frank had come to terms, that he had put the animosity behind him. I really couldn't believe Peter could kill Frank.

But if he hadn't, then who had? Who had a reason to kill Frank? As well as the opportunity?

I pulled on my robe, then headed to the kitchen for coffee. The loft seemed awfully quiet and I figured Sheridan was sleeping in until I saw the sticky note stuck to the counter.

Left early to do some research.
Won't be home for dinner.
Love, S.

I plucked the note off the counter and tossed it in the trash, wondering what kind of research you could do this early in the morning. And if the research involved the man with the tattoos and the motorcycle. I didn't like where my thoughts were headed. The terrible twos had nothing on the later teen years. I only wished my biggest worries about Sheridan had to do with potty training and how to wean her off a pacifier.

I pushed those thoughts aside and replaced them with ideas for today's shoot. I still had four shots with cats. At least there were no dogs involved today. I carried my mug of coffee to the light table and spread out the layout for the shots. Connie had drawn a picture of two cats curled up in a basket of yarn on one layout. That should be easy enough, although I wondered how Miss Kitty felt about kitty tranquilizers.

Lionel had assured me he'd assembled all the props indicated in the layouts plus some extras in case of emergencies. The next layout showed a group of kittens, each one in a Christmas stocking. A few weeks ago I would have ooohed and aaahed at that, but now it looked like a nightmare. Did Connie think I was Anne Geddes? Maybe I could shoot the kittens right after they'd eaten and they'd be nice and calm. Especially if I could put some tranquilizers in the food. Or maybe the food would make them overly energetic. Crap. Maybe Anne Geddes had the right idea. Babies were more predictable than kittens. At least Jerry would be there to handle the kittens.

Jerry. With the big strong hands and the willingness to do anything his mother told him to. I wondered again if he was really capable of strangling a man. He was such a sweet person. But would he do *anything* his mother told him to? He'd said he would. He obviously believed he had to do what his mother told him to do. What*ever* his mother told him to do. And Miss Kitty wasn't shy about her hatred for Frank. I guessed I'd hate anyone who killed my soul mate, too. Of course I'd never considered a cat as soul mate material. I mean, I like animals. Cats, dogs. Even wild animals. But a soul mate? Good grief.

I chugged the rest of my coffee and headed to the bedroom to get dressed only to be interrupted by the phone. I snatched the instrument off the kitchen counter hoping and praying it wasn't someone calling with a problem about the shoot. I just wanted to get it done and over with. Of course it could be Sheridan calling because she'd been in a motorcycle accident. Worse yet, it could be the hospital calling because she'd been in an accident. I didn't want to think such negative thoughts. Maybe it was just Bobbi Jo calling to tell me to come and get my mother. I told myself to get a grip and picked up the phone.

"Hello?"

"Skye, Scott here."

Like I wouldn't recognize his voice. Scott had one of those voices that could be sweet and sexy at the same time. Not when he was interviewing suspects, of course, but when he was talking to me. It sent shivers across my back and made me a little tongue-tied. I cleared my throat and hoped my voice wouldn't be a high-pitched squeak.

"Hi, Scott. What's up?"

"Nothing since you aren't here. What are you doing today?"

I think I had a hot flash. I wanted to tell him I was doing anything he wanted me to do today. Fortunately I came to my senses and played it cool.

"Shooting cats and kittens. Unfortunately, I'm only using a camera."

"Sweetheart, you are a sick and perverted woman."

"I thought that was one of the things you liked about me."

"Oh, it is. It is."

I laughed. "So, what are you doing today?"

"Actually, this is kind of business related. Have you heard from Peter?"

"No. Well, I saw him yesterday at the shoot. But I haven't talked to him since then. Why?"

"I've been trying to reach him since last evening, but he's not answering his phone or his door."

"That seems strange. Doesn't he still have the dogs

with him?"

"Yeah, I guess. I wanted to let him know he could return them to the kennel, but now I'm wondering if he's skipped town."

"You mean you think he murdered Frank?"

"No. I don't mean anything except that I'm wondering why he'd leave town."

"Well, maybe he didn't leave town. Maybe he just went somewhere."

"Wouldn't that be leaving town?" Scott asked.

"Not necessarily. Maybe he spent the night with a girlfriend."

"Then why didn't he answer his cell phone?"

"Maybe he was busy. You know, with his girlfriend?"

Scott chuckled. "I could understand that."

"I'm sure you could." I remembered more than one evening when Scott had turned off his cell phone when we were together. I wouldn't be at all opposed to having some of those evenings again.

"Still, I don't like it. If you hear from him, tell him I need to talk to him."

"Sure."

"You busy tonight?"

"Actually, I don't know. With my mom in town, it's kind of hard to say what I'll be doing."

"Maybe I could take both of you out to dinner," he

suggested. "And Sheridan, too."

"No." I took a deep breath. "I mean, I don't know if Mom has plans either. And Sheridan's already at school and left me a note that she won't be home for dinner."

"Well, why don't you ask your mom? I'll hold on."

"I can't. She's staying at Bobbi Jo's."

"So, you have the loft all to yourself?"

A warm tingle spread from the phone down my arm and into my belly. I could simply ignore the shoot and spend the morning with Scott. We could have breakfast together, and talk, and maybe have more makeup sex. Then a shower together. And lunch. I'd love to go out to a long lunch. Somewhere with good salads and nice wine. After lunch we could take a drive up the gorge maybe. I'd enjoy a leisurely walk up to Multnomah Falls. I hadn't done that in years. A long walk would give Scott and me time to talk.

Because although we were on friendly terms again and we'd had the one bout of makeup sex, we still hadn't talked about what had caused us to take that giant step back several months ago. Scott wanted a more formal commitment. And I didn't blame him for that, but geez, the ink was barely dry on my divorce papers. I wanted time to enjoy being single. I liked having my own home. I liked not being responsible for getting dinner on the table every night. I loved being able to decide what to do with my free time without having to consult someone else. I also loved Scott. I loved being with him. I loved the conversations we had. I loved the fact that he was perfectly capable of getting dinner on the table. But did I love it enough to take the relationship to the next level?

What the hell was I thinking? I didn't have time to think about dinners on the table and next levels.

"If that's an offer, I hate to turn it down, but I've got cats and kittens waiting to be shot."

"Fine. You know, it's rather emasculating to be shoved aside for cats and kittens."

"You're man enough to handle it."

"Sure. Call me if you can do dinner. With or without your mother."

"I'll see what I can arrange," I said. Hopefully, without my mother. I hung up the phone and pulled some clothes out of the closet. Cargo pants, long sleeved T-shirt, and a V-neck sweater, tastefully accessorized with sneakers and wool socks.

I fought my way through the traffic on I-26, which only gave me more time to think about the murder investigation, Bobbi Jo's pregnancy, Sheridan's latest amour, having to introduce Scott to my mother, and why my life was so damned complicated. I arrived at the arena building to find Lionel waiting at the door sucking on one of his ever-present cardboard cups of coffee, a paper shopping bag at his feet.

"Hey, I was beginning to wonder if you'd found

something better to do," Lionel said.

"Better than this? You've got to be kidding." I pulled out the key Peter had given me and opened the door to the training arena, trying to push aside thoughts of things I could be doing with Scott, not to mention the other parts of my life that were spinning out of control.

"Yeah, kidding. What could be better than garnering multiple wounds from pissy cats?"

"Did you put some antibiotic cream on those scratches?" I asked.

Lionel shoved the sleeves of his stained sweatshirt up to his elbows and held his forearms out for inspection.

"Yes, Mom."

"Smart-ass." I looked at the angry scratches on his arms, pleased that they appeared to be superficial. Still red, but no signs of infection. "Cat scratches can be very bad."

"No kidding. I mean, do you know where those claws have been?" Lionel frowned. "They've been covering cat feces with sand. Or gravel. Or whatever they use."

"Try not to think about it," I advised.

"Easy for you to say. I don't see any scratches on your arms."

He had a point. One I didn't really want to argue.

"Miss Kitty and Jerry should be here soon with the kitty talent. Do we have everything we need for the

Thanksgiving shot?"

"Check." Lionel followed me into the arena with his shopping bag. "The fake turkey is already here, along with the straw bales and pumpkins. I've made little feather headbands for the cats and a black pilgrim hat." Lionel set his shopping bag on the prop table. "You know, I don't get any points with chicks when I tell them this is what I do all day."

"Deal with it. I'm just glad we don't have to do dogs and cats together today."

"You know, we should do the October shot soon, too. Those pumpkins aren't going to last forever. And it cost a fortune to get them. March isn't exactly pumpkin season."

"Good point. Do you need to carve one of the pumpkins before the shot?"

"Yeah. I could do it after we do this shot. I mean, how hard could it be? Just cut some holes out of the pumpkin, right?"

"Lionel, have you never carved a pumpkin?"

"Not really. But like I said, how hard can it be?"

I had an instant flashback to the first time Sheridan had carved a pumpkin. I still felt a heavy load of guilt about letting her use a kitchen knife. We'd ended up in the emergency room for three hours and left with four stitches in Sheridan's finger and a stern lecture from the attending physician about letting children play with knives. The following year, I'd found one of those safe-for-children kits. I still felt guilty. And I could only imagine having to drive Lionel to the emergency room.

My imagination was cut short by the arrival of Miss Kitty, her son, Jerry, and a load of cats safely imprisoned in their cages.

"Miss Kitty, I'm so happy to see you. Today should go much better."

"Well, I should hope so. I don't know that I could stand another day like yesterday. Having my precious kitties attacked by those awful dogs . . ." Miss Kitty shook her head, then motioned toward her son.

"Jerry, bring the crates in and set them up over there." She turned back to me. "We aren't having any dogs today, are we?"

"No," I assured her. "No dogs. Just cats today."

"Well, that's a huge relief." Miss Kitty swished off to direct Jerry in exactly where and in what order he should arrange the cat cages.

I turned to Lionel. "Set up the Thanksgiving shot."

"Sure. No problem. Think you could give me a hand with the sheet? I mean, backdrop? Or seamless. Whatever we're calling it."

"Of course." I pulled the orangey beige sheet off the ironing board and carried it to the setup Peter had rigged for us. Between Lionel and myself, we got it hung and adjusted so there were no folds. Through the lens of my camera it looked as good as real seamless. Okay, maybe not as good, but I thought it was good enough. If Connie didn't like it, then she should have been here to say so. Lionel dragged the straw bales to the platform and got them into place. There was a lot of grunting and groaning but he managed. He added cornstalks and some decorative squashes, then placed the Pet Place products.

"Hey, Skye, can I get some help with these hats?" Lionel held two miniature pilgrim hats by their stretchy strings and a tiny headband with three feathers attached.

"See if Jerry can help you with them. I still need to check the lights and I'm sure he'll be more help than me."

"I'll be glad to help, if you'll tell me what to do."

I looked up to find Peter standing a few feet away and remembered that Scott wanted to talk to him.

"Hi, Peter. I didn't expect to see you today." I adjusted one of the reflective umbrellas. "Did Scott Madison get in touch with you?"

"The detective?" Peter shook his head. "Not in the last few days, but I've been at the coast since yesterday."

"You should give him a call. He said something about it being okay to put the dogs back in the kennel."

"That's good news. I took them to the coast because my condo was just too small for that many dogs. It'll be a relief to have them back in their home again."

"I was wondering if I need to do anything differently now that you own the business rather than Frank?"

Peter shrugged. "I really don't know, but I don't think so. The business will bill your agency for the animal talent. I have an appointment with Frank's accountant later this week to see what I need to do."

"Probably need to see a lawyer, too. Just to get everything transferred to your name," I suggested.

"Yes, I've got that appointment set up, too. But I'm thinking that I'm just going to sell the business anyway. Or maybe sell the dogs individually to other animal agencies."

"Really?"

"Well, Frank was only doing the talent business and I've never been that interested in that part of it. He didn't really own any show dogs other than Captain."

"I didn't know he showed Captain. I thought he was just a companion dog."

"Captain was both. He regularly won at dog shows. It's always been a pleasure to show him."

"Frank had you show his dog? Why didn't he do it?"

"Frank never had the patience for dog shows. There's a lot of politics and more than a few backstabbers. But he liked having the ribbons and the bragging rights, so he let me show Captain."

"Couldn't you keep the business and turn it toward what you like?" I asked. "You still do the agility training and the show dogs."

"The accountant says the business isn't doing very well. And I only got the business, not the house or kennels or the arena. Which means I got the dogs and some wardrobe pieces." Peter shrugged. "So there's no real point."

"That's too bad. Did you expect it to be in better shape?" I asked.

"Not really. Frank's strong point wasn't running a business, and he was always complaining about how bad business was. I kind of expected it."

I'd thought that Peter was inheriting a good business. One that he'd been cheated out of years ago. And that would have made him a suspect, but now it looked like there was no real reason for him to want Frank dead. I was relieved because I liked Peter.

Peter followed me to the next light and watched as I adjusted the angle of the light reflector. "Were you asking because I'm a suspect?" he inquired.

"What?" I turned away from him, hoping to hide my surprise. "Why would you ask that?"

"Skye, it's all right. Detective Madison told me I was a suspect."

"He did? Oh. Did you tell him that you knew the business wasn't worth much?"

"Not really. He didn't ask and I never thought of it. You think it makes a difference?"

"It should. I mean, that would be your only motive, wouldn't it?"

"Even if the business had been booming, it wouldn't have been a motive to kill Frank."

"Of course not. I'm sorry. I'm putting this the wrong way."

Peter grinned. "Don't worry. I know what you meant. And yes, I guess that would have been the only motive. I'll go call Detective Madison about getting into the kennel, and I'll be sure to let him know about the business."

"Good idea. See you later."

Peter waved and pulled his cell phone out as he walked to the door. I turned back to the task at hand to find that the set was ready and Jerry was cuddling three of the kittens we were going to use for the Thanksgiving shot. Lionel was desperately trying to hold on to the other two.

"All right. It looks like we're ready to shoot," I called. Lionel quickly dumped his two kittens on the platform, and Jerry gently placed the three in his arms next to them, shooting my stylist a frown.

"Jerry, could you do something to get them playing together?" I asked. Jerry nodded and pulled a length of yarn from his pocket. One end was tied into a loopy knot, which the kittens lunged for as soon as he dangled it over them. I clicked off shots from the camera on the tripod, then grabbed my digital camera and snapped another dozen or so.

After an exhausting few hours, I'd finished the Thanksgiving shot and two others when Miss Kitty announced that the cats were all fatigued and had to be taken home to rest. It was already late enough that I didn't argue with her. Lionel helped me pack up the cameras and tear down the set while Jerry packed the kitty cages into Miss Kitty's van.

The door to the arena opened, casting a shaft of late afternoon sun across the floor. I looked up to see the dark outline of a man standing in the doorway.

"Can I help you?"

"Maybe. I hear Frank was killed." The man walked across the arena and stopped a few yards from me.

"Yes, I'm afraid he was. Was he a friend of yours?"

"Hardly." The man shuffled his feet. "I been Frank's neighbor ever since he bought the place. Used to be real quiet and peaceful until he brought all them dogs here. Since then, it's been nothing but barking and whining all hours of the day and night."

"I see." I didn't know what else to say and hoped the man would enlighten me as to his purpose for being here.

"Name's Taylor Hudson." The man pulled a ratty hat off his head and stepped forward to offer me a beefy, calloused hand.

"Skye Donovan." I shook his hand. "Did you want something?"

"Not really. Just wondered about all the activity over here. What with Frank gone and all." He shoved the hat back on his head and stuffed his hands in his pockets. "Actually, we all been hoping that things would get a mite quieter now. But that don't seem to be the case."

"I'm sorry if we're disturbing you. I'm just shooting some photographs for a pet calendar and I hope to be finished in a few more days."

"It's not you. It the dogs. Barking all night. Howling all the time. It's enough to drive a man to drink, if he was inclined to that kind of thing. Which I'm not."

"Have the dogs been barking more lately?" I asked. He nodded. "I see. I think it's probably because the kennel was off-limits to everyone while the police investigated the murder. But I understand they've released the crime scene. I'm sure Peter will take care of the dogs now, so you shouldn't be bothered much longer."

"Well, I hope that's the truth. Most of the neighbors have had about as much as they can take. Can't say I'm surprised someone would kill Frank. He never seemed to care if he was inconveniencing anyone else. We complained plenty of times about the noise, but he just told us he was within his rights."

"Oh." Well, what could I say? It sounded like Frank was a class A jerk.

"Like nobody had rights except him." The man shook his head. "Wouldn't surprise me if one of the neighbors finally had enough of him and the noise and took matters into their own hands."

I nodded mutely, at a loss for anything to say.

"Well, I'll be getting back to the house now. *Wheel of Fortune* is coming on in a bit and I hate to miss it."

"*Wheel of Fortune?*" I asked.

He nodded. "I got satellite so I get it several times a day. The missus likes to see what Vanna's wearing every day. Me, I'm fond of the puzzles. I can get most of them before the contestants do."

"I see. That's good."

"'Course, it'd be easier if they'd show the damned board longer. The contestants, they get to stand there and stare at it for the whole show. Viewers like me, we just get to catch a glimpse. I think they do it on purpose."

"Probably," I agreed.

The man turned and left without any further words. Which was fine with me as I'd found the entire conversation more than a little unsettling. I was still pondering whether he'd wanted me to do something about the barking dogs when my cell phone jingled. I pulled it out of my pocket and felt a little thrill when I saw Scott's name on the display.

"Hi, Scott."

"Hi, gorgeous. You about done with the cats and kittens?"

"I am *so* done with the cats and kittens."

"So, we can have dinner?"

"Dinner sounds wonderful. What did you have in mind?"

"What I have in mind has nothing to do with dinner, but if you insist on eating, how about the Chart House?"

I swallowed hard at his innuendo and took a breath. "I'd love to go to the Chart House."

"I thought you would. Will your mother be joining us?"

"No!" Then I realized maybe that had sounded a little forceful. "I mean, she's at Bobbi Jo's, and I think she said something about them shopping for the baby tonight." Okay, she hadn't said anything of the kind. In fact, I hadn't even talked to her today. But no way was I going to let her visit disrupt whatever Scott and I were trying to put back together.

"Should I meet you at your place or do you want to pick me up?" I asked.

"I'll pick you up at seven."

"Perfect. I'll see you then." I closed the cell phone and carried my bags to the truck. After loading everything in the back, I slid behind the wheel, put on the headset to my cell phone, and punched in the speed dial number for Bobbi Jo's home phone.

"Hello?"

"Hi, Lily, it's Skye. Is my mother there?"

"Thank the Goddess, no."

"Oh. That doesn't sound good."

"Sorry. It's just that she and Bobbi Jo are driving me crazy. Fortunately, they've gone to the hospital."

"Oh, my God! Is Bobbi Jo in labor? Why didn't someone call me?"

"No, it's not that. Bobbi Jo's Lamaze teacher has been telling all the women to go take a tour of the labor and delivery ward. Of course, Bobbi Jo didn't want to do it, but your mother managed to talk her into it."

"That's a relief. Why didn't Bobbi Jo want to take the tour of the ward?"

"How the hell would I know?" Lily asked. "Sorry. I don't think I'm really cut out to be a doula, you know? I mean, I thought I could do it. And I probably could for a normal mother-to-be. But Bobbi Jo is high maintenance."

"I'm sorry. And now you have my mother to deal with, too."

"Oh, your mother is the only thing saving my life right now. Probably saving Bobbi Jo's life, too. If I had to deal with her alone, I'm not sure I could be held responsible for my actions."

"Well, I'm glad to hear my mother isn't adding to your stress. I'm also glad to hear she's occupied. Scott and I are having dinner tonight, so tell her that I'll talk to her tomorrow."

"Dinner? Are you two working things out?" Lily asked.

"Maybe. I'd like to. But we still have some major issues."

"You'll figure it out."

"Thanks, Lily. I have to run. I'm home and I need to take a shower and get ready."

"Have fun, Skye. I'm going to go have a glass of wine in blessed quiet and solitude. While I can."

I pulled the truck into my parking space and pulled the headset off. I had an hour and a half to get gorgeous for Scott.

CHAPTER SEVEN

"Va-va-va-voom!"

I turned toward my open bedroom door and grinned at Sheridan. "Stop that. I haven't finished dressing."

Sheridan eyed my black bra, matching thong, and thigh-high stockings. "I should hope not. But, really, Mom, the only reason to wear underwear like that is to have someone look at it."

She was right, of course. I'd purchased the under garments a couple of months ago in the hope of having a chance to wear them for Scott. But, I wasn't going to admit that to Sheridan.

"Scott is taking me to the Chart House tonight. I thought I should dress up, and this is my only black bra."

"You have a black sports bra." Sheridan snickered. "Why not wear that?"

I grabbed a pillow off my bed and threw it at her. She dodged the pillow, picked it up, and placed it back on the bed, making sure it was straight, then smoothed a wrinkle from the bedspread.

"Scott, huh? You two seeing each other again?"

"Well, we're having dinner. I'm not sure where it will go from there."

"You've already had sex with him." Sheridan nodded.

"Sheridan! You don't need to speculate on my sex life."

"I don't have to speculate. It's written all over your face."

I don't know why or how, but Sheridan and my best friends always seem to know when I've had sex. They all say it's written all over my face. If I could figure out which part of my face it's written on, I'd erase it.

"Well, I think it's great that you two are back together. I know you've missed him."

How could she know that? I didn't confide in Sheridan about my relationship with Scott because I didn't think it was appropriate. Was I that transparent?

"What are you doing tonight?" I asked in an effort to change the topic.

Sheridan turned and headed for the door. "Hanging out with Zack."

"You've been seeing a lot of him lately, haven't you?"

"Is that a problem?"

"Of course not. It's just that he's quite a bit older than you, isn't he? I thought you'd be more interested in boys your own age."

"That's exactly the problem, Mom. The boys my own age are boys. Besides, Zack is only ten years older than me. You've dated men that much older than you."

Sheridan was referring to a gentleman I'd dated twice after Scott and I had taken a break. But it was only an effort on my part to put Scott behind me. That turned out to be impossible because I still loved him. And the gentleman wanted a plaything more than he wanted a relationship.

"I know, but the difference between eighteen and twenty-eight is a lot different from the difference between forty-two and fifty-two."

"Mathematically, that doesn't make any sense. Besides, I like Zack. We have fun together. He's really cool."

I wanted to tell her she couldn't see Zack anymore. I wanted to tell her she was grounded until she was thirty-five. I wanted to lock her in her room. But, of course, I knew better than to attempt any of those. I knew that any negative feedback from me would send her running straight to him, convinced he was the only one for her. I decided to play it cool.

"Well, as long as you're having fun."

"Oh, we are," Sheridan assured me in a tone that

made me wonder just how much fun they were having. And what kind. And if she was doing something about birth control.

"Are you using birth control?" I blurted out the question before I had time to think. I was afraid Sheridan would think I was prying into her personal life, but she was only eighteen. Okay, she was a few weeks away from nineteen, but still. She was a baby as far as I was concerned. Better to make her angry because I was prying than to have her announce an unplanned pregnancy in a few months.

Sheridan burst out laughing.

"Are you?" I demanded.

"Mom, you can trust me. If I need birth control, I know how to use it."

I debated asking her if she needed it, but decided that really was prying and I probably had no right to ask.

"Are you?" she asked.

"What?"

"Are *you* using birth control? Because with that kind of underwear, you should be."

I arched an eyebrow and gave her my best Mom Glare. "Don't you have somewhere to go?"

She laughed and waved on her way out the door. Fifteen minutes later I was dressed in a black cocktail dress that Bobbi Jo had insisted I buy because it was on sale. And because I looked really, really good in it. I'd touched a little perfume to my pulse points the way I'd learned from fashion magazines when I was in my twenties, which was probably the last time I'd read a fashion magazine. I applied a rosy lipstick and wished I had time for a quick manicure, but settled for some lightly scented hand lotion. The doorbell rang just as I was rubbing the lotion into my cuticles. I wiped my hands on a towel and hurried to press the buzzer to let Scott in, sending up a little prayer that I didn't look as anxious and hopeful as I felt.

"Wow. You look terrific," Scott said when I opened the door.

"Thanks. You look pretty good yourself."

Scott turned and modeled his dark blue suit for me. "Is the tie right?"

"It's very nice." I made a mental note to buy him a new tie for the next small gift-giving occasion.

We chatted amiably in the elevator and in his truck on the way to the restaurant. It was just across the river in Vancouver, Washington, right on the riverbank with a lovely view of the river and the lights of downtown Portland. Scott pulled up to the front door and handed his keys to the valet, then watched as the young man drove it away. Minutes later we were seated next to a floor-to-ceiling window sipping our drinks.

"How's the shoot going?" Scott asked.

"Great. Good." I laughed. "Actually, it's awful. I've

never had a shoot with so many problems. But I only have a few more days. Oh, I saw Peter this morning. Did he call you?"

Scott nodded. "I told him he could take the dogs back to the kennel. We're finished in there."

"Good. I know that's got to be a relief for him. He said he took the dogs to the coast because there were too many of them cooped up in his condo."

"Yeah. He stayed in a big house on the beach that a friend of his owns. Lots of room for the dogs and he could let them run on the beach."

"That's nice," I said.

"He also told me that he had no reason to kill Frank."

"Really?" I wasn't sure whether I should mention I'd suggested Peter do exactly that.

"He seems to think that because he knew the business was practically worthless, I should see he didn't have a motive."

"Well, he wouldn't have a motive, would he? I mean, I thought you thought that his motive was to get the business back from Frank. If the business isn't worth anything, then there's no motive, right?"

"Hard to say. For one thing, I only have his word that he knew the business wasn't worth much. And that doesn't account for any animosity he might have held for Frank stealing the business from him when it was worth something."

"Peter wouldn't lie about that."

"How do you know?"

"Well, he just wouldn't. You know, your job makes you suspicious of everyone."

"Can't argue with that." Scott picked up a menu and I did the same, happy to let the matter go. At least for now.

"The Alaskan king crab legs look good," Scott said.

"I was thinking of a steak."

"Then you should have the filet mignon. It's excellent."

"You've been here before?" I asked, disappointed somehow that he'd shared this place with someone else.

"Couple of days ago. Irene wanted to take me to dinner to discuss the case."

"Irene Knutson? Really? That seems odd."

"Odd? I don't think so. She's the mayor so it stands to reason she'd want to know what was happening with the case. A small town like Hillsdale doesn't get many murders."

"No, I mean that she'd take you to dinner. Especially to a place like this." The Chart House was an elegant restaurant. A beautiful view, comfortable seating in cozy arrangements, soft lighting that encouraged intimacy, delicious and pricey food. It was a date restaurant. Not a business dinner restaurant.

"It's just a restaurant," Scott said.

The waiter appeared and took our order and silently disappeared. I decided to take the high road and forget about Irene Knutson. Well, not mention her anyway.

"So, how is the case going? Any suspects besides Peter? Oh, wait, that reminds me, I had an unusual visitor at the arena today."

"Who?"

"One of the neighbors. His name is Taylor Hudson, and he said that all the neighbors had a problem with the dogs barking."

"Really?"

"Actually, he said he was surprised someone hadn't killed Frank sooner. Evidently, Frank wasn't very sympathetic about the barking keeping his neighbors up at night."

"Taylor Hudson. I'll make a point of talking to him." Scott waited while the waiter placed our salads before us. Chilled baby greens tossed with a Green Goddess dressing, sprinkled with croutons and sliced almonds, and served on a chilled plate with a chilled fork.

"Thanks," Scott said after the waiter had disappeared.

"For what?"

"Telling me about Taylor Hudson. Could be an important lead."

"I thought interviewing the neighbors would be

standard procedure for a murder." I grinned at him. "That's how they do it on television."

"Of course. And detective training for the Portland Police Bureau requires eighty hours of watching television crime drama." He shook his fork at me and a smile played around his mouth. "And that doesn't include commercial breaks."

I laughed at his joke, happy we were keeping the conversation light.

"Actually, we have interviewed the neighbors. But none of them said anything about having a problem with Frank or his dogs." Scott shrugged and took a bite of salad. "Of course, when people talk to the police, they don't always mention every little detail."

"I suppose they don't. At least now you have a suspect besides Peter."

"Peter's not my only suspect."

"Who else do you suspect?" I asked.

"Well, there's your helper, Lionel."

"Lionel? He didn't even know Frank. If he's a suspect, you might as well put me on the list, too."

"Evidently, Lionel was going to buy a puppy from one of Frank's bitches. Then the bitch won a championship and Frank reneged on the deal. Wanted to charge Lionel more money. A lot more money. Lionel seemed pretty pissed off about it."

"He never mentioned anything to me. Besides,

Lionel was with me the entire morning that Frank was killed."

"The coroner hasn't established time of death yet, but he thinks it will be around midnight. Was Lionel with you all night?"

"Of course not. We didn't meet at the arena until nine."

Scott nodded. "So, he had plenty of time to kill Frank before you arrived."

"Scott! Lionel is a friend. How can you possibly suspect him of murder?"

"He's not my friend. And everyone who has ever committed murder was friends with someone."

I took a bite of the salad and chewed energetically. It didn't calm me down so I tore off a chunk of bread and slathered butter on it.

"You're upset," Scott observed.

"Well, Lionel is a friend. And an associate. And Peter is kind of a friend. And you think both of them murdered Frank."

"Actually, only one of them could have done it. Probably. I mean, there's no reason to think they were doing it together."

I bit into the bread, chewed, and swallowed, creating one of those painful lumps in my chest. How dare Scott imply that my friends were murderers? I took a gulp of wine to ease the lump of bread down my throat and almost choked on it.

"Skye, you need to stay out of my investigations." Scott's tone was gentle but insistent.

This had been an argument before. On more than one occasion. It wasn't my fault. He'd tell me about some case he was working on, and I'd find it interesting. What was I supposed to do? Just ignore it? Besides, this case involved my friends.

By the time I'd cleared the bread from my throat, I was beginning to see his point. He was a detective with the Portland Police Bureau. His job was to find murderers. Probably other people, too. Showing an interest in his work didn't mean I got to butt my inquisitive nose into it. Still, these were my friends. Didn't I have a right to feel something? Didn't I have an obligation to give him my opinion?

"I'm sorry. I know this is your job. And I know I shouldn't get involved, but it's hard not to when I know the people you're investigating."

"I know." Scott laughed. "As I recall, you got very involved when Bobbi Jo was a suspect." His blue eyes darkened. "And in a way, I'm glad you did. Otherwise, I probably wouldn't have gotten to know you. Not biblically, anyway."

I blushed at his reference to sex. He must have noticed because he reached for my hand and lowered his voice.

"What are you wearing under that gorgeous dress?"

"It's hard to describe, there's so little of it."

"Maybe you could show it to me later," he suggested.

"Maybe," I agreed.

Scott forked some salad into his mouth. "This is delicious."

He was right. The salad was delicious. So was the warm bread that was served as a tiny loaf on a wooden board. And the filet mignon with roasted potatoes and grilled asparagus. We passed the meal with talk that didn't lead us into anything we might argue about. I didn't know what he was thinking about, but I was wondering how much of the meal I could eat without making my stomach stick out. We'd finished our meal and refused dessert when Scott's cell phone buzzed. He pulled it out of his pocket, looked at the display, and smiled apologetically.

"Sorry. I really need to take this." He spoke briefly then pocketed the phone.

"I hate to do this, but I need to go to the station."

I probably didn't do a very good job of hiding my disappointment. I'd had visions of us sharing our own personal dessert at Scott's apartment.

"I thought you were off duty."

"Police detectives are never really off duty," he said.

Didn't I know it. This wasn't the first evening to be aborted because of his job.

"I'll drop you off at my place. This will only take a

few minutes. You can get comfortable while I'm gone."

I watched an old movie for a couple of hours, then decided to discard my dress and pose prettily on the bed in my new underwear. After an hour of that, I tossed the underwear on top of the dress I'd draped over a chair, pulled on one of Scott's T-shirts, and crawled under the covers. Scott didn't get home until after four in the morning. I'd been asleep for several hours, and he was exhausted, so the night of unbridled passion I'd envisioned was reduced to some cuddling before we both fell asleep. We woke shortly before seven, and I pulled on my dress and stuffed the underwear in my purse while Scott took a shower. We drove to an espresso stand for coffee on the way to my loft, then he went back to the station. He hadn't even gotten a glance of my fancy lingerie. I'd barely taken my dress off, pulled on a robe, and headed for the shower when the phone rang.

"Skye?"

"Hi, Peter."

"I need to cancel today's shoot. A couple of the dogs have some kind of stomach problem."

Ewwww. I could only imagine trying to photograph dogs while they were puking. Or worse. "Can we shoot some of the other dogs?" I asked. This shoot was already taking a lot longer than I'd scheduled. I didn't have another job coming up for a couple of weeks, but Steinhart would expect me to be available for studio work.

"Probably not a good idea. If two of the dogs are sick, there's a good chance that they'll all be sick before the day's out."

"Right. Like kids in school. One of the kids gets a virus and by the end of the week, they all have it."

"Exactly. I'm hoping it's just something they ate, and they'll all be okay by tomorrow. But it might be a virus and that could mean several days. Maybe a week."

"Those poor dogs. I hope it's something that passes soon."

"Well, that's one way of putting it." Peter laughed. "Believe me, they're passing a lot right now."

Ewwww, again. "I'd offer to help, but it would be a lie, and I'd never really do it."

"I understand. A lot of my friends love dogs, but they all disappear when you tell them you have a dozen dogs throwing up and crapping all over the kennel."

I could see their point. I wished him the best with the dogs and hung up. Now I had an entire day of freedom. To be honest, I was more than ready for a day without photographing dogs or cats. I quickly phoned Lionel to let him know the shoot was cancelled, then poured myself another cup of coffee and considered what to do with my free day. There was no shortage of things that needed to be taken care of. It was merely a matter of deciding what to do first.

My first thought was Scott, but he was still working

and probably wouldn't even get off early in spite of having worked most of the evening. Sheridan was already at school, not that I thought another conversation would change her mind about dating an older man. That left my mother and Bobbi Jo. Suddenly photographing dogs didn't sound so bad. Even sick dogs.

Finally I decided I'd take care of some much needed housecleaning and laundry before I went to Bobbi Jo's. It wasn't like I needed to spend the entire day there. I finished my coffee, threw on a pair of jeans and an old T-shirt, and grabbed a bucket of cleaning supplies from the utility room.

After three hours of scrubbing, polishing, picking up, sweeping, mopping, and dusting, I felt like I was wearing all the dirt I'd cleaned up. But I also felt relaxed and happy. Something about cleaning reduces my stress level. Maybe it releases endorphins. Maybe it gives me a false sense of control over my life. I just know it works and that's good enough for me.

The Northwest was enjoying one of those unseasonably warm days that occur in the spring. The weather announcer had predicted a high close to eighty degrees. This kind of weather was more than welcome after a long, wet winter, but we all knew it would last a day or two, then we'd be cold and damp again for a few more months. The sun was shining through my freshly washed windows, so I opened them for some fresh air and spent a few minutes enjoying the clutter-free, spotless environment I'd created.

But before long, I remembered my intention to go see my mother and Bobbi Jo. Besides, it was simply too beautiful to stay indoors. I took a quick shower, pulled on clean clothes, and drove over to Bobbi Jo's. Usually Bobbi Jo hears my car and has the door open by the time I get to the walkway. And my mother has an annoying habit of knowing exactly when I'm going to show up. But the door was closed so I rang the bell.

No answer.

I waited a few minutes and rang it again. Still no answer. I should have called. They could be out shopping for some baby item Bobbi Jo decided she couldn't live without. Although from what I'd seen in the nursery I couldn't imagine what was left. I walked over to the garage and stood on tiptoe to look in one of the high windows on the door. Bobbi Jo's Escalade was parked next to her little foreign sports car. She had to be home. Maybe napping. I walked to the side of the garage and opened the gate. I could just go around to the back and go in the sliding glass door. Bobbi Jo rarely locked that door except at night when she turned on the alarm system. I didn't want to wake her up if she was resting, but at least I could leave them a note that I'd dropped by.

When I turned the corner and stepped onto the patio that led to Bobbi Jo's spacious backyard, I saw a naked

Bobbi Jo reclining in a chaise lounge. The sunlight glinted off her short red curls and her face had turned pink.

"Bobbi Jo, what are you doing out here?"

She turned her head as far as she could and I saw tear stains on her pink cheeks.

"I'm stuck!" she cried. "It was such a pretty day with all the sun and it was so warm for March. I thought I'd feel better about myself if I got a little color."

"You're naked," I said.

"I know! I didn't have a swimsuit that I could get into, so I thought while your mother was taking a nap, I'd just lie down out here. Now I can't get up." Bobbi Jo burst into tears.

I saw the problem. Bobbi Jo had reclined the chaise and was wedged between the arms. With her tummy muscles stretched to their limit over the baby, she couldn't sit up and the arms of the chaise prevented her from getting out of the side.

"I tried to turn it over and crawl out, but the damn thing's too heavy."

I hurried over and held my hands out to her, bracing my feet against the legs of the chaise. "Here, take my hands."

Bobbi Jo grasped my hands and pulled against me. Her back lifted a few inches off the chaise, and then her hands slipped and she fell back, arms flying out to the side.

I laughed. I didn't mean to and I tried to stop. But,

really, it was funny.

"Don't laugh at me!"

"I'm sorry. I'm not laughing at you, I'm laughing with you," I said.

"Right. That's what people always say when they're laughing at you."

"I'm sorry, Bobbi Jo, but you have to admit it's pretty funny."

Bobbi Jo scowled, then her mouth quirked. "I must look like a beached whale." She looked down at her swollen belly and long legs. "A big pink whale."

"How long have you been out here?" I asked. Her skin had turned an unhealthy shade of pink, and I knew she'd be really miserable in a few hours.

"About an hour, I guess. I was hoping your mama would wake up and find me before I got baked into a crispy critter."

"Hey, is anyone home?" a man's voice called out.

Bobbi Jo and I stared at each other for a second. I turned to see Chase standing at the edge of the patio holding a shopping bag.

"Chase. What are you doing here?"

"Lily wanted me to come by with these samples for her to look at. Are you two all right?"

"My robe! My robe!" Bobbi Jo whispered urgently. "Skye! Give me my robe."

I should have already thought of that, but I'd been

too shocked by Chase's appearance. I picked up the robe and threw it over her. Bobbi Jo spread it to cover most of her body.

"Do you need some help?" Chase asked and moved closer to where Bobbi Jo and I were. When he reached our side of the patio, he stopped and stared at Bobbi Jo.

"Oh."

"Bobbi Jo, this is Chase. He's helping Lily remodel the apartment." I didn't know what else to say, and an introduction seemed to be appropriate.

"Hi, Chase. It's so nice to meet you. Lily tells me you're doing a wonderful job on her apartment."

"Thanks. It's nice to meet you, too." Chase looked a little perturbed. Probably because he couldn't figure out why a sunburned pregnant woman was lying in a chaise on her patio. I hadn't been able to get Bobbi Jo up, but I was certain Chase could. If Bobbi Jo would let him.

"I don't want to interfere or anything," Chase said. "But it looks to me like you could use some help."

"Oh, no, I'm fine. Lily just stepped out for a minute. I'm sure she'll be back soon. You can go wait for her inside, if you'd like." Bobbi Jo was pretending nothing was wrong, but I didn't think that was going to get her out of the chair. And she really didn't need to be in the sun a minute longer.

"Actually, we are having a problem. Bobbi Jo can't get up."

"I thought as much," Chase said.

"I can get up. I just need a minute." Bobbi Jo shot me a glare.

"I tried to pull her up but she's so—I'm not strong enough." I wasn't about to mention how big Bobbi Jo was. She was already humiliated.

"I can pick her up," Chase said and set his shopping bag down. "Looks like it's about time for you to get out of the sun anyway."

"No, you can't pick me up," Bobbi Jo said. "I'm pregnant."

"I won't hurt you or the baby. I promise."

"But—well, it's just that—I don't have any clothes on. Under the robe, I mean."

"I promise I won't look."

Bobbi Jo started to cry and Chase knelt down beside her. "Now, sweetheart, there's nothing to cry about. I'm going to have you out of this contraption in no time and then you can just forget this ever happened." He stood and leaned over, slipping one arm under Bobbi Jo's knees and the other behind her back.

"Be careful. I'm just huge. You could hurt yourself," Bobbi Jo said.

"A little thing like you? I don't think so. Why, you're no bigger than a minute." With that, Chase easily stood up, lifting Bobbi Jo as if she weighed nothing at all.

"Oh." Bobbi Jo looked at me and I thought she

blushed but it was impossible to tell with her face already pink. "You can put me down now. I can walk to the house."

"I don't think so." Chase shook his head. "It looks to me like you've been stuck in that chair for a while. I'd bet your back and legs are going to be stiff and sore, so I'll just carry you inside."

I picked up his shopping bag and followed them into the house. Chase didn't stop at the kitchen or living room but marched up the stairs with her.

"Which one is your bedroom?" he asked.

"At the end of the hall." Bobbi Jo pointed the direction.

Chase carried her to the bedroom and gently deposited her on the bed.

"I can't thank you enough," she said.

"Oh, don't think anything of it. You take care of yourself, now." He turned, took the shopping bag from me, and walked out. Bobbi Jo stared after him for a moment, then pushed the robe off.

"I'm sunburned. *Gawd!* I'm such an idiot. You don't think I hurt the baby, do you?" She rubbed her belly and looked like she might cry again. "I'd just die if I did anything to hurt the baby."

"I don't think sunburn would hurt the baby. He or she probably enjoyed the warmth. Come on, let's get some lotion on you." I stepped into the bathroom and opened a cabinet. She had an array of lotions to choose from. I read the ingredients on each one, finally settling on a light green bottle that claimed to have aloe and vitamin E in a natural lanolin base. I slathered her with lotion, then helped her into a loose robe.

"I could bring you something to eat, if you want to stay in bed," I offered.

"Thanks, but I've had enough of lying down for a while." We started for the kitchen and Bobbi Jo hesitated at the top of the stairs. "Do you think he's still here?"

"I don't know. Do you want me to go check?"

"No, I guess not. But, Skye, he picked me up naked. And I'm all ugly and pregnant and huge."

"It didn't seem to bother him at all," I said.

"Well, it bothered me."

"Why?"

"Skye, I haven't had a man's arms on my naked body since the night I got pregnant. It felt funny."

"Funny, how?"

"Funny, like I started thinking things a pregnant woman shouldn't be thinking."

"I wouldn't worry about it. I'm sure every woman who sees Chase starts thinking things she shouldn't."

"He's awful cute, isn't he?"

"Did Lily tell you she thinks he's been flirting with her?" I asked.

"No! Really?"

"Yes. And I'm not sure she's completely wrong about it. But he's so nice to everyone, it's hard to be certain. Anyway, that's why she wanted him to meet her here. She's afraid to be alone with him." I had to laugh a little at Lily being afraid of anything.

"Does she think he'll do something?" Bobbi Jo asked.

"No. Well, nothing really. Lily told me she's always had a problem with saying no to a man."

"Well, we all knew that, didn't we? I mean, she was married to one man and living with another and considering adding a third one to the group."

"She's not ready for a relationship right now."

"How could any woman not be ready for that man?" Bobbi Jo wondered. "Well, come on, let's go downstairs. Now that I know he's smitten with Lily, I don't feel so bad about the whole thing."

I wasn't sure what that had to do with it, but I was happy Bobbi Jo had rationalized away her embarrassment. When we got to the kitchen, Mom was perched on a stool at the breakfast table with Chase next to her. Lily had returned home from shopping and the teakettle was whistling on the stove.

"Lily, I'll leave these flooring samples for you to look at. Like I said, I'm partial to the rosewood, but let me know which one you want." Chase stood and gathered the samples, placing them back in the shopping bag. "I should be going now."

"Thank you again, Chase," Bobbi Jo said.

"No problem. I hope the sunburn isn't too bad. If it starts to hurt, I could give you a remedy my mother used to use on us kids."

"Why, thank you. That is so kind of you," Bobbi Jo said. Chase walked to the patio door, then turned back. "I'll close your gate on my way out."

"Bye, Chase, and thanks for bringing those samples to me," Lily said.

"Hi, Mom." I gave her a hug. "Have you been enjoying staying with Bobbi Jo?"

"Well, that's something to ask with Bobbi Jo sitting right here, Skye."

"What?" What had I done now?

"Well, if I wasn't enjoying myself, I'd hardly say so in front of my hostess," she said.

"Oh, Ruby Lee, are you not having a good time here?" Bobbi Jo asked.

"Of course I'm having a good time, Bobbi Jo. I was just pointing out to Skye that she shouldn't have asked that kind of question."

"Oh, well, I'm so relieved you're happy here. I can't tell you how much I'm enjoying your visit. And if there's anything you want or need, you just let me know."

Mom waved one hand and took a cup of tea from

Lily with the other. "Honey, it's pleasure enough just spending time with you."

Lily and I rolled our eyes at each other. Bobbi Jo and my mother had developed some kind of mutual admiration society that Lily and I weren't members of. Not that we wanted to be.

"We haven't seen you in a couple of days, Skye." Lily handed me a mug of fragrant tea. "Busy with the shoot?"

"It's not that I thought this shoot would be easy." I shook my head. "I knew it would be different with animals, but I thought with no human models to deal with, no weather problems since I'm shooting indoors, it would be easier than it has been."

"Nothing's ever as easy as you hope it will be," Lily said.

"We didn't shoot today because some of the dogs got sick. But Peter called and said they were better so we can start shooting again tomorrow. Between that and the dogs and cats fighting, and dealing with Miss Kitty and Connie not being here, it's just been one problem after another."

"Well, with that man getting killed, it was bound to all go south," Mom said.

"I don't like to speak ill of the dead," Lily said. "But if anyone had it coming, it was Frank Johnson."

"You knew him?" I asked.

"I knew of him. A couple of years back he was charged with cruelty to animals. Of course he beat the charge, but a group of us from the animal shelter protested. It didn't do any good, but at least it got him some bad publicity."

"Frank? But he loved dogs," I said.

"He loved that mangy mutt of his. But the rest of his dogs were nothing more than a paycheck to him. He kept them in kennels that were too small and none too clean, either," Lily said.

"Men like that shouldn't be allowed to own dogs." Mom shook her head.

"Well, they made him give the dogs bigger kennels and clean up the place. I thought they should have done more than that, but at least it was better for the dogs." Lily poured another cup of tea and handed it to Bobbi Jo.

"No, thanks, Lily. I've just worn myself out. I think I'll crawl into bed for a little nap." Bobbi Jo tied her robe again and waddled toward the stairs. I watched her climb them, one hand braced against her lower back, and remembered how tired I was at the end of my pregnancy. She was close to her due date and I hoped she'd have the baby on schedule. I didn't know how much more of this she could deal with.

"Did your boyfriend find the murderer yet?"

I turned to my mother. How did she know that Scott and I were seeing each other? Damn. Bobbi Jo probably told her all about our relationship. How we met, how long we dated, why we took a break. Oh, well. It wasn't like I could have kept it a secret forever.

"No. But he has a long list of suspects. I found out that my photo stylist was going to buy a puppy from him, but Frank reneged after the puppy's mother won a championship."

"Is that reason enough to kill a man?" Mom asked.

"You'd be surprised," Lily said. "If he wanted to show the dog, it could have been a big deal. Some of those people are a little over the top."

"And one of Frank's neighbors said he was surprised someone hadn't already killed the man."

"He actually said that?" Lily asked.

"His exact words," I said. "Evidently the dogs were loud, and Frank ignored his neighbor's complaints."

"Still, you'd have to be crazy to kill someone because his dogs bark," Lily said.

"If you ask me, anyone who kills another person is crazy. I think that whole business about temporary insanity is a bunch of crap." Mom picked up the cup of tea Lily had poured for Bobbi Jo and sipped it.

"I learned that his former partner, Peter, already knew the business was failing, so I don't think he had a reason to kill Frank. Although Scott doesn't necessarily agree with me." I grinned at Lily. "You better not let Scott find out you were a part of that protest; he might add you to his list."

"I can't say I'm sorry to see the man dead. If you ask me, Frank Johnson was the real dog."

CHAPTER EIGHT

Scott called on my way home and invited me to dinner again. Instead of going out, he offered to cook, which was a plus on several levels. Scott was an excellent cook and after so many years of preparing all the meals, I considered having someone else cook and serve a meal to me to be truly luxurious. He'd also promised no interruptions. Big plus. I knew Scott would probably be in jeans and a sweater but I wanted to look special, so I chose my best jeans that fit just right and a silk blouse. I wore the black bra and thong in the wild hopes that someone besides Sheridan would get to see them. After checking my reflection out from every angle, I drove to the liquor store and purchased two bottles of wine. One red and one white, since I didn't know what he was cooking. While I was checking out, two men were checking me out, which made me feel I'd made the right choice with clothes, hair, and makeup.

I took a deep breath, straightened my shoulders, and knocked on Scott's apartment door. I wasn't disappointed. Scott opened the door, let his eyes roam over my body for a few seconds, then wrapped his arms around me, pulling me inside. I kicked the door closed with my heel and after a few minutes of kissing and nuzzling, pulled back to look at him.

He must have wanted to look a little special, too, because he was wearing beautifully tailored wool slacks in dark charcoal and a sweater of the same color with a thin thread of blue that matched his eyes. He took the bottles of wine from me, and I admired his form when he walked back to the kitchen, then settled myself on a stool at the bar that separated the kitchen from the living area.

"Let's save the wine for dinner." Scott opened the refrigerator and pulled out a bottle of champagne.

"Are we celebrating?" I asked.

"Absolutely." Scott unwound the wire from the cork and placed a dish towel around the bottle. The cork emerged with a soft pop and a wisp of champagne mist. Scott poured the elixir into two tall fluted glasses and handed me one.

"What's the occasion?" I asked.

Scott appeared to consider for a moment, then lifted his glass. "To life." We each sipped the champagne. "Without interruptions," he added.

"I'll drink to that." I took another sip, enjoying the tickle of bubbles against my nose and flowing down my throat. "But how can you be assured of no interruptions?"

"I left strict orders. Unless there's a mass murder, I'm not to be called, paged, or otherwise summoned."

He turned back to the pots and pans on the stove, giving one a quick stir, then replacing the lid. Soon salad plates appeared with spring greens, slivered nuts, and a scattering of raisins and dried cranberries. He spooned blue cheese dressing over the salad and set a basket of crusty French bread and a dish of butter on the bar. I didn't want to eat too much, but the smooth, salty tartness of the dressing mixed with the crisp greens, crunchy nuts, and slightly sweet fruit was too much to resist. At least I only ate half a slice of bread.

We chatted while he removed the salad dishes and replaced them with heaping plates of chicken Alfredo with mushrooms, spinach, and fettuccine pasta. I managed to just nibble at mine, keeping in mind my black thong.

"Something wrong with the food?" Scott asked.

"No, it's wonderful. I just don't want to get too full."

"Are you expecting to be engaged in some kind of vigorous activity later?" Scott grinned and waggled his eyebrows.

"I'm hoping it's a possibility."

"Oh, it is. It definitely is a possibility. In fact, I'd say it's practically a sure thing."

Scott refilled our glasses with champagne and carried them to the coffee table. I sat close to him and the champagne was left untouched as we indulged in what I would have called necking in high school. It had been fun as a teenager, and it was even better now. Within a few minutes Scott had removed my jeans and was admiring my thong. Between murmurs and softly enticing touches, my blouse floated to the floor. I got Scott's sweater off and let my hands admire his muscled chest and broad shoulders.

Then the doorbell rang.

"Ignore it," Scott urged, nibbling on my shoulder and pushing my bra strap off.

"What if it's important?" I asked.

"It isn't. There's nothing more important than this."

"But you don't know who it is." I couldn't concentrate on Scott or what we were doing knowing someone was at the door.

"It's probably someone who wants to convert us to their particular brand of Christianity. I don't want to read their pamphlets or discuss the Bible with them. I don't even want to have to tell them to leave."

But Scott must have known I was too distracted to continue with someone ringing the doorbell and now knocking on the door. He bit my neck gently, sighed, and rolled off me.

"Go in the bedroom. I'll get rid of them."

The bedroom sounded like a good idea, since that's where we were headed anyway. I certainly wasn't dressed to greet anyone. Besides, the bed would be more comfortable than the sofa. I grabbed my jeans and blouse and gave Scott a quick kiss, then scooted into the bedroom and closed the door, tossing my jeans and blouse onto the chair in the corner. The bedroom was cool and I stood inside the door, shivering in my sexy but skimpy underwear. I left the door open a crack so I could hear what was going on, hoping it wasn't something that would cut my night of passion short.

"Irene." I heard the surprise in Scott's voice. "What are you doing here?"

"Well, I tried to call, but you must have your cell phone turned off. I wanted to ask you about the investigation."

Come on. It was already past nine. Surely she could wait until tomorrow morning. Besides, I didn't believe for one minute that she came to Scott's apartment just to talk about the investigation. Just like I didn't believe she'd taken him to the Chart House just to talk about police business. The beautiful, blond mayor of Hillsdale had her sights set on Scott and nothing would convince me otherwise. I really didn't need that when we were just getting back together. I nudged the door open another inch so I could hear better.

"We talked earlier today. Nothing new has come up. But I'll be glad to talk to you again tomorrow morning. Why don't you call me then?"

I opened the door another inch or two and peeked out to see that Scott had his hand on Irene's arm guiding her toward the door. Irene giggled.

"Oh, did I catch you at a bad time?" Her hand moved to his chest. "I don't see anyone else around."

I gasped when I saw her hand petting his chest. That was *my* chest and she needed to keep her grubby paws off it. Unfortunately, Irene heard my gasp and turned toward the bedroom door. Evidently my constant nudging of the door had opened it enough for her to see me because she looked me right in the eye, then let her gaze fall down my skimpily clad body. She still hadn't taken her hand off Scott's chest, which was also unfortunate.

"Ha, I found you!"

I jerked my eyes to the doorway, where a tall, beefy man stood with his fists propped on his hips.

"Who are you?" Scott asked.

"I'm her husband, that's who I am. Take your hands off my wife."

I thought that was a bit strange because Scott clearly didn't have his hands on Irene. The man took his fists off his hips and cracked his knuckles, which must have startled me because I hit the door, causing it to creak loudly. They all three turned to look at me, still in my skimpy undies. This was not what I'd had in mind when I put them on. I jumped back into the bedroom and slammed the door. Scott's black terry robe hung on the back of the door. I grabbed it, shoved my arms into the sleeves, and tied the belt around my waist. At least I was covered up. When I opened the door, Irene's husband still appeared to be angry. Not that I blamed him. I was a little pissed off at her myself.

"Thought you could sneak away and meet your boy-friend, didn't you?" he asked.

"Arnie, that's ridiculous," Irene said. "I'm here on official business. Scott is the detective investigating Frank's murder."

"Then why doesn't he have any clothes on?" Arnie eyed Scott's bare chest.

"That's none of your business," I said as I walked into the room, trying to be as dignified as I could wearing a man's robe that engulfed me and knowing they'd all just seen me in my thong and lacy bra. "Scott and I were having a quiet evening when your wife showed up. Un-invited." I probably didn't need to add that, but I wanted her to know I wasn't happy with the interruption.

"I didn't mean to interrupt anything. I just wanted to know if you'd arrested anyone for Frank's murder yet. The entire town is upset about one of our most beloved citizens being murdered in his bed."

"Beloved?" Arnie asked. "Maybe by you, but certainly not by the rest of the town. Frank was a bastard. Always voting against everyone else on the city council, pissing people off with his barking dogs. Face it, Irene, you were the only one who loved him."

"It's a sin to speak ill of the dead!" Irene said.

"Well, it's a sin to be an adulteress, too," Arnie spat back.

"Look," Scott said. "Obviously, I wasn't having an illicit meeting with your wife. I'm here with my girlfriend."

I felt a little tingle at hearing Scott call me his girlfriend.

"Why don't you two go home and work out your problems?" Scott maintained a soft, reasonable tone although I knew he had to be angry. I certainly was.

"Come on, Arnie. You can follow me home to be sure I don't stop to see anyone else." Irene pushed past her husband and walked down the hall toward the front door of the building.

Arnie followed her out without even a nod of apology. Scott closed the door on their bickering and looked at me.

"Now, where were we?"

"Did you hear that? Arnie thinks Irene was having an affair with Frank."

"Yeah, I heard. I like the way you look in my robe." He pushed it off one shoulder and toyed with my bra strap. "But I like the way you look out of it even better."

"But if he really thought his wife was having an affair with Frank, he might have been the one who murdered him. You said once that strangulation was usually a sign of anger in a murder."

"Yes, it is, and yes, Arnie is going to the top of my list of suspects. Tomorrow. Tonight, I only have one suspect and you won't believe what I suspect you're capable of doing."

There was no point in trying to pursue the discussion with Scott in an amorous mood. And, to be perfectly honest, I had no desire to change his mood.

Outside of the surprise visit from Irene and her husband, Scott kept his promise of no interruptions for our evening together. But it ended at the crack of dawn when he got a call. I accepted his offer of a travel mug of coffee for my trip home, assured him I had several things to attend to myself anyway, and drove back to my loft.

I'd scheduled the shoot for the afternoon. Peter thought it might be best if we waited a few extra hours to be sure all the dogs were in tip-top condition. So,

I didn't really have many things to attend to, but I was hoping I might get a little quality time with my daughter. I made a pot of coffee, took a shower, and changed into my work clothes of cargo khakis, long-sleeved T-shirt and a multipocketed vest. Already dressed for work, I could hang out with Sheridan until I had to leave for the shoot. But Sheridan was still asleep and I remembered that her first class didn't start until eleven. I couldn't come up with a good excuse to wake her up so I drank more coffee and waited.

By nine, I was wondering what I could do that would accidentally wake her up when my phone rang. I let it ring four times, hoping it might get Sheridan out of bed, then finally answered it before it could go to voice mail.

"Oh, good, you're home," Lily said.

"What's up?"

"Chase is coming over to talk about the flooring. I was wondering if you could be here."

"Lily, don't you think you're being a little over the top about this? I mean, you can't really be sure he's even flirting with you." That's what I said, but I had to agree that his attention to Lily was unusual.

"I don't know. I can't think rationally right now. I only know that I don't want to be alone with him."

"But Bobbi Jo and my mother are there. You won't be alone. Just make sure one of them is in the room with you. Tell them you want their opinion on the flooring."

Neither of them were hesitant about voicing an opinion so I doubted they would demur.

"That's just it. They're gone. They went to a whole foods market this morning and then there was some talk about having a late breakfast somewhere. I don't think they'll be back for hours. And Chase is on his way now."

Lily sounded desperate. I understood desperate. I didn't like it, but I certainly understood it. Besides, it didn't look like Sheridan was going to roll out of bed in time to have any kind of quality time with me.

"I'm on my way. See you in twenty minutes." I poured the remainder of my coffee down the drain, rinsed the cup, and took my camera cases since I was pretty sure I'd have to go directly to the shoot after playing chaperone for Lily. I was never sure how my life got to be so complicated. I'd just come to expect it. I drove to Bobbi Jo's and parked in the driveway next to a beat-up old truck I assumed belonged to Chase. Lily opened the door mere seconds after I rang the doorbell.

"Skye, what a nice surprise. Did you come by to see your mother? She and Bobbi Jo are out right now, but I'm expecting them any minute. Come on in."

Like I had a choice. I followed Lily to the dining room, where Chase had spread out a selection of flooring choices over Bobbi Jo's plush carpet.

"Hi, Chase. I guess you and Lily are trying to choose

from all these," I said.

"Hi, Skye. Which one do you like? I'm kind of partial to the rosewood and Lily likes it for the living area, but she's leaning toward a natural stone for the kitchen."

"I thought the slate would be easier to care for in the kitchen," Lily said.

"I don't know a lot about flooring, but it makes sense to me."

"I was just about to tell Lily that slate is really no easier to care for than wood. They have finishes that make wood a viable alternative to tile or stone in the kitchen, and I think she'll be happier with the continuity of the wood flooring throughout the space. I know I would."

"Oh. Well, now that you say that, then I think the rosewood is fine," Lily said. "Is there anything else?" Lily began picking up the various slabs of wood and stone flooring.

"Well, we need to decide which wood to use," Chase said. He took the samples from Lily, placed the stone into a stack, and added more wood samples from a bag. "The kitchen cabinets you chose have a rosewood finish, but the wood is white oak. So, we have several choices that will coordinate with them."

Lily gave me a look that screamed for help. I'd never seen her so distressed, so I tried to pay attention and help move the selection process along.

"So, what are the choices?" I asked Chase.

Chase proceeded to tell us all about how different woods take different stains and the advantages and disadvantages of matching the wood type with the stain or choosing something that would contrast with the cabinets.

"Of course, a lot of people are going with laminate these days. It's not wood and it's not my first choice, but it's easy to take care of and they've really improved the product the past few years, so it looks much more like real wood than it used to." Chase added some sample boards of laminate flooring to the selection.

"I like wood," Lily said.

"I'd have to agree. I think the laminate lacks a certain depth that you get with the real wood." I wanted to help Lily out by being there for her, but I also didn't want her to end up with something she didn't love. I walked around the samples.

"This looks like a perfect match for the cabinets," I said. "I like the idea of the flooring and the cabinets matching. What do you think, Lily?"

"I like it, too. We'll go with that one. Excuse me, I need to check on something." Lily raced out of the room. I was a little stunned at her abrupt departure, but Chase didn't seem to notice.

"I'm glad you agree. I really wanted her to go with the continuous flooring rather than the stone for the kitchen. I think she'll be happy she did."

"Yeah, I think so, too." I watched Chase pick up the samples and tuck them into three big brown shopping bags.

"I kind of expected this decision to be made by committee." Chase grinned.

"Committee?"

"You, your mom, Bobbi Jo, and Lily," he explained. "I got the impression you all hang out here at Bobbi Jo's house."

"We do hang out here a lot, but Bobbi Jo and my mother went shopping."

Chase nodded and glanced at the stairs Lily had disappeared up. "She seems really stressed out."

"She is stressed out. It's been a difficult time for her. I think she just needs things to be as normal as possible right now. You know, no new developments in her life."

"Oh, yeah. You're probably right. I hope everything turns out good for her."

"I'm sure it will. It looks like Lily might be a while. Did you need anything else from her?"

"No, not at all. I'll be on my way. Nice to see you again." Chase picked up his shopping bags and carried them out to his beat-up truck. Moments later, Lily reappeared.

"Is he gone?"

"Yes, he's gone. Lily, you've got to get a grip about this. I might not always be available to run over here."

"I know. And I'm really grateful that you could do it

this time." Lily sank onto one of the dining room chairs. "What did you think? I mean about what he said?"

"The flooring? I agreed with you. You're getting the white oak with the rosewood stain. You're all right with that, right?"

"Yes. I guess. At this point, flooring is the last thing on my mind. What do you think he meant when he said I seemed stressed out?"

"I think he's been paying attention. You are really stressed out. That's why I tried to gently let him know you probably don't need any more stress in your life right now."

"Thank you. I swear, this is driving me nuts. Why can't I just stand up and say what I want?"

Yeah, I was really the one to answer that question. I pulled a chair up next to hers and put an arm around her shoulders. I didn't really have to say anything. And I didn't really have anything to say. It was enough to just be there for her. But I couldn't hang out forever. I still had a shoot to attend to.

"I need to go. Are you going to be all right?"

"I'm going to be fine." Lily patted my hand. "I don't know what I'd do without you."

"You don't have to," I assured her.

I left Lily fussing about in the kitchen, calm in the knowledge that I would be there for her. And that her encounter with Chase was ended—at least for today. And that she had another couple of hours before Bobbi Jo and my mother returned. I drove to the arena building hoping all the dogs had really recovered from their illness.

The shoot for today would begin with our March layout, which had a theme of spring cleaning. The layout called for assorted cleaning supplies in bright colors and two dogs. No cats, which was a relief. I arrived at the arena building before anyone else. I let myself in, turned on the lights, and began setting up my equipment. Before I was finished, Lionel arrived with the props and started setting up the shot.

"Lionel, you never told me you had a relationship with Frank," I said as he placed a red bucket on the set.

"I knew him but I wouldn't call it a relationship. What about it?" He shrugged, but I could tell he was tense.

"Was there any reason you didn't mention it?"

"Not really. I mean, I didn't like the guy. He'd promised me that puppy, then raised the price so much I couldn't afford it."

"I heard that. What kind of puppy was it?"

"She was a malamute. I've always wanted a dog I could go hiking with. A friend brought me over to Frank's. Well, here, actually. Anyway, he had a litter that was just a couple of weeks old. One of them marched right up to me and licked my hand." He shrugged again and grinned. "I guess it was love at first lick. Anyway, Frank agreed to sell her to me for a couple hundred dollars."

"And then he changed his mind?" I asked.

"Yeah. Seems the mother dog won a championship a few weeks later and he decided the puppies were worth more. He wanted a thousand dollars for Maggie."

"Maggie?"

"That's what I named her. I'd come by several times a week and play with her. Frank had a rule about not letting the puppies go until they were three months old. Something about them needing to be with their litter-mates in order to socialize."

"When did he raise the price?"

"About a week before I was going to take her home. I mean, I was so attached to her by then. And she loved me, too. But how was I going to come up with that kind of money?"

"I'm sorry. It must have been hard."

"That's not even the worst of it. I borrowed the extra money from a couple of friends, but when I showed up to pick her up, he'd already sold her to a breeder."

"Oh."

"Yeah. Pissed me off."

"When did all this happen?"

"About six months ago. Why?"

"Lionel, did Scott tell you that you're a suspect in Frank's murder?"

"Yeah, he told me. I mean, I was here the day he was killed. And it's not like I was in someone's sight all the time. I guess he figures I could have done it."

I nodded, unsure what to say.

"I didn't kill him. You know that, right?"

"Of course, I know that." But did I, really? Lionel and I had worked together on several shoots, but I didn't know anything about him personally. Still, he'd always been even-tempered and easy to work with. I didn't see anything in his personality that made me think he could ever kill someone. "The set looks great. Do you know which dogs we're using today?"

"Peter said we're using Spot and Lady Peaches. Dalmatian and a Cocker Spaniel."

"Black and white. That will look great with all the color."

Lionel had arranged the red mop bucket along with a rag mop with a bright yellow handle, a bright green oversized sponge, and a purple-handled scrub brush in the center of the set, which was covered with a bright pink sheet functioning as seamless.

"Skye? You here?" Peter called from the doorway.

"Over here." I waved at him to indicate our location.

"We've got a problem."

"Another one?" I asked. Was there no end to the problems on this shoot? There was a part of me that still blamed the accumulation of problems with the shoot on Connie and the Rastafarian who had lured her into some island-voodoo marriage. It was entirely unreasonable of me, but I didn't care.

"Spot is sick. I think he got into some trash last night. Or maybe a dead animal. Anyway, he can't make it. Can you do the shoot with just Lady Peaches?" Peter paused to remove the leash from Captain's collar, then did the same with the other two dogs with him. "I brought Lady Peaches, of course, and I thought Herman could stand in for Spot."

I watched the three dogs stand quietly while he did that, then they all settled down on either side of him. My shot could work with only one dog, but it wouldn't be as visually interesting, and I was sorry to lose the black and white element that Spot, the Dalmatian, and Lady Peaches, the black cocker spaniel, would bring to the shot. Herman was a black and tan German shepherd. A handsome dog, by anyone's standards, but hardly black and white.

But what about Captain? He was white, which fit in with the color scheme. And I really liked the way his dreadlocks mimicked the strands of the rag mop we were using. I doubted Frank would have approved, but then Frank wasn't here to object, was he?

"Can we use Captain?" I asked.

Peter considered my proposal for a moment and nodded. "I guess so. He's not really trained for acting, but he's obedient. I could probably get him to do what you need him to."

"Great. Lionel, let's get the shot set up." I directed my stylist to tie the bright blue bandana around Lady Peaches's glossy black head, then had Peter position her on the set next to the red bucket and the green sponge. She was small for a cocker spaniel and seemed to know how pretty she was, posing nicely while Peter got Captain up onto the set and settled next to the mop. I started clicking off shots, unsure how long Captain would put up with our foolishness. I had a good number of shots when Captain got restless. I took a few more for good measure, then Captain decided to pick up the mop by the bright yellow handle. Lady Peaches must have sensed his restlessness and started to squirm. Her left foot came up and then landed squarely on the oversized green sponge that had been sitting in a puddle of soapy water.

I just barely managed to get a couple of shots of it before they started playing and romping around on the tiny set. I kept clicking off shots until Peter ran over and got them both under control.

"Did you want to try again?" Peter's voice sounded upbeat and cooperative, but I could tell from the look on his face that he figured the dogs had done the best they could and I probably wouldn't get much more from them.

"No problem. I've got what I need." I just hoped those last few shots turned out as good as I wanted.

Peter clipped leashes on the dogs, which somehow seemed to settle them down. He led them off the set and over to where Herman lay on the floor looking morose because he hadn't been chosen. I couldn't help feeling sorry for him. And a little guilty that I'd chosen Captain over him.

Lionel got busy clearing the set while I leafed through the layouts. We were shooting photographs for an eighteen-month calendar, so six of the months required two shots. And they had to be different. We'd already done a Thanksgiving shot for November, but I had another one that was based on Veteran's Day. The layout called for a dog in an army hat. I glanced at the German shepherd.

"Peter, could Herman pose for this shot?"

Peter left the dogs and joined me at the table where I'd spread out the layouts. He looked at the layout for a moment.

"Sure, but the dog in the picture is small. Herman is kind of big."

"Lionel, what do you have for the Veteran's Day shot?"

"You mean props?" Lionel asked. I nodded. "I haven't finished them yet. I have an army hat and a rifle, but I was going to cut the hat down to fit the dog and try to find a smaller gun. Other than that, I've got everything here."

"Perfect. See if the hat will fit on Herman." I let Peter and Lionel take care of that while I set up my lights for the shot.

The hat was a perfect fit and the rifle would work. Lionel set about draping the large flag in the background, and Peter took the dogs out for a potty break while we finished up. When he came back, Herman walked up the ramp onto the set and stood perfectly still while Lionel placed the hat on his head and propped the rifle beside him. I got my shots in record time, thanks to Herman's stalwart professionalism.

"That's it for the day," I announced. I was elated that the shots had gone so well. Both of them promised to be excellent and we were finished early. Lionel packed up the props and I packed away my cameras.

"Lionel, we're shooting the exotic pets tomorrow." I walked to the door and turned back. "See you at nine?"

Lionel waved his agreement, and Peter walked the dogs back to the kennel. I tucked my cameras into the rear of the Escape and headed home, hoping I could sneak in a quick nap before I called my mother. Last night had been wonderful but tiring. And I was emotionally worn out from thinking about who might have murdered Frank. It was bad enough that Peter was a suspect, and I really didn't think he killed Frank but I couldn't seem to convince Scott to see my reasoning. Now Lionel was a suspect and that was even more distressing. I'd worked with Lionel on numerous shoots and I didn't think there was a bad bone in his body. Of course, he'd been angry about Frank not selling him the dog, but he wouldn't kill because of it. But, again, Scott only wanted to look at the facts and ignore the nature of the people involved.

I still thought there were a lot of better suspects. Like Taylor Hudson. He'd admitted that all the neighbors hated Frank. He'd even said he wasn't sorry Frank was dead and he was surprised no one had killed him before. That seemed pretty strong to me. And there was Arnie. He obviously suspected Irene of having an affair with Frank. And the way she was always flirting with Scott led me to think that Arnie might have good reason to be suspicious of his big blond wife. Arnie was certainly strong enough to have strangled Frank. Probably without even breaking a sweat. But I didn't seem to have any influence with Scott in the matter of viable suspects. Just thinking about it made me even more tired and I pressed my foot on the accelerator thinking that the sooner I got home, the sooner I could have that nap.

I turned the corner and pulled into a parking space in front of my building. I'd be leaving well before it became a no-parking zone at seven, so there was no point in parking in the garage. I got out and headed for the door eager to get started on that nap when I heard my name. I turned to see Arnie Knutson across the street. It wasn't looking good for the nap.

CHAPTER NINE

What was Arnie Knutson doing in front of my building? I flashed on the fact that he'd seen me in my thong and bra last night and cringed. But it had only been a nanosecond and his face hadn't registered any emotion at the time. Of course, at the time, he was angry with his wife.

"Sorry to drop by like this, but I didn't have your phone number."

"But you have my address?" I asked.

Arnie ducked his head and shuffled from one foot to the other. "You're listed."

"With my phone number," I said.

"Sorry. I just wanted to speak with you in person. I don't really like phones. You can't tell what someone's thinking if you can't see their face."

"What did you want to speak about?"

"Irene and your boyfriend."

I waited for him to continue because, really, what could I say? That although I thought his wife was more than capable of adultery, I had complete faith in Scott?

"First of all, I'm sorry I busted in on you guys last night. It's just that I was afraid Irene was having another affair."

"If she is, I'm pretty certain it's not with Scott," I said.

"Yeah, probably not. But I know something's been going on. She's always going somewhere, and then she's not where she told me she was going."

"You've followed her?" I wasn't surprised that a spouse who suspected something was going on would follow the other one, but somehow it came across as creepy and scary.

"Of course I follow her. I have to. How else would I know she's cheating?"

"But maybe she isn't cheating on you. Maybe she had a good reason for not being where you expected her to be."

"No." Arnie shook his head. "It's happened too often."

"I see." I didn't, but what was I going to say? I still wasn't sure why Arnie wanted to talk to me. It seemed to be about more than merely apologizing for last night.

"I guess I deserve it, though. When I met Irene she was married. We had an affair for two years until her husband found out."

"So, you're afraid she'll do the same thing again?"

"I'm sure of it. I mean, it's in her nature, right? If she cheated on her first husband, what's to make her not cheat on me?"

"I don't know, but if you're married to someone, shouldn't you trust her? Or at least try to?"

"I can't. I know she'll cheat eventually. It's just going to kill me when it happens. I love her more than anything. I'd do anything to keep her from going to someone else."

I thought he should consider counseling. The man certainly needed professional help as far as I was concerned. Arnie looked like he was about to break down and cry. I didn't need this. I didn't want to be his therapist or even a shoulder for him to cry on. I didn't want to have anything to do with him.

"I'm not sure what to say."

"I know. I shouldn't have come here. Just keep an eye on your boyfriend. Irene can be very determined when she wants something. Or someone."

"I don't think I need to worry about Scott."

"It's not him. Worry about her." Arnie turned and opened his car door, then fished a card from his pocket. "Call me if anything happens."

I took the card and stared at him as he pulled away. Call him if anything happens? What did he mean by that? Did he expect me to call him every time Scott and Irene talked? I didn't want to be a part of his paranoia, and it bothered me that he'd found me so easily. I hadn't thought about having my phone number and address unlisted when I'd moved in, but I was going to arrange for that immediately.

My cell phone rang and I looked at the display. I didn't recognize the number but flipped it open and said hello.

"Skye Donovan?" a man's voice asked.

"Speaking."

"This is Harold Vanderbilt. I'm the attorney handling Frank Johnson's estate."

"Hello, Mr. Vanderbilt. What can I do for you?"

"Mr. Johnson's son, David, has decided to sell the property and wants to put it on the market as soon as possible. I understand you're doing some kind of photography in the arena building?"

"Yes, I'm shooting photographs for a calendar. Mr. Johnson was supplying the dogs for the photography and offered to let us use the arena building for the shoot."

"I see. Do you know how long it will take? My client wants to be able to show the property, including the arena building, to prospective buyers."

"I see. I still have a few more shots to get and it's difficult to say how long that might take. I should be able to wrap everything up some time next week."

"That would be wonderful. My client has arranged to show the property the following weekend, so if you could be finished by Wednesday, that would give him a couple of days to get everything in order."

"Wednesday? I guess I could do that." Could I? My mind raced through the shots we still had left. It would be tight, but I could do it. Besides, this gave me a deadline. I might have to work hard to keep it, but at least by Wednesday it would be done.

"Thank you for being so cooperative. I'll let my client know."

I regretfully gave up on my idea of a nap and headed upstairs to change clothes. My mother had been here for almost a week and I'd hardly seen her or spent any time with her. I took the elevator up to my loft. Sheridan wasn't home yet, so I wrote her a message on a sticky note that I was going to Bobbi Jo's for dinner and to see my mother. I might have indicated that it wouldn't hurt her to come over and spend some time with her grandmother. Hopefully, she'd come home and see it rather than spend the night with her new tattooed, motorcycle-riding, older boyfriend who might have a drinking problem. Not that she'd spent the night with him yet. And I knew that she could go to bed with him during the day and still be home at night. It was just the idea of my baby girl staying out all night. She hadn't done it yet and I wasn't at all sure I was ready for it. She was only eighteen years old. Still a baby in my mind. And in my heart.

I stuck the note to the refrigerator where I was sure she would see it—if she came home—and went to the bedroom to change clothes. I didn't need my mother commenting on the amount of dog hair that clung to my pants and shirt. The unusually warm weather we'd been having had disappeared so I dressed in khaki pants and a T-shirt and pulled an oversized flannel shirt on. An outfit that even my mother couldn't object to. I grabbed a bottle of wine from the fridge and headed out the door.

My cell phone rang as soon as I got in the car. I looked at the display. Bobbi Jo's cell phone number. I flipped open the phone.

"I'm on my way now. Should be there in about twenty minutes," I said.

"No. Don't go to the house. I'm in labor. Meet us at the hospital."

Bobbi Jo's voice was rushed and a little breathless. Still, I wondered if it was really labor or just Braxton-Hicks contractions again.

"Let me talk to Lily."

"She can't talk. She's driving," Bobbi Jo gasped.

"Is my mother with you? Let me talk to her."

"Hello, Skye," my mother said.

"Mom, do you think Bobbi Jo is really in labor?"

"How would I know that, Skye? She's having contractions and they seem to be pretty hard. I don't understand why you'd question it."

"Well, she thought her water had broken once and it was just that the baby had pushed on her bladder and she'd wet her pants."

"That happens sometimes," Mom said. "But there's no point in taking a chance. Just meet us at the hospital."

"Fine. I'll be there in twenty minutes." I closed the phone and made the next left onto Burnside Street, which would take me to the 405 Highway, and then it was only a few miles to the hospital. I parked in the visitor lot and ran to the entrance. The receptionist directed me to the labor and delivery floor, informing me that Bobbi Jo was in room three-twelve. I took the elevator up to the third floor thinking that if they'd admitted her, surely she was really in labor this time. I was so happy to be there for the birth, but at the same time I was really hungry and I couldn't help thinking about the meal Lily would have prepared. Lily is an excellent cook. Everything from stew to meat loaf turned into a gastronomic delight at her hands. I'd skipped lunch and I'd been looking forward to one of her meals for hours. But Bobbi Jo was having her baby. That was more important than my stomach right then.

I rushed up to the nurses' station and waited impatiently for the nurse to finish his phone conversation to ask directions to room three-twelve. He was speaking at length about whether his child should play a video game or attend to his homework. I tamped down an urgent desire to inform him that it was a no-brainer. Homework first. Always. He continued to talk, trying to convince the child that was the case. Maybe I'd been a mean mommy, but Sheridan knew homework always came first.

"Skye!"

I turned toward the sound of Lily's voice.

"We're over here. The doctor is examining Bobbi Jo, so we had to leave the room."

I abandoned the nurse. He obviously wasn't going to give me the information I wanted, and Lily seemed to know what was happening with Bobbi Jo.

"Is she really in labor?"

Lily shrugged. "Maybe. She was having contractions. How can you tell if they're real or not?" She leaned toward me. "I don't think it was real. She wasn't in enough pain for it to be real." Lily took me by the hand and guided me to a sitting area. "You want some coffee? No telling how long we'll be here."

"Sure. Coffee sounds good." Actually food sounded good, but the cream and sugar counted as food, didn't it? I sat down next to Mom on the green vinyl settee while Lily went off to secure a cup of coffee for me.

"It's her first baby," Mom said.

"I know."

"First time, it's hard to tell if it's really labor or not."

"Do you think it's real?" I asked her.

"Hard to say. She seemed to think it was real."

"But what do you think?"

"Doesn't matter what I think. The doctor will tell us soon." Mom continued to work her crochet hook, pulling yarn from a ball tucked inside her voluminous purse.

"That's beautiful yarn." I reached over to finger the string that extended from her needle.

"It's a blend of lamb's wool and hemp. Hemp is from the marijuana plant, you know. It has a lot more uses than just getting high. Lily took me to a shop on Hawthorne called the Stitching Witch."

"What are you making?" I didn't want to get into a discussion about marijuana with Mom, and I was more than a little surprised that she'd ventured into a shop call the Stitching Witch. Mom had always been ultraconservative when I was growing up but she seemed different now. When had that happened? And how had I not noticed?

"A blanket for the baby. Bobbi Jo has bought so much for the baby, but I thought it would be nice to have something handmade."

"That's nice. You're using blue and green yarn."

"Blue for a boy and the green just in case it's not." Mom stopped crocheting and patted my hand. "It's good that you came. It's important to Bobbi Jo."

"I know."

Lily came back with a paper cup of what could only jokingly be referred to as coffee and handed it to me. I took the cup and sipped, burning my tongue.

"How long has the doctor been in there?" I asked.

"A while," Lily said. "He should be out soon"

As if she'd made a proclamation, the doctor stepped out of a door and walked down the hallway. All three of us stood up.

"Is she okay?" I asked.

"Is she in labor?" Lily asked.

Mom just clutched her half-finished blanket and waited.

"She's not in labor. Just normal Braxton-Hicks contractions. She was asking for an epidural but we didn't give her one," he said.

How many times were we going to have to go through this? And she was asking for an epidural for Braxton-Hicks contractions? At this rate Bobbi Jo would need morphine to get through the actual delivery.

"She's getting dressed now." The doctor looked back at the door as if he might question that statement. "You can go in and give her a hand, if you like."

Yeah, I knew what he meant. The doctor wanted her out of the hospital as soon as possible. He was probably hoping and praying he wasn't on duty when Bobbi Jo really went into labor. The three of us tromped down the hallway and knocked on the door to room three-twelve.

Bobbi Jo had a pair of stretchy pants on, pushed below her swollen belly, her hands behind her back wrestling with the fastener of her maternity bra. She gave up and flopped down onto a stool. "I guess I shouldn't have taken the damn bra off. But I was so sure it was really labor this time. I figured I'd need to have the stupid gown on."

"Here, honey, let me get that for you." Mom lifted the expensive linen maternity top off the hook on the back of the door, walked over, and efficiently fastened the bra for Bobbi Jo, then handed her the top. "How you feeling, dear?"

"Oh, Ruby Lee, I just feel like shit. Pardon my French."

Bobbi Jo had never pardoned her French before. But that's the effect my mother had on people.

"Now, you just don't mind about any of this. Happens to every woman."

Mom shot Lily and I a glance that told us we should not, under any circumstances, deny her statement. Not that either of us were inclined to do so.

"Now, let's get you home and tucked into bed. Unless you're hungry. Maybe you should eat a little something before you go to bed. Might make you sleep better."

"I'm really hungry," Bobbi Jo said. "I can't seem to eat more than a couple of bites and I'm so full I'm about to bust open. Then twenty minutes later, I'm starving again. That's just wrong. Why can't I eat a meal like I used to?"

"Oh, it's the end of the pregnancy. The baby's taking up all the room your stomach used to have. You simply need to eat whenever you're hungry. Don't matter if it's every two hours or every twenty minutes." Mom put an arm around Bobbi Jo's back and guided her toward the door. "Skye, get Bobbi Jo's bag."

I picked up the bag and Lily and I followed them out of the room, down the hall, and took the elevator to the ground floor.

"I'll go get that monster truck of Bobbi Jo's and bring it around," Lily said.

"I'll stay here until you get back, then I'll get my car." I patted Bobbi Jo's shoulder. "Are you okay, Bobbi Jo?"

"Oh, gawd. I guess I am. I'm so embarrassed. I mean, I was so sure it was really labor, you know? I was so afraid the pain was going to get worse and worse that I started screaming for something to make it go away."

"Don't worry about it, Bobbi Jo. It's okay." I patted her shoulder again because I didn't know what else to do.

"Well, don't think I'm not gonna want some drugs when the time comes," Bobbi Jo said. "I mean, this hurt bad enough. I can't even imagine what it's gonna be like when it's real. Oh, my gawd, if I don't get some drugs,

I'll probably die. Then my baby will be an orphan."
Bobbi Jo burst into tears. My mom came to the rescue
with the no-nonsense tone I'd heard all my life.

"Now, Bobbi Jo, you're being silly. You aren't going
to die whether you get drugs or not, and there's no reason
to think you won't get them." Mom put her arm around
Bobbi Jo's shoulder and gave her a one-sided hug. "This
is perfectly normal behavior at the end of a pregnancy.
Your hormones are all out of whack, you've been carrying
around another human being for months, you can't sleep,
can't eat." Mom shook her head. "Let's get you home.
You need something to eat and a good night's sleep."

Bobbi Jo calmed down immediately and let us hand
her into the Escalade Lily had brought around. Mom
decided to ride back to Bobbi Jo's with me. We chatted
mostly about Bobbi Jo, and I was more than a little
relieved that Mom didn't seem to be in the mood to give
me the third degree about my life. When we arrived
at the house, Lily had Bobbi Jo settled on the sofa, and
I heard cooking noises coming from the kitchen. It
was a welcome sound because I was starving. I figured
everyone else was hungry, too, so I left Mom to entertain
Bobbi Jo and went to the kitchen to help Lily.

"It's almost ready." Lily poured soup into a tureen
then pulled a pan of rolls from the oven. "Put these on
the table, and I'll throw the salad together."

I carried the soup tureen to the dining room table

then went back for the basket of warm rolls. The yeasty smell made my mouth water. Lily was quickly chopping vegetables to add to the salad bowl.

"I'll get the butter and salad dressing, then set the table," I said.

"Good. We should be ready to eat in a few minutes."

By the time I had the soup bowls and salad plates on the table, Lily brought in the salad and called everyone in to dinner.

"So, when am I going to meet your beau, Skye?" Mom asked.

I almost dropped my soup spoon. How did she find out about Scott? I cast a suspicious glance at Bobbi Jo. She was trying to look innocent, but I wasn't buying it.

"Well, I don't know that I'd call Scott my beau. We go out occasionally, that's all."

"Is that a euphemism for having sex?" Mom asked.

"Mom!"

"What?"

"Do you have to ask me about my sex life?"

"Evidently, it's the only way I'm going to find out anything. So, are you doing it with this Scott?"

Bobbi Jo burst out laughing, and Lily had a smirk on her face. My mind worked frantically for a reply, but I was at a total loss. The only thing I could think to do was change the subject.

"You'll never believe what happened last night. I was at Scott's apartment and Irene Knutson showed up. Apparently, she wanted to ask Scott some questions about the investigation and decided it couldn't wait."

"Why didn't she just call him instead of showing up at his door?" Bobbi Jo asked.

"He'd turned off his cell phone." I glanced at my mother, who was nodding like she knew what that meant. "Anyway, right after she showed up, her husband, Arnie, arrived. He accused Scott and Irene of having an affair."

Lily laughed. "Sounds like an overly jealous husband. That's something I'd never put up with."

"Those are the kind of men who end up killing their wives or girlfriends because they're so worried they'll lose them," Bobbi Jo said. "Which makes no sense at all. I mean, if you kill someone they're more gone than if they'd simply left you for someone else."

"Well, Arnie also showed up at my loft this afternoon. I think the man is seriously deranged. He was going on about how he just knew Irene was going to have an affair. Evidently, she was married when they met so he figures it's only a matter of time before she does the same thing to him."

"He's probably right," Mom said. "If she did it with him, she'll do it to him."

"I think Arnie might have killed Frank Johnson,"

I said. "I mean he certainly has a motive. He thought Irene was having an affair with Frank, too."

"What does Scott think?" Bobbi Jo asked.

"He's considering it, of course. Along with other people who I really don't think could or would have killed Frank. He still thinks Peter is a suspect, but Peter didn't have a reason to kill Frank. And he's investigating my stylist because Frank agreed to sell him a dog, then raised the price so much that he couldn't afford to buy her."

"This Frank sounds like a real asshole," Mom said.

I was a little surprised by Mom's language lately. When I was growing up, she'd never let words like *asshole* or *sex* slip out even accidentally. She'd changed after my dad passed away several years ago. When I'd told her Craig and I were getting a divorce because he was gay, she'd wanted to know all the details. I didn't even know the details, nor did I want to.

"Well, Scott must have his reasons for suspecting those people," Mom continued.

"Yes, of course he does. I only wish he'd listen to reason some times," I said.

"Skye, you're not insinuating yourself into his investigation, are you?" she asked.

"No, of course not. But I have an opinion and I don't think it would hurt him to listen to me."

"Sounds to me like you're trying to tell him how to do his job. Men don't like that, you know."

I really didn't want relationship advice from my mother. Especially when she wasn't on my side. But I knew part of this was because she hadn't met Scott. Once she met him, she'd relax and stop asking me questions and telling me what to do. At least I hoped so. In any case, I wouldn't get any relief until she met him, and setting that up would distract her from asking me questions.

"Would you like to have dinner with us this weekend?" I asked. "We can go out or I can cook at home. Whichever you want."

"And Scott will be there?" Mom asked.

"Yes, Mom. Scott will be there. Just promise me you won't start asking him questions about our sex life."

"Oh, so you *are* having sex with him," Mom said.

CHAPTER TEN

The next day I tried to concentrate on work and forget about the impending dinner with my mother and Scott. We would be shooting the December and January layouts in the morning and then the exotic pets at the end of the day. January called for the party hats that I'd promised Lionel I'd help him with and had totally forgotten about. It also called for dogs and cats together. I wasn't really looking forward to it and hoped to avoid any cat and dog fights this time. The December layout involved a Santa Claus and a lot of dogs. I'd scheduled our human model who would play Santa Claus to arrive at eleven so I'd have two hours to get the New Year's Eve party shot completed. I didn't think I could take more than two hours of the dogs and cats together anyway.

"Hi, Skye," Peter called from the door of the arena building. "We're shooting the party today, right? And Santa Claus?"

LIZ WOLFE

"Right. Thanks for accommodating our schedule. I know you usually need to have your afternoons free."

"No problem. I thought we'd use Geoffrey, Sammy, and Latasha. They're all really good with cats, so hopefully we won't have a problem."

"Great." I finished setting up the lights and walked over to Lionel's worktable, where he was still assembling party hats.

"You need some help?" I asked.

"Thanks, but I've got it handled." Lionel grinned at me. "I knew it was too good to be true that you'd help."

"I'm really sorry. I've just been so busy."

"It's okay. I don't mind. The hats turned out to be easier than I'd thought they would be. I don't know how easy it'll be to get them on the cats, though."

As if on cue, Miss Kitty and her son walked into the building. Jerry carried a large crate that contained two cats. He walked the crate over to a spot far away from the dog crates and knelt down in front of it. He put his fingers through the wires and petted the cats, speaking softly to them. Miss Kitty watched for a moment, then made her way over to me.

"Hello, Skye, how are you today?"

"I'm fine, Miss Kitty."

She glanced at the dogs. "I hope we won't have a problem with the dogs today."

"I want to thank you for trying this again. I know the last time must have been upsetting for you."

"Oh, it was. It was. But this time, I've brought two cats that have been around dogs, so as long as the dogs behave themselves, we should be fine."

"How have you been?" It seemed polite to ask and I hoped it would divert her attention from the dogs.

"As well as can be expected, I suppose." She shook her head. "Oh, I can't complain. A little tired, but I think that's to be expected at my age. And, sometimes, it's difficult with Jerry, you know."

"Really?"

"Well, he's not difficult, of course. Bless his little heart, he does anything I tell him to."

Yeah, I'd noticed that. I was still wondering how far it might go.

"But he's involved in the Special Olympics. Oh, it's a wonderful program and he loves it so much. But it means a lot of running around for me. I'm always taking him to some event or promotion."

"I'm glad he has something he loves so much," I said. "What does he do with the Special Olympics?"

"Well, he's won a lot of regional events. He's really kind of a star for them. And that means they like to have him go to promotional events. Why, we were at one shortly before the last shoot we did with you." Miss Kitty leaned toward me and lowered her voice. "Frankly, I think that was part of the problem. You know, with him grabbing the dog that day. Jerry was still a bit exhausted from the event, and I don't think he was as considerate as he usually is. He didn't even seem to have his mind on the cats, and he's usually so attentive to them."

"Oh, what event was it?" I asked.

"It was a luncheon at the Park Hotel, in Eugene. We drove down the morning of the luncheon and stayed overnight to visit with my sister and her family. Then we drove back the morning of the shoot. He really enjoyed himself. They gave him a medal for having competed in so many events. He has a lot of medals. We display them in a glass case in the living room. But the trip was tiring for him."

"I'm glad he had such a good time." That meant Miss Kitty and Jerry would have been out of town when Frank was killed. So much for my theory that Miss Kitty instructed her son to strangle Frank. I was more than a little embarrassed I'd ever even considered the possibility and very happy I hadn't mentioned it to Scott.

"Now, I know we'd agreed on three cats for this, but I decided it would be better if I only brought two. That way, Jerry and I can each handle one so we don't have a problem with those dogs." Miss Kitty looked over at Jerry and nodded at the way he was calming the cats.

"I'm sure two cats will be fine." I wasn't sure Miss Kitty even heard me because she'd turned away to stride across the arena floor to wrap Peter in a warm hug. I checked the layout again and helped Lionel carry the props to the set. We sprinkled glittery confetti on the floor and strung streamers so they would hang just above the largest dog's head. I'd chosen a black sheet for the background and set the lights so it would bounce off the silver and gold streamers. Lionel set up a small table with two champagne flutes and a champagne bottle in a silver bucket.

"Skye, I think it might be best if we get the dogs in place on the set first. Then Miss Kitty and Jerry can put the cats in place right before you take the photograph."

"Good idea, Peter." I would have agreed to anything that might make the shot go smoothly. Peter brought the dogs out of their kennel crates and guided them up the ramp to the set. Lionel placed the party hats on the dogs and sprinkled more confetti on them. The dogs were real troupers and stood still through it all.

"You think one of the dogs would hold this in their mouth?" Lionel asked Peter. He held out a noisemaker he'd altered so it looked permanently inflated.

"Sure. I'll put it in Latasha's mouth right before the shot. Are you ready, Miss Kitty?"

Miss Kitty and Jerry each picked up a cat and placed one of the tiny party hats on their heads. The cats appeared to be pretty calm about everything. So far. I took my place behind the camera, adjusted the focus, and gave the signal to begin.

Miss Kitty and Jerry placed the cats on the set in between the dogs, and I clicked off shots as fast as I could. To my amazement one of the cats leaned closer to Sammy and rubbed her cheek against his shoulder. It was a perfect shot. Then the cat reached up and smacked Sammy with her paw. Sammy yelped. Latasha barked, which upset Geoffrey, and he snapped at her. Miss Kitty grabbed the cat and Jerry scooped up the other cat and they put them back in the crate. I supposed the shot was over. Hopefully, I'd gotten enough for Connie to work with. Lionel's cell phone chirped and he pulled it out of his pocket and walked over to the prop table. Miss Kitty got the cats settled and Peter returned the dogs to their crates.

"Bad news, Skye," Lionel called from his worktable.

"What?"

"Santa Claus can't make it. He's in the hospital with a heart attack."

"Can't they send another model?" I asked. I really needed to get these shots done. Now that Frank's son had put the property on the market, we had to be done by next Wednesday. I doubted my Santa model would be out of the hospital by then.

"Not one who looks like Santa Claus."

Connie had been very specific that she didn't want a fake-looking Santa. No shiny fake beard and hair, no pillow to make him look chubby. She insisted on the real thing. There simply weren't that many older, white-haired, chubby models available in Portland. I silently cursed Connie for falling in love on her vacation and leaving me to handle this shoot. Then I called her office.

"Hi, Karen? Skye Donovan. We've run into a problem with the layouts for the Pet Place calendar." I explained the situation and asked if there was anyone who could provide a different layout I could shoot from. I was pleasantly surprised when she said she'd have one of the layout artists come out and art direct a shot on the spot. I almost jumped with glee when she said he'd be there in half an hour.

"Lionel, Karen is sending a layout artist over to art direct a different Christmas shot. What kind of props do you have that we can use?"

Lionel looked around. "I've got a couple of boxes wrapped in Christmas paper, some evergreen garland, and red velvet bows. A couple of strings of bells. And a useless Santa Claus suit."

"I could get you a tree," Peter offered.

"A Christmas tree?" I asked.

"Fully decorated." Peter nodded. "Frank had a fake tree professionally decorated, then he covered and stored it each year. You want to take a look at it?"

"Absolutely." I wasn't holding out a lot of hope that the tree would be useful, but I was desperate. I needed as many props as I could get my hands on. I followed Peter out of the arena building and across the lawn to the house. He opened the door with a key and led me down a back hallway.

It felt a little weird to be in the house where we'd found Frank's body. I knew it was a silly reaction, but it was there anyway. Peter didn't appear to be bothered by it, which also seemed a little creepy. At the end of the hallway he opened a door with another key. The room was stuffed full of items draped in dust sheets. He walked to the rear of the room and carefully lifted a sheet from a conical object.

The tree was beautiful. A perfect Christmas tree decorated with old-fashioned ornaments interspersed with red velvet bows tied to the tips of the branches. The kind of tree you saw pictures of in decorator magazines.

"It's got lights, too," Peter said. "I don't know how that would work with the photography, though."

"I love it. I don't know if we'll be able to use it. That will be up to the layout artist. But it's really very lovely."

"Is there anything else you could use?" Peter asked. "I think Frank had some candle holders and some garland."

"We have garland, and I don't want to take a chance with candles around the animals." I stood back and sized up the tree. It had to be eight or nine feet tall and almost that wide. "How do we get the tree to the arena building?"

"It's on wheels," Peter said. He reached a hand into the tree and pulled it from its corner. The tree moved easily.

"That's good for in here, but I don't think it's going to roll over the ground."

"I can take it the long way around. There's a sidewalk that goes from the house to the arena."

"Perfect. Do you need help?"

"Nope. You go back and wait for your artist. It'll take me a while to get the tree there."

I was so happy, I could have kissed him. Of course, I didn't. I was dating Scott, after all. Great. That made me think about the dinner I'd promised Mom. I'd better call Scott and get his agreement. I pulled my cell phone from one of my many pockets and punched in his speed dial number.

"Hey, gorgeous."

My heart skipped a beat. You have to love a man who answers the phone like that when he knows you're calling.

"My mother wants to meet you. I was thinking dinner Saturday night. Are you free?"

"For you, I'm always free. Well, reasonably, anyway. Do you want to go out, or should we cook something at home?"

I wasn't sure if he meant my home or his. But it was a moot point. I'd already decided going out would be better. If I cooked, that would leave Mom with entirely too much time with Scott alone. If Scott cooked, then Mom would complain she hadn't really had any time with him at all. But at a restaurant, they would have plenty of time together, and I'd be right there to monitor the conversation. Plus, I wouldn't have to cook. Sounded like a win-win situation to me.

"I was thinking we could go to Hurlihy's Steak and Brew."

"Sounds good to me. Should I pick you up or meet you there?"

"Why don't you meet us there? Mom is staying at Bobbi Jo's, so I'll pick her up. Is seven all right with you?"

"Perfect. I can't wait to meet the mother who raised such an incredible woman."

I think I actually blushed. Scott was being very nice to me. Attentive, generous, compromising. All of the things I really loved about him. But we still hadn't hashed out where our relationship was going. Or how fast it should get there. It wasn't that I didn't want to marry Scott, or even live with him. I simply needed a little more time to stretch my wings as a single woman. I'd gone from living with my parents to living with my husband, so I'd never had the experience of being completely on my own. And I was thoroughly enjoying it. With Sheridan in college, I wasn't expected to do any cooking or cleaning for anyone unless I wanted to. I had only myself to take care of, and it was an exhilarating experience.

"Flattery will get you everywhere," I said.

"I'm counting on it. See you tomorrow night. And I'll be on my best behavior." Scott made a smooching sound and hung up. I was hoping my mother would be on her best behavior, too. But I didn't have time to dwell on the possibilities right at the moment.

The door to the arena building opened, and I turned to greet the layout artist Karen had sent over.

"Hi, Skye. I didn't know you were a photographer until Karen told me. Sheridan never mentioned it."

I'm pretty sure my mouth was hanging open as I started at Zack, Sheridan's boyfriend. It wasn't that there was anything wrong with him being a layout artist, I just hadn't expected it. Sheridan hadn't told me much about him and had resisted my gentle probing for information. Evidently, she wasn't saying much to Zack about me, either. Then I remembered she'd told him I was her roommate. Which I suppose was accurate in a way. We did live together. And technically she was an adult. Still, she was my baby girl and it rankled that she didn't want him to know I was her mother. It wasn't like I was a monster or anything. Was I?

Then it occurred to me that she might want to appear older and more mature than her eighteen years. I wondered if Zack even knew her age—her *real* age, that is. By referring to me as her roommate, it appeared she was more independent than an eighteen-year-old who still lived with her mother. I could deal with that. I remembered how much I'd wanted to be treated like an adult at eighteen.

"Oh, hi, Zack. I didn't know you were an artist, either. Sorry to drag you away from work, but I need some help with this shot. Did Karen explain what's going on with it?"

"Nope. She just said to come out and art direct a shot."

"Well, Connie had done this layout." I pulled her original layout from the stack and placed it on top.

"Nice," Zack said. "The traditional Christmas scene is always a winner."

"Yes, but Connie insisted on someone who really looked like Santa. No fake beards or hair, no pillows to make him look chubby. We found a model who was perfect, but he's in the hospital now and I only have a few more days to get this shoot wrapped up."

"Yeah, I heard you'd had a few problems."

That was an understatement. Zack looked over the props Lionel had assembled, then set his layout pad on the table and pulled some markers from his pocket.

"Oh, we have another prop. A big Christmas tree. Peter should have it here soon."

"Good, I can work that in." Zack made some swift strokes on the pad. "How big is the tree?"

"Probably eight feet or more," I said.

Zack pulled more colored markers out and continued drawing. After a few minutes, he stood back and pointed at the pad. "Will that work?"

He'd drawn a big Christmas tree with two big dogs in front and a small dog sitting inside a box covered in holiday wrapping paper. The big dogs had enormous red ribbons around their necks. Scattered about in front of the dogs were a variety of doggie Christmas gifts that the Pet Place sold.

"It's perfect." I was impressed with Zack's ability to size up the situation and the props and put it all together in a matter of moments. "I'll have Lionel set it up."

Zack and I helped Lionel carry the props to the set, and the three men managed to get the giant Christmas tree up on the platform. Peter brought in several dogs for Zack and me to choose from.

"I like the Akita and the golden Lab," Zack said.

"How about the Yorkshire Terrier and the miniature Dachshund in gift boxes?" I asked.

"That'll work," Zack agreed. "No, wait. Look at the Chihuahua." He pointed to the tiny dog standing behind two of the larger ones. One ear stood up and the other bent a little halfway down. His brown eyes were bright and curious. I had to smile at him. He wagged his tail and did a little dance. I laughed and knelt down to get a better look at him, and he bolted straight to me and jumped. Before I knew it I was holding him, and he was licking my nose.

"That's Speedway," Peter said. "A friend of mine saw him get hit by a car out by the Portland Speedway and rushed him to the Humane Society. They had to remove his jugular." Peter pointed to a faint scar that ran down the side of the little dog's neck. "I'm amazed they were able to save him. Doesn't take long for a little dog like that to bleed out."

Speedway seemed to want to stay with me while Peter put the other dogs in their kennel crates and got the four we'd chosen up on the platform. Lionel attached the big red velvet bows to the dogs' collars and placed the products around them. I handed Speedway to Lionel to place in one of the open gift boxes, checked the shot, adjusted the lights, and started clicking away. Everything went smoothly, and we were finished in no time.

"I really appreciate you coming out to help with this," I said to Zack. "It made my life a lot easier." I removed the lens from my camera and packed it into the case.

"No problem," Zack said. "I guess I should get back to the office. I'll see you tonight, probably. I'm picking Sheridan up at seven."

"You're going out again?" I could have bitten my tongue. I didn't want to sound like I was prying and I knew that's exactly what it sounded like. Because that's exactly what I was doing.

"Is that a problem?" Zack asked.

"No, of course not. I mean, why would it be a problem?"

Zack grinned. "Relax, Skye. Sheridan is just helping me with my singing. We aren't actually dating."

"Your singing?"

"I'm going to audition for *American Idol* this year. I sing with a rock band and that's about all the singing I've ever done. I wanted Sheridan to help me with some other types of songs. You know, like country and motown and blues."

"I see."

"And I know you're her mother even though she introduces you as her roommate."

"You do?"

"The resemblance is unmistakable." Zack grinned. "And I know Sheridan's only eighteen. I like her a lot but only as a friend."

I was so relieved I wanted to hug him. Suddenly, his buzzed head and tattoos didn't appear to be threatening at all. Now that he wasn't interested in my baby.

I changed the film in my camera, then helped Lionel pack up some of the props we'd used. "I know we don't usually shoot on the weekends, but I'd like to work to-morrow if you're available."

"Sure. The sooner we get this done, the better." Lionel closed the box and picked up a brush to clean the dog and cat hair from the set. "It's been fun working with the dogs, but I'll be happy when it's over. The whole murder thing was a total bummer."

He was right. It was a bummer. Probably more so for him since he was one of the suspects. I had to wonder why Scott hadn't told me about Lionel being a suspect. Probably he was reluctant to upset me.

"I'll make sure Peter can make it. I guess we need to get ready for the exotic shot now." I tried to sup-press a shudder. The parrot didn't bother me, but the iguana and the snake gave me the heebie-jeebies. Lionel got busy with the jungle foliage for the background and I checked the lighting until Peter came back from return-ing the dogs to the kennel.

"Speedway cried when I put him back in the ken-nel," Peter said.

"He's a sweetheart. If I was going to have a dog, it would be one like him."

"He's available if you're interested."

"Doesn't he belong to K-9 Stars?"

"Well, not technically. I took him in because my friend who rescued him couldn't have a dog at his apart-ment. The intention was to find him a good home. I just kept him here because I already have two dogs."

"I'm not in the market for a dog." I shook my head. "He's adorable, but I don't have the time and energy to devote to an animal right now."

"I understand. I'm not trying to pressure you. It looked like you got some good shots," he said.

"I think so, too. Could you possibly work tomorrow? Frank's son wants me out of here by Wednesday, and I'm more than a little worried about getting all the shots finished by then."

"Yes, his lawyer called me with that news, too. He said I need to have the dogs all moved as soon as possible."

"I hadn't thought about that. What are you going to do with them?"

"I have a friend with a kennel. She's agreed to keep them for a while. Until I decide what's going to happen to them."

"So, you aren't going to continue with K-9 Stars as a business?"

"I haven't decided yet. Frank had booked some of the animals, and I'll certainly honor those contracts. Maybe by then I'll come up with a good idea. But in answer to your question, sure, I can work tomorrow. I don't have anything planned."

"Great. How about nine? We should be able to get several shots done in a few hours and that will only leave a few for Monday. Then if any of the photos aren't working, I can reshoot them on Tuesday."

Peter nodded. "How late do you think we'll be tomorrow?"

"Not past four. I'm having dinner with Scott, so I'll want some time to clean up."

"Detective Madison? I didn't know you two were an item," Peter said.

"It's been off and on."

"Well, put in a good word for me, okay?" Peter laughed.

I tried to laugh with him, but I was still a little concerned about him being a suspect. What if Scott didn't find anyone better? Would he arrest Peter? Or Lionel? See, this was why it was so hard to stay out of Scott's work. If it involved my friends, I wanted to know what was happening. And I thought I had a right to give him my opinion, too.

The snake and lizard handler and the bird woman arrived right on schedule. Lionel had created a credible-looking jungle scene with lots of green foliage and a few well-placed orchids along with a bamboo frame for the parrot to perch on and a couple of big fake boulders. He'd even fashioned a mini-waterfall.

"How did you do the waterfall?" I asked. "It looks great."

Lionel picked up a five-gallon bucket the water had

cascaded into and carried it around to the back of the set, then replaced it with an identical empty bucket.

"I got the idea from a water feature I saw in a home and garden store. The setup was right, but I needed a faster flow of water, so I just dump the water from a full bucket onto the top, and it flows down to the empty bucket."

"Very smart," I said.

"You look surprised." Lionel grinned.

"Oh, I am. I had no idea you were this smart, and I've never seen you be innovative and proactive." Of course, Lionel knew I was only teasing him. "Really, I appreciate all the extra work you've done for this shoot."

"Only for you, Skye."

"Well, let's get the animals into place and get this over with." I didn't want to have to be around the snake and lizard any longer than necessary.

The reptile handler carried the iguana to the set and placed him on one of the fake boulders, then took the enormous snake from around his shoulders and let him curl around part of the bamboo stand.

"I fed the snake this morning, so he'll be docile," he said. "And it's cool enough in here that both of them should be fairly lethargic."

I looked at the snake and saw a lump in his body. I didn't want to know what it was. I motioned for the woman with the brightly colored parrot, and she walked over with the bird perched on her forearm, which was covered with a strip of leather. Looking at the claws on the bird, I could understand why. As soon as she placed the bird on the perch and stepped out of the shot, I started clicking the camera. Lionel poured the water from the top of the waterfall and through my lens it looked really great. I clicked off as many shots as I could while the water was running down. Lionel came around to the front of the set with the empty bucket.

"Do you want me to do the waterfall again?" he asked.

I was about to say yes when the snake decided he wasn't feeling lethargic at all. He lifted his head and stretched out toward the parrot with his jaws gaping open. The bird squawked and flew off his perch, leaving a few feathers behind on the foliage. The noise seemed to alert the iguana to the fact that something was happening and he scurried to the edge of the platform. The handler barely managed to grab him before he jumped to the floor. The parrot's owner was running around the arena cooing and clucking to the bird, who had perched on one of the rafters. The snake hissed at being denied a taste of the parrot.

"No, I don't think so. I got enough shots. We're good."

CHAPTER ELEVEN

The photo shoot on Saturday went without a hitch. I got all the photos I'd planned plus an extra one, so Monday I'd only have two more to do. Then I could get them developed and check that I had a selection of good shots for each calendar page. Connie would be back at the end of the week. I didn't want to disappoint her even though I felt like she'd abandoned me. I considered Connie a friend as well as a valuable client. I couldn't stand the thought of losing her business or her friendship because I hadn't been able to do the job she expected.

I pushed the thought aside in favor of worrying about dinner. When I was a teenager, I'd worried about introducing a boy to my parents because I was afraid they wouldn't like him. Now I was worried Scott wouldn't like my mother. Not that she was unlikable. But she tended to speak her mind at the strangest times, and I never knew what would come out of her mouth.

After a long, hot shower, I took my time applying makeup and styling my hair. Hurlihy's Steak and Brew wasn't fancy at all and I didn't want to overdo it on the makeup, but I still wanted to look nice. For Scott and because it made me feel more confident. I could use a little extra confidence tonight. I changed outfits three times before I found one I thought was just right. Finally, I couldn't put it off any longer. I had to drive over to Bobbi Jo's and pick up my mother.

Mom had dressed in tailored pants and a silk blouse. I was surprised and pleased she'd not worn one of the velour jog suits she usually favored for cold weather.

"You look very nice, Mom. I like that color on you."

"Were you afraid I'd wear something inappropriate?" she asked.

"Of course not." Already I was on the defensive. "Why would you ask that?" Damn. It sounded like I was doing the same passive-aggressive thing she always did to me.

"Oh, I know how much you hate the clothes I normally wear. But I know how to dress when I have to."

I chose to not say anything because everything I thought of could be turned around and I was pretty sure that's exactly what she would do. Mom didn't seem to have that effect on anyone but me, and I often wondered if it was because I was her daughter. And I wondered if

I was also doing it to my daughter. Hopefully not, but I was going to ask Sheridan anyway.

"Are you nervous?" Mom asked.

"No." Should I be?

"Oh. I thought you might be. Having your mother meet your beau and all. You always used to get nervous when you brought boys home in high school."

"That's because I was worried you and Dad wouldn't like them."

"Really? Did it mean that much to you?"

"I suppose it did." I didn't add that I figured I wouldn't be allowed to see the boy again if Mom and Dad didn't approve. I turned into the parking lot of the restaurant and pulled into a parking space close to the front door. Scott was waiting for us in the entryway.

"Mom, this is Scott Madison. He's a detective with the Portland Police Bureau. Scott, this is my mother, Ruby Lee Donovan."

"Mrs. Donovan, it's a pleasure to meet you." Scott held out his hand and Mom placed hers in his palm.

"Now, you just call me Ruby Lee like everyone else does. And I'm sure it's going to be a pleasure meeting you, as well." Mom glanced at me and winked, which I took as a sign of approval. That had to be good. If she liked Scott, I figured she was less likely to cause a problem.

"Our table is ready," Scott said. He took Mom's elbow and guided her to the back of the restaurant. She was all smiles and a few giggles as he settled her into one side of the booth, then turned to let me slide in before he took his seat next to me.

"The food here is wonderful." Scott picked up menus and handed them to Mom and me.

"What kind of food do they serve?" Mom asked. "I'm not a picky eater by any means, but I don't care for overly fancy food."

"I couldn't agree more," Scott said. "They have a very good porterhouse steak and if you like fish, they always have a fresh catch of the day. The waitress said they have wild salmon and yellowfin tuna tonight."

"I don't care much for fish," Mom said. "I'm more of a beef or chicken girl, myself."

I thought Mom's tone was a little belligerent and hoped it wasn't going to continue all evening. We ordered drinks and dinner, and I realized we were at the point where we needed to have some kind of conversation until the meal arrived. That made me nervous. Very nervous.

"So, you're a detective," Mom said. "That must be interesting work."

"It has its moments, some more interesting than others. Mostly, it's a lot of footwork and paperwork."

"So, who do you think killed this Frank person?" Mom asked.

I almost choked on my wine. I didn't think this

was where I wanted the conversation to go. Scott and I already had an issue with how much he could or would tell me about his investigations and about how much I had a right to know.

"Mom, I don't think Scott wants to talk about his work."

"That's okay, Skye. I don't mind."

That statement stunned me into silence.

"I try not to decide who I think committed a murder—or any crime, for that matter. It's usually best to let the evidence speak for itself. If you start thinking one person or another is guilty, it's too easy to overlook some evidence that could point you to the real criminal." Scott chuckled. "Of course, it's easier said than done. We're all human and we all have opinions."

"You sound like a good cop," Mom said.

"Thank you. That means a lot to me."

We were briefly interrupted when the waitress delivered our soup and salad along with a basket of freshly baked bread and a small bowl of whipped butter.

"Skye tells me you moved to Arizona about ten years ago. Green Valley, right? Do you like it better than Portland?"

"Oh, my, yes. I never did care much for all the rain we have up here and the gloomy winter days. In Green Valley, it's summer almost all year long. I have a little house in a planned community. We have a big community center and there's always something going on."

"Sounds like a good place. I'm sure you have a lot of friends there," Scott said.

I breathed a sigh of relief that the conversation was on this track. "Mom square dances three times a week, right, Mom?"

"Oh, yes. I love to dance. If I hadn't met Skye's father, I'd have moved to New York City and tried out for the Rockettes." Mom took a bite of her salad and reached for a roll. "I'm always busy at home, what with the dances and then going to bingo with the girls and playing cards twice a week. Pinochle and euchre are my games. Truth be told, I'm starting to miss everyone back there a bit. But I promised Bobbi Jo I'd stay until she has the baby."

That was encouraging news. Bobbi Jo couldn't stay pregnant forever. The rest of the evening turned out to be blessedly uneventful. Mom seemed to enjoy Scott, and she didn't bring up the subject of his job again. After we'd had coffee, I drove Mom back to Bobbi Jo's.

"Your man is a nice fellow," Mom said in the car. "I don't know why you were so reluctant for me to meet him."

"I wasn't reluctant, Mom. It's just that Scott and I had stopped seeing each other for a while, and I'm not really sure where we stand right now."

"Well, if you'll stop interfering with his work, I think you'll be fine. He might even ask you to marry him."

I wasn't about to tell her I'd already turned down his offer of marriage.

"Or, you could live together. In some cases, it makes sense. Harvey and Madge moved in together about five years ago. They thought about getting married, but after a while, Madge decided that if it wasn't broke, it didn't need fixing."

When I dropped Mom off I went in to say hello to Bobbi Jo and Lily. They were both in the living room. Bobbi Jo was turning the pages of a book on pregnancy, and Lily was doing needlework. Mom settled into a chair and brought out her crochet.

"You want some coffee, Skye? I was about to make a pot." Lily put her needlework aside and stood.

"Oh, I want some, too," Bobbi Jo said. "With cinnamon and vanilla."

Lily's shoulders heaved slightly, and I could tell she was holding in a sigh. "I'll make two pots."

I followed her into the kitchen. Her steps were heavy and her shoulders a little slumped.

"Are you all right, Lily? You look exhausted. Or depressed," I said.

"Hard to tell which most of the time." Lily turned the water on and filled the coffeepot. "You know I love Bobbi Jo, but I swear, the girl's running me ragged." She spooned coffee into the basket and turned the coffeemaker on, then filled a kettle with more water. "Her hormones are crazy so she's all happy one minute and crying the next. Every time she feels a twinge, she thinks it's labor. And it's get me this and bring me that all day long."

"Oh, Lily, I'm sorry. I wish I could be around more to help."

"Well, thank the Goddess your mother is here. She seems to have a calming effect on Bobbi Jo."

I wished I could say she had a calming effect on me, but that had never been the case. Lily poured boiling water into a French press pot, then pulled coffee cups from the cupboard.

"I'd make decaf for everyone, but coffee puts me to sleep and I could use a good night's sleep."

"Coffee puts you to sleep?"

"Always has. My mother used to give me a little in my bottle at night. I have no idea how she discovered it worked like that." Lily shrugged. "I think it's a southern thing. Back when I was a baby, mothers put iced tea and cola in baby bottles." Lily handed me the tray she'd set with cups and cream and sugar, then picked up the French press pot and the coffee decanter, and we carried everything into the living room. I motioned Lily to sit down and poured coffee for everyone.

"Mom, do you want regular or decaf?"

"Oh, decaf. Regular coffee would keep me up all night."

I took a cup of regular since the French press pot only held two cups of decaf.

"So, what did you think of Scott, Ruby Lee? Isn't he a handsome thing?" Bobbi Jo asked.

"More important, he's a nice man. I have no idea how Skye managed to snag a man like him. Nothing like her first husband," Mom said.

"Mom! You always liked Craig. And why wouldn't you think I would be attractive to a man like Scott?"

"Oh, for heaven's sake, Skye. Can't you take a joke? Of course I always liked Craig. Still do. I even like that boyfriend of his. Did I tell you they came over to see me yesterday?"

"No, you didn't mention it." I was surprised she hadn't mentioned seeing Craig and Danny. And surprised Craig hadn't called to tell me, either.

"Oh, yes. They came by with a big bunch of flowers and some cookies that Danny had made. He's quite the baker. Said he likes to make all kinds of breads and pies and cakes. And the cookies were delicious. They had caramel and nuts and chocolate."

"If anyone's hungry, I could bring them out," Lily

offered.

"Well, actually, they're all gone," Bobbi Jo said.

"Bobbi Jo, did you eat all those cookies? My Goddess, there must have been over a dozen left in the box." Lily shook her head. "Mark my words, you're going to regret eating like that."

"Oh, leave her be. It's the end of her pregnancy. Probably the only time a woman can eat a box of cookies and not worry about it. She'll take all the weight off after the baby comes."

"I'm fat?" Bobbi Jo burst into tears. "Oh, gawd! I'm fat and pregnant and no man is ever going to want to look at me again."

I leaned over and patted Bobbi Jo's arm. "You're not fat. Every woman gains weight during pregnancy."

"Now, Bobbi Jo, just shush. You don't want to upset the baby, do you? You'll take all that weight off right after the baby comes. And new mothers are always beautiful. You'll have men following you all over town."

"Oh. I hadn't thought of that," Bobbi Jo said. "I don't think I'll have time for men. At least not for a while."

Lily rolled her eyes. I put my cup down and stood up, thinking I'd best get out of there while Bobbi Jo was still in a good mood. "I've got to go. It's late and I need to get to bed." I gave Bobbi Jo a hug, then hugged Mom and Lily.

"I guess I'd better go to bed, too," Bobbi Jo said. "It's just so hard to get to sleep, and then it seems like fifteen minutes later, I have to go pee."

Bobbi Jo was starting to sound a little whiney again, and I hustled out of the house before it could become a full-blown episode of tears.

I was home around eleven and expected Sheridan to be studying or watching television, but the loft was dark. I checked her bedroom to see if she'd gone to bed early, but the bed was neatly made. Then I saw the note on the refrigerator.

Out with Zack. Home late. Don't wait up.

I was less worried now that I'd talked to Zack and discovered she was coaching him on his singing. Still, she was my baby girl, and I couldn't give up worrying about her completely. I wondered if Mom ever worried about me? And would I still be worrying about Sheridan when she was in her forties? I was too wired from the coffee to sleep, so I poured myself a glass of wine and settled in to watch some television. The weather forecast promised some sun tomorrow, but it was late March and I knew the sun could be accompanied by rain, hail, or snow—or all three. Normal spring weather for the Pacific Northwest. After the weather, I switched from wine to milk and watched half of a movie I'd already seen twice. I was rinsing the glass when Sheridan came home.

"What are you doing up?" she asked. "You weren't

waiting up for me, were you?"

"Of course not. I had coffee at Bobbi Jo's after dinner and I was too wired to sleep. How was your evening?"

"Great."

"What did you do?"

"Went to a movie. Then had a late dinner," she said.

"Really? Zack told me you were coaching him in singing."

"Oh, yeah, he told me he met you yesterday at the shoot. He's a good artist, isn't he?"

"Yes, he's very good. He helped a lot with getting an impromptu shot exactly right."

"Great. Well, I'm going to bed. See you in the morning."

"Sheridan, are you only coaching Zack, or are you also dating him?"

"Why do you ask?"

"Just curious. I guess I got the impression from Zack it was only vocal coaching." I held my hands up. "I'm not prying. I'm just trying to stay current on your entirely too busy life."

"Well, of course we're dating. I mean, I'm also coaching him with the singing, but that wouldn't take this much time, you know?"

"No, I wouldn't have any idea how much time you'd

spend coaching him. He simply didn't specifically mention that you were dating."

"Oh, well, we are. But it's no big deal, it's just casual. Is that a problem?"

"No, not at all."

"Okay. See you in the morning."

It was definitely a problem. Zack had told me he wasn't interested in Sheridan. So, was he lying? I didn't think so. I thought that Sheridan was enamored with him. And either he didn't know it, or he was using it to get some free vocal coaching. Either way, my little girl had a good chance of getting her heart broken. I wasn't going to let that happen. Connie was my friend. She'd fire him if she thought he was taking advantage of my daughter. If she ever came back from her Bahamian honeymoon.

I turned the lights out and crawled into bed with vengeful, angry thoughts about Zack. Then I realized I was acting like a controlling, overprotective mother hen. The same way my mother had been when I was a teenager.

I slept in fits and starts and had just drifted into a deep sleep when the phone rang three hours later. I groped for the phone and mumbled a groggy and disgruntled greeting.

"Skye, this is Lily."

"Is everything all right? Is Bobbi Jo in labor?"

"She seems to think so. But I'm not certain. We're taking her to the hospital, just in case."

"Okay. I'll be right there. I only have to get my clothes on." The thought of getting out of bed, getting dressed, and driving to the hospital made me want to cry.

"You sound exhausted."

"That's because I *am* exhausted."

"Listen," Lily lowered her voice, "I don't think Bobbi Jo is in labor. She's had a few Braxton-Hicks contractions and she lost her mucus plug. But I told her that the plug comes out two weeks before real labor sometimes."

"You really don't think it's labor?" I asked and tried to keep the hopefulness out of my voice.

"No, I don't. We're going to take her to the hospital just to be sure. But even if it really is labor this time, you don't need to get up now. Let's wait and see what the doctor says. If it's labor, you'll have plenty of time to get here."

"Well, I'm only twenty minutes from the hospital. Do you think Bobbi Jo will mind?"

"Let me take care of that," Lily said.

With another assurance that Lily would call immediately if Bobbi Jo's labor was real, I hung up the phone and snuggled down to get whatever sleep I could before Lily called again.

That turned out to be until eight in the morning. And it was only because the sun came in my window. Evidently, I'd managed to turn the alarm clock off rather than hitting the snooze button. I lurched out of bed, took the fastest shower of my life, and pulled out of the parking garage in half an hour. Wet hair, no makeup, and mismatched clothes, but I could still make it to the arena by nine if I ignored the speed limit, and there was no traffic.

Those hopes were dashed when I saw Arnie leaning against the trunk of his car, which was parked right next to the parking garage exit. He jumped in front of my Escape waving his arms. I stopped and pressed the button to lower my window.

"Arnie, what are you doing here?"

"I just wanted to apologize," he said. "I mean for the other day. I know I had no business coming here and talking to you."

But somehow it was okay that he was doing it again?

"I didn't want you to think I'm some kind of nut."

Too late. I was already certain he was some kind of nut. Possibly the kind of nut who would kill a man because he thought his wife was having an affair with him.

"Anyway, I wanted to say that I'm sorry, and I won't do it again. It's not like I think you'd call me if you thought Irene was having an affair with your boyfriend. Would you?"

"Arnie, I really don't think Irene and Scott have any interest in each other. It's just that they're involved in the investigation."

"Yeah, it's important to Irene. She thinks that if she can solve the case and arrest someone for Frank's murder, it'll be good for her campaign."

"She's running for mayor again?" I asked.

"No. She's going to run for state representative. She says she needs all the good publicity she can get."

"Well, see? There's no way she'd jeopardize an election by having an affair, is there?"

Arnie took a moment to think. It probably always took Arnie a moment to think. He didn't look like thinking was his strong point.

"Yeah, I hadn't thought of that. Well, I'm sorry again. Thanks for everything."

"No problem, but I'm late. I really need to run." I pulled out before Arnie could agree or disagree with that and headed for the arena. I thought I did pretty good. I was only fifteen minutes late, and I didn't get a speeding ticket.

CHAPTER TWELVE

In spite of a slightly late start, I finished up the last two photos before noon. I packed my cameras away and took down the lights while Lionel gathered up his props. Peter had told us not to worry about leaving it spotless, which was nice. There was a significant accumulation of dog hair on the floor, and I didn't relish the idea of sweeping such a large area. Probably Peter figured Frank's son could worry about it since he had inherited the place.

"I'm all packed up, Lionel. Want some help with getting all this out to your car?"

"Sure."

Before I could pick up a box, my cell phone chirped and I pulled it from my pocket to see Scott's name and number on the display. I flipped it open.

"Hi, Scott."

"Hey, Skye. Are you still shooting the dogs?"

"Just finished, why?" Maybe Scott was in the mood for a little afternoon delight.

"I need a photograph taken. The chief wants a photograph of me and Irene to put in the regional newsletter. Something about encouraging cities to work together."

"Sure, I could do that. What kind of shot is he looking for?" I didn't really want to take a photograph of Irene and Scott together. I didn't like the way she had to *stay in touch* with him all the time. Even though I'd tried to assure Arnie that his wife wasn't having an affair with Scott, I didn't trust the woman. Given half a chance, I thought she'd be on Scott like a duck on a june bug.

"I think it's just a grip and grin shot. I guess Irene is going to present me with some kind of award or something for helping with the investigation into Frank's murder. I'm guessing it's some tacky frame with a piece of paper printed on a deskjet."

"Seems a little early for that, doesn't it? I mean, you haven't arrested anyone yet, have you?" I was kind of hoping he had arrested someone, because he hadn't had time to arrest Peter since he left and Lionel was with me. If it wasn't one of them, then I didn't really care who it was.

"Nope. No arrest. I think the chief is hoping we'll have a collar before the newsletter comes out. In any case, it's what he wants."

"No problem. Where do you want to take the photo?"

"Actually I was hoping you'd have an idea."

"I could do it at Steinhart's if there's a bay free. What's a good time for you?"

"There is no good time. I'm swamped. But I was thinking we could do it tonight after work if that's all right with you."

"Sure, that would be fine. It'll be easier to do it at the studio after hours, too. How about seven?"

"Great. I'll call Irene and let her know. Maybe we can grab a bite to eat later?"

"I'd love that. See you then."

By the time I hung up, Lionel had gotten all his boxes into his car without my help. I closed up the arena building, locked the door, and dropped the keys through the mail slot on the door as Peter had requested. When I turned around, Speedway came running across the ground from the kennel building, yapping wildly. I knelt down, and he jumped into my arms.

"Hey, little boy, where did you come from?" I let the dog nuzzle my neck and give me a nose kiss. He must have gotten out of the kennel when Peter was putting the other dogs away. Unfortunately, Peter had already left. I pulled my cell phone out, punched in his number, and listened as I walked across the grounds to the kennel building. In a second, I heard a recording telling me Peter's cell phone wasn't currently in service. I checked the door of the kennel, but as I'd expected, it was locked. The dogs all started barking and howling and I immediately thought of the neighbors since Taylor Hudson had told me the barking bothered them.

I trotted back to my car with Speedway under my arm. He seemed perfectly happy to let me carry him around. And to be honest, it felt good to have the little guy in my arms. But what was I going to do with him? I couldn't get him back in the kennel, and I couldn't reach Peter.

I'd have to take him home with me. For a brief moment, I wondered if Peter had let the little dog out on purpose and now wasn't answering his phone. He'd suggested that I take Speedway. No, surely he wouldn't do that. He wouldn't know I'd find the dog, and he'd never leave a dog where it could get lost or hurt. Speedway nuzzled my neck again and blinked at me.

I had planned to drop the film off to be processed, then go home for a short nap before I had to meet Scott and Irene. Now, I had to add a trip to the store to that. Speedway would need food and dishes for food and water. And a leash for when I took him out to do his business. Maybe a bed to sleep in. Then I remembered Bobbi Jo. Lily hadn't called back so I assumed Bobbi Jo hadn't really been in labor. But Bobbi Jo had been unreasonable, demanding, and difficult the past couple of weeks, and I was fairly certain she would be outraged that I hadn't come to the hospital. A phone call wouldn't be enough. I needed to go see her. It wasn't looking good for that nap.

It was too bad that Lionel had already left. I could have gotten everything I needed for the little dog from the products we used in the photographs. Although I was pretty sure the Pet Place expected to have their products returned unused. I dropped the film off to be processed, then stopped by the Pet Place. The shop window had a big sign announcing that pets were welcome, so I picked Speedway up and we went shopping. I had no idea what to feed him, so I asked a clerk for advice, then Speedway picked out a small fluffy bed, and I chose two red dishes for his food and water and a red leash. Half an hour and fifty dollars later, we were back in the car headed for Bobbi Jo's. Maybe she would be distracted by Speedway and not be angry at me for not showing up at the hospital last night.

When I arrived at Bobbi Jo's, she was taking a nap. Lily was at her shop and my mother was watching a soap opera on Bobbi Jo's enormous television in the family room.

"What's that?" Mom picked up the remote and muted the television.

"This is Speedway. He's one of the dogs we used in the photographs. When I was leaving, he got out of the kennel somehow and I couldn't reach Peter, so I brought him with me."

"He's a cute little bugger." Mom got up and walked

over for a closer look at the dog. Speedway greeted her with a nose kiss.

"Is Bobbi Jo angry with me?" I asked Mom.

"Off and on. You remember how it is at the end of a pregnancy. Hormones on a roller coaster. She'll be fine once she has the baby."

"I probably should have gone to the hospital, but Lily was pretty sure she wasn't really in labor, and I was so exhausted."

"Well, I'm sorry if I'm such an inconvenience to everyone."

I turned to see Bobbi Jo standing in the doorway. She looked like she'd just lost her best friend. I handed Speedway to Mom and hurried over to wrap my arms around her. She stood stiffly, refusing to return the hug.

"You're not an inconvenience, and I'm really sorry I didn't go to the hospital with you last night. But I was only twenty minutes away and Lily would have called me if you'd been in labor."

Bobbi Jo burst into tears and put her head on my shoulder. "I just need you there. I don't think I can go through this alone."

"You won't have to. I promise. I'll be there no matter what."

"Really?" Bobbi Jo lifted her head and wiped the tears off her cheeks.

"Absolutely."

"But what if I call and you can't answer your phone? Like you're in a meeting or in the middle of a shoot or something? I mean, I call you all the time and you might think it's just a regular phone call from me."

"Text me. I promise I'll keep the phone on all the time, and I can always look at a text message. That way, I'll know immediately and I'll drop everything and run to the hospital."

"Oh, where did that cute little dog come from?" Bobbi Jo pushed me aside to get to Mom and the dog. Speedway nuzzled her neck and pawed at her belly. "He's adorable." I guessed that the text message idea was all right with her.

"It's only temporary," I said and explained how I happened to be in possession of the dog.

"You want some ice cream?" Bobbi Jo asked. "I've been craving ice cream for weeks now. My gawd! I'm going to be a mountain by the time I have this baby." She scratched Speedway's tiny head. "I bet you'd like some ice cream, wouldn't you?"

"I don't think dogs are supposed to have ice cream, but I'd love some," I said. I hadn't had lunch, and ice cream had protein in it, right? Sounded good to me.

"We need a code," Bobbi Jo said.

"What kind of a code?"

"You know, something short that I can text to you when I'm in labor. I mean, I'll be busy with the breathing and everything. I won't have time to text a really long message."

"All right," I said. "How about some numbers. Like nine-one-one."

"No, we need something different." Bobbi Jo pulled her cell phone from her pants pocket and flipped it open. "I'll text two-two-two-nine. That spells baby."

I agreed, and Bobbi Jo dished up the ice cream. Either the ice cream or the text idea had put Bobbi Jo in a good mood. I was happy to see her laughing and joking again. Mom was right about the hormone roller coaster. I remembered being completely unreasonable at the end of my pregnancy.

I left after the ice cream and after confirming I knew what the secret code would be and promising once again I would not miss her delivery no matter what.

I drove home and hauled my doggie purchases up to the loft. Speedway danced around and yipped until I realized he probably had to take care of business. I clipped his leash to his collar and we took the elevator down to the ground floor. Outside, Speedway found a suitable bush and christened it, then left a solid deposit a few yards away. I needed to pick it up, but I hadn't brought anything with me. We walked over to the Dumpster, where I found a plastic bag, then went back to clean up. I made a mental note to keep all my plastic grocery bags, then went back upstairs to take a shower before I met

Scott and Irene at the photo studio.

Sheridan wasn't home, and I mentally ran through her schedule. Mondays she had morning classes and was usually home in the afternoons and then gone for her vocal lessons in the evening. Maybe she was doing her homework at the library. Or at Zack's house. I just couldn't let go of the Zack issue. I worried that he was using her. I worried that she'd get her heart broken. I didn't want her to pin her hopes on a man who wasn't interested in her. And I didn't want her to get involved with a man who only wanted her for singing lessons and sex. There, I'd thought it. I was worried Sheridan was having sex with a man who didn't give a hoot about her. Knowing it probably happened to the majority of American girls didn't make me feel one bit better. I should be able to protect her somehow. But I knew that telling her my thoughts would be met with a wave of her hand and assurances that she was an adult and could take care of herself, thank you very much.

I pushed the thought out of my head and replaced it with thinking about what to wear. Normally, I wear cargo pants and a multipocketed vest to the studio. But Irene was going to be there. With Scott. I wanted to look really nice. There was no rule that a photographer couldn't dress up. Of course it would help if I had a more extensive wardrobe.

I pulled several items from the closet and laid them

on my bed. Speedway immediately jumped up on the bed and nosed around the clothes. The lavender-gray palazzo pant outfit was one of my favorites, but it was entirely too dressy, so I hung it back in the closet. I really liked the emerald green sweater I usually wore with khaki pants, but the sweater made me look chubby. Speedway jumped on the sweater and rolled around, leaving beige hairs all over it. I took that as an omen and tossed the sweater into the laundry hamper. That left my basic black outfit. I'd owned it for several years, but it was so basic it would never go out of style. The fabric was some kind of slinky knit that makes any woman look good. The pants were neither wide-legged nor narrow, and the simple design of the open jacket draped just right. I had a choice of a black and white sleeveless top or a red silk camisole to wear with it. I held up the black and white top and Speedway growled. I showed him the red camisole and he jumped around and barked. I had to agree with him; besides, it didn't feel like a time to be holding back. I pulled a pair of black heels from the closet and tossed them on the bed, then I headed for the shower.

I took a little longer than usual with my hair and makeup. Okay, I took an hour and a half as opposed to the fifteen minutes I usually devoted to the process. After my hair was partially dry, I put it up in some rollers. The kind that are made of the loopy part of Velcro. I sprayed it with a liberal amount of hair spray, then got to work on my makeup. I wanted a natural look that was better than my look naturally. Fortunately, I'd watched some of the best makeup artists in Portland apply make-up to models for the past year. Moisturizer first, then a light application of foundation mixed with more moisturizer done with an artist's brush. After that had a few minutes to set, I got out the mineral makeup Bobbi Jo had talked me into buying. I dipped the brush into the silky powder, tapped it on the counter of the vanity to work it deep into the brush, then buffed it over my face. I checked the results in the mirror.

Too much.

I pulled a tissue from the box and patted my face and neck. Yeah, that was good. Next came the eye shadow in a dark sage green and eyeliner in soft brown. So far, so good. I didn't think I really looked like myself, but I looked pretty good. Mascara was one of the few items I used on a daily basis, so it was quick and easy to apply. After coating my eyelashes, I brushed the almost dry wand across my eyebrows. Just enough to darken them. The final step was lipstick. I pulled out four. A dark red lip gloss, a coral matte, burgundy with a little frost in it, and a deep, clear red. The coral matte looked awful. I wiped it off and rubbed some cream on my lips to get the last of it off. I tried the burgundy but thought I looked like a streetwalker. Speedway whined. Not only was he cute, he seemed to possess a good fashion sense. I was down to the clear red and the gloss.

Did women really go to this much trouble? Even for special occasions? I chose the gloss and swiped it across my lips. The good thing was that all the lipstick removal had made my lips swell up a bit, and it looked great.

I spritzed on a little of the perfume Scott had given me last year and headed to my car. Then I came back and gathered up my cameras and Speedway and took them with me.

I just hoped Scott was worth all that trouble.

My cell phone rang the instant I got into the car. The display showed the string of numbers that had shown when Connie called. I checked my watch and saw I was early. Well, ten minutes, but it was long enough to talk to Connie. Especially since she kept hanging up on me when she called.

"Hi, Connie?"

"Hi, Skye, how's everything going?"

"I finished up the photo shoot today." I doubted she really wanted to know about Bobbi Jo's false labors or Sheridan falling for Connie's tattooed, motorcycle-riding layout artist or the crazy bitch who was the mayor of Hillsdale or the fact that my mother was visiting. I was surprised Lily didn't have some drama going on in her life that required my attention, then I remembered the situation with Chase. "When are you coming home?"

"Just a few more days. Tyreese and I are enjoying

our honeymoon. You know, it's so warm here at night, you can sleep on the beach with just a blanket."

Oh, dear God. Connie was sleeping on the beach with her Rastafarian husband. I doubted the marriage was even legal in the States. But maybe that would turn out to be a good thing.

"So, did you actually marry him?" I asked.

"Oh, Skye, it was the most beautiful wedding. If you hadn't been busy, I'd have flown you down to take pictures of the ceremony. My gown was gorgeous. All gauzy and filmy and floating on the ocean breeze. Tyreese wore a sarong."

"Your husband wore a woman's dress?"

"No. Down here, men and women wear a sarong. It's a length of fabric. The men wear it wrapped around their hips and woman wrap it up higher to cover their breasts."

I could just see it. Connie in a homemade gown of gauze and her Rastafarian groom in a garish piece of fabric wrapped around his loins. They probably toasted the nuptials with a bong rather than champagne. Not that I had the nerve to ask her that.

"And after the ceremony, all the women of the village did a beautiful dance. Tyreese said it was to encourage fertility. Isn't that wonderful?"

"I guess. If you want to be fertile, that is." I didn't know what to say. Connie was in her midthirties and she'd always said she didn't have time for children. Or a husband, for that matter. I guessed she'd found time for at least the husband while she was on vacation. "So, when are you coming home?"

"Soon. Tyreese is trying to arrange everything now."

"Arrange everything?" I asked. That sounded ominous.

"Well, there's paperwork that has to be completed and some deal he says has to be wrapped up before he can leave."

Some deal? Like what kind of deal? Probably he was trying to smuggle some ganja onto the airplane. Oh, God. Connie could end up in some Caribbean prison.

"What kind of deal?" I asked even though I was afraid to hear the answer.

"I have no idea. To be honest, my mind tends to wander when he starts talking about deals with all of his buddies. But, don't worry, I'll be home soon. Besides, you've finished the photo shoot. I knew you could do it without me."

"I had to change the Christmas layout."

"I'm sure it'll be fine. I trust your artistic judgment, Skye."

"Well, thank you. I just hope I don't disappoint you."

"You won't. I'm sure of it. I've got to run. Tyreese is back from some meeting about his deal."

Dial tone.

I sighed and closed the phone. Right then I didn't have time to worry about Connie. I had to take a photo of Scott and Irene. After that I had to worry about Sheridan and Bobbi Jo. Not to mention Lionel and probably Peter, too. I'd worry about Connie when she got home again.

Benjamin Steinhart's studio was dark when I arrived a few minutes before seven. All the other photographers had finished their shoots and left for the day. I opened the building and turned on the lights, leaving the door unlocked for Scott and Irene's arrivals. At least I hoped it would be separate arrivals. If Scott and I were going to have dinner after the shoot, I didn't want to have to drop Irene off somewhere, and I really didn't want her to join us.

Speedway sniffed around the studio, then ran over to me and jumped around. I thought he probably wanted me to hold him.

"Sorry, little boy. I'm busy. You'll have to entertain yourself for a while." Then I realized that having Speedway with me could be a problem. I couldn't take him with us to a restaurant. What had I been thinking? I should have left him at home.

I barely got my camera set up and the lights adjusted around a swath of gray seamless when I heard Irene's voice.

"Hey, is anyone here?"

"Back here," I called. I walked to the door and stuck my head out. Irene was walking down the hall.

Tall, blond, gorgeous. She had on a light blue suit that brought out her blue eyes. Her long blond hair looked thick enough to cover several heads and hung in waves no curling iron or perm could duplicate.

"I came early so I'd have time to freshen up my makeup," she said. "Where should I go?"

I knew exactly where she should go. But I merely directed her to the mirrored counter and chairs that our makeup artists used. She pranced over to perform her fluffing and buffing routine while I continued to work with the lights.

Speedway ran over and growled at her. Irene jumped and backed up, eyeing the little dog with apprehension. Instead of praising him, which is what I wanted to do, I made a clicking noise and said, "No." Speedway looked disappointed that he wasn't allowed to bark at her but sidled up next to my leg and sat quietly.

"You're very dressed up tonight. Got a hot date later?" Irene asked.

"Scott and I are having dinner after the shoot," I said. I looked up to gauge her reaction, and I wasn't disappointed.

"Oh, I didn't realize you two were close."

"We've been seeing each other for about a year," I said.

"Scott never mentioned it. I wonder why?"

I seethed. To the point that I was surprised steam

didn't come out of my ears.

"There you are."

I turned to see Scott standing in the doorway. Tall, handsome, virile. Okay, you can't really tell if a man is virile by his looks, but still.

"Is this all right?" Scott stepped into the photography bay and turned around. He wore a dark blue suit with a white shirt and conservative striped tie.

"Perfect," I said. Speedway ran over to him yipping and jumping like he was an old friend.

"Who's the little rat?" Scott asked.

"Speedway," I said, then explained how I'd taken him with me when he escaped the kennel.

"Oh, you look so handsome in that suit, Scott." Irene sashayed across the bay to greet him. "Why, I had no idea you cleaned up this well." Her hand reached up to rest on his chest.

"Irene, I need you over here to do some light readings." It wasn't entirely a lie. I needed a human to stand still while I took some readings, and it was a good way to get her away from Scott.

"Oh, let's both go," Irene said to Scott.

He pulled back and shot me a glance.

"That's okay," I said. "Scott will be fine because his outfit is in high contrast." I eyed Irene in a critical manner. "But yours is a little muddy. I'd hate for you to look all washed out."

Irene looked torn. I could tell she wanted to stay with Scott, but I figured she was vain enough to want to look good in the photograph. Vanity won out and she sauntered across the floor, making sure Scott had a good view of her hips whipping side to side. I turned away and rolled my eyes. For revenge I made her stand under the hot lights for fifteen minutes while I fussed with the light meter and tweaked the light an inch this way and an inch that way. By the time I finished, little beads of sweat had popped out on her forehead and her hair looked a little deflated.

"All right, the lights look good for you. Did you want to freshen up a bit before we take the shot?" I asked.

"Do I need to?"

I shrugged. "Not really. The natural look is very popular these days."

Irene took some quick little running steps back to the makeup counter. Her face almost crumbled when she looked in the mirror. Scott and I talked while she fussed with her hair and applied powder to mop up the sweat.

"Did you really need her to stand there that long?"

"Of course I did. Are you insinuating I had an ulterior motive?"

"Well, I don't know about a motive for that, but surely there's some motive to the outfit you're wearing."

"Just trying to look professional. And I didn't know where we might go for dinner. I didn't want to be underdressed."

"But I like you underdressed." Scott's eyes twinkled. "Oh, wait. That's not it. I like you *un*dressed."

"Maybe we could make that happen after dinner," I said.

"Maybe we could make that happen instead of dinner," he replied.

"I'm ready. How do I look?" Irene asked.

She looked like Amazon Barbie.

"Perfect," I said. "If you two would stand over there." I pointed to a spot on the seamless that I'd marked with masking tape. "And shake hands." Scott had said a typical grip-and-grin shot. I hated grip-and-grin shots. I thought they looked stupid and posed and revealed nothing of the situation or the participants. But if Scott's chief wanted a grip-and-grin, then that's what I'd give him. Besides, I didn't mind taking a photo of Irene looking stupid.

"Oh, wait. I have something." Irene minced over to her oversized purse and pulled out a picture frame covered with intricate gold scrolls. "I had this made just for you, Scott."

Scott took the frame from Irene and looked at it. "Guest Detective of the Year."

"Wow," I said. "You don't get that every day." I motioned them back to the center of the seamless and focused my camera. "Irene, why don't you hand the plaque to Scott and, Scott, you put your hand out to take it."

Scott held out his hand as Irene pushed the plaque toward him. I clicked off two shots, then, in a lightning-fast move, Irene snuggled close to Scott and laid her head against his shoulder, her free hand wrapping around him to rest on his shoulder. I clicked off a few more shots of Scott's horrified expression, trying not to snicker.

"Let's try one shaking hands," I said. "I understand that's what the chief wants, right, Scott?"

"Yes. He specifically asked for that." Scott inched away from Irene and she followed.

"If you two could move back into position?" I asked.

Scott inched back toward the center of the seamless, but Irene refused to move, causing them to become very close. They grasped hands, and I clicked off more shots.

"Could I have a few for my own use?" Irene asked.

"Of course," I said.

Irene must have taken that as permission to change her pose. She got as close to Scott as possible, tossed the plaque to the floor, and laid her hand on his chest, leaning her face close to his. I was a little surprised she didn't kiss him.

I clicked off a few shots. Later I'd tell her the camera malfunctioned, and the shots didn't come out. No way was I going to give her pictures of her cuddling with my man. *My man?* Where the hell did that come from? I'd never been a jealous or possessive person. Not even in my marriage. But something about Irene set off alarms for me.

"That should do it."

Irene didn't move, but Scott gently disentangled himself.

"I'll have these to the chief soon," I said. I fussed with winding the film and removing the camera from the tripod. "I'll be right back." I took the camera to one of the closet-sized dark rooms and removed the film, placing it in a black plastic cylinder and marking the contents and date on the white label. When I came out, Irene was standing as close to Scott as possible without actually melding her body to his. He looked uncomfortable. That was nice.

"Skye, you ready to go?" Scott asked, trying to disentangle himself from Irene's grip.

"Ready when you are," I said.

"Irene, can Skye and I walk you to your car?"

I almost laughed at the way her face fell. Then she brightened.

"I thought maybe we could spend some time going over the Frank Johnson case. It's important that I stay up-to-date on everything." She smiled at me. "Some of my people don't understand the need to have a detective from Portland take over a murder case."

Some of her people? Geez.

"There's nothing new on the case, but I'll be happy to meet you tomorrow morning if you like."

"Oh. I see. Well, that would be fine. How about breakfast? We could meet at the IHOP in Beaverton. They have wonderful pancakes."

"I might be busy for breakfast. How about I call you around nine?"

Irene's face fell again. She took a deep breath and reached for her bag. "That would be fine. I'll be waiting for your call." With that, she swiveled her hips out of the building.

I turned and looked at Scott. His face was a mixture of horror and relief. He shook his head. "She is the strangest woman I've ever met."

"Really? You've never had a woman have a gigantic crush on you before?"

"You think she has a crush on me?" he asked.

"You don't?"

"Never really thought about it, I guess."

"Scott. She's so obvious. Leaning on you. Laying her head on your shoulder. Trying to get you to go with her instead of with me." Could he be that oblivious?

"No. I don't think so. I just think she's a little uncomfortable in social situations, and she's really obsessed with this murder case."

Could a man be that stupid? I was poised to question him further, but he changed the direction of our conversation.

"Where do you want to have dinner? You're all dressed up. Does that mean you're expecting something special?"

"Well, not as far as dinner is concerned," I said.

Speedway yipped and jumped, placing his front feet on my leg. I leaned over and picked him up. "Besides, I can't take this little guy into a restaurant."

"We could leave him in the car," Scott suggested.

Speedway whined.

"Let's get some Chinese and eat at my place," Scott suggested.

CHAPTER THIRTEEN

Scott and I managed to get through an entire evening without being interrupted, which had resulted in some vigorous activity followed by a brief amount of cuddling and hours of blissful sleep. For some reason, I always slept like a rock when I was with Scott. For a while I thought it was due to the feeling of safety that came from having a man around. But then I realized that sleeping with Craig had never had any effect on how I slept. Mostly I was unwilling to explore the reasons any further.

When I woke, I could hear Scott in the kitchen and smell coffee. Possibly there would be a luscious omelet or perhaps bacon and eggs along with the coffee. Speedway was still curled up on the blanket Scott had put on the floor for him. I threw back the covers and stepped into the bathroom to brush my teeth. One look in the mirror made me decide to take a quick shower while I was there.

After I toweled off, I pulled a light blue shirt of Scott's off the hook on the back of the door. When we'd been seeing each other last year, he'd kept that shirt on the hook for me when I came over. I could still smell the faintest hint of my cologne on it and got a little thrill of pleasure that he'd kept it just as I'd left it.

"Hey, lazybones, breakfast is ready," Scott called from the modest kitchen.

I sauntered into the living area and was rewarded by a lascivious look from Scott. He waggled his eyebrows, which made me laugh. It was easy being with Scott and I was enjoying every minute of it. But I was still concerned that we hadn't really talked about the reasons we'd stopped seeing each other last year.

"I took the dog out when I got up," Scott said.

Damn, I'd already forgotten about Speedway. "Thanks. That was nice of you."

"How long are you going to have him?"

"Until I can get in touch with Peter, I guess."

"You don't want to keep him?" Scott asked.

"I don't have time for a dog. He's really sweet, but I'm working all the time and dogs need to have someone around."

"Sheridan could help with that," he suggested.

I had to admit that Sheridan would probably fall in love with the little dog. In fact, it might be hard to get him away from her once she'd seen him.

"I'm starving." I hopped up on a stool at the counter that separated the kitchen from his living area. Scott slid an omelet from a large frying pan onto a plate and cut it in half. He must have used half a dozen eggs because it was huge. Swiss cheese oozed from where he'd cut it and I saw bits of onion, tomato, and spinach. My mouth watered and I picked up a fork in anticipation.

Scott set the plate on the counter followed by steaming cups of coffee for us and came around to take the stool next to me.

"So, what's on your schedule today?" I asked.

"Talking to possible murderers."

I shook my head. "I guess I never thought of your job that way."

"Actually, I don't usually think of it that way, either. I was trying to be funny." He forked some omelet into his mouth and chewed for a moment. "But, really, it's something you need to think about."

"Why?" I had a bad feeling about where this conversation was going.

Scott put his cup down and placed a hand over mine. He stared at the plate of omelet and rubbed the back of my hand for a moment. "Because when you involve yourself in my investigations, that's exactly what you're doing. Talking to possible murderers."

"Scott, it's not like that."

"Well, yes, it is. Exactly like that. Take this investigation, for instance. I don't know who killed Frank yet, but I'm fairly certain it's one of our suspects. It could be Lionel, or Peter. We don't know. So, you'd be better off if you limited your exposure to them."

"Well, that's all well and good. Except I really believe neither of them could have killed Frank. And I can't just not do my job because someone is a murder suspect. Especially when it's ridiculous for them to even be considered a suspect in the first place."

"You finished the job, right?" Scott asked.

"Yes. I finished yesterday."

"Then you don't need to be around Lionel or Peter." He picked up his coffee cup and took a sip. "And there's no reason for you to be around any of the other suspects, either."

I decided to let the topic drop. I didn't really have a good defense. I didn't have a defense at all. Other than I really, really didn't believe either Lionel or Peter could ever kill someone. And Scott's reasons for suspecting them were flimsy at best. I didn't tell Scott that, either. Part of me wanted to but another part didn't want to destroy the fragile reconnection we'd made.

We ate in silence for a few minutes, letting the tension fade. Then Scott glanced at the clock.

"I'd better jump in the shower. Don't want to be late for my nine-thirty meeting."

"I'll clean up," I offered.

He dropped a kiss on my lips. "You don't have to. But I'm not saying it isn't appreciated if you don't have to leave right away."

"I've got plenty of time."

Scott went to the bathroom, and I ran hot water in the sink and squirted dish detergent into it. The dishes were done in only a few minutes. Scott was a neat cook, messing up only what he needed and cleaning as he went along. After I dried the last plate and placed it on the shelf, I went to the bedroom to get dressed. Scott stood at the closet door. Naked. I let myself enjoy the view for a moment, then took my clothes off the chair and started dressing. Speedway curled into a tiny ball on his blanket and snoozed. We took advantage of our state of partial undress to share a few kisses and caresses. But Scott's meeting loomed, so it didn't go past that.

On the way home, I got a call from Lionel. I pressed the *speaker* button and felt both guilty and rebellious.

"Hey, Skye, I've got a problem."

"What's up, Lionel?"

"I left a box of props at the arena, and I'm in classes all day. Any chance you could pick it up for me? Steinhart will nail my hide to the wall if I lose his props."

"No problem. I'm more or less free today, anyway."

"Thanks, I really appreciate it."

Well. Now, I'd talked to Lionel and I also had to talk to Peter. More rebellion and guilt warred for dominance. Rebellion won. Besides, I needed to see Peter to return Speedway to the kennel. I glanced at the little dog curled up on the seat next to me and felt guilty. He had to be unhappy in the kennel. Of course there were other dogs to keep him company, but how much human companionship did he get? I punched Peter's number into the phone and listened to it ring.

"Skye, nice to hear from you," Peter said.

"Hi, Peter. I need to get back into the arena building. Lionel left a box of props inside, and if Benjamin discovers props missing, he'll have a fit."

"Sounds like a very understanding boss."

"He's got talent and clients. He doesn't need to be understanding to photographers and stylists."

"No problem. I was going to go by the arena this afternoon anyway."

"Also, I have Speedway with me."

"I knew you'd like him, but how did you get him out of the kennel? I locked up when I left."

"He must have sneaked past you," I said. "He came running over to me right as I was about to leave. I called you, but a recording told me you were out of the service area."

"Would it be possible for you to keep him a few more days? I don't know how he got out of the kennel, but I'd hate for it to happen again when no one's around. I'm moving all the dogs to my friend's kennel later this week."

I resisted. I really did. Then I looked at Speedway. He opened his dark brown eyes and blinked at me.

"I guess I could. My daughter would probably love taking care of him."

"Great. Do you want to meet me at the arena building, say, around two?"

"That sounds perfect. I'll see you then."

When I arrived at the loft, Sheridan was hunched over a book and a pad of paper covered in numbers and symbols. She looked tired and frustrated.

"You don't look happy," I said.

"I'm tired."

"Did you stay up late?"

"Kind of."

"Studying?"

"Not really. I went out with Zack last night. Where were you?"

"I stayed at Scott's. Did you see my note on the refrigerator?"

"Oh, right. So, are you and Scott together again?" Sheridan laid her pencil down and settled back on the sofa.

"Maybe. I think it's too soon to tell."

"You guys haven't talked about it?" she asked.

"He's a man." I shrugged. "Generally they avoid talking about things."

"Don't I know it." Sheridan yawned. "I'm getting

nowhere with this math."

"Are you having trouble with it?" When she was in high school I'd always known how she was doing in her classes. But now that she was in college I didn't see report cards or notes from teachers, and at eighteen, my daughter seemed to think she was an adult who didn't need to confide in her mother.

"No. Not really. It's never been my best subject, but I'm doing okay. I'm just tired from being up late."

"What did you and Zack do last night?" I couldn't help it. I knew I shouldn't pry, but I really wanted to know what was going on with them. How else would I know when the crash would happen and Sheridan would experience her first heartbreak? And I was more and more certain it was coming.

"Nothing. I mean, nothing special. We hung out at his place for a while, then went to get a bite to eat. The usual."

"Is he a good singer? Do you think he can make it on *American Idol*?"

"Absolutely. He's got great range. It's just that all he's ever sung is rock. If he's going to even get to the final ten, he'll need to be able to sing a lot more than that."

"I guess so." I enjoyed music, but it wasn't a passion of mine. I couldn't sing or play a musical instrument. I didn't understand the nuances of the art. And I had no idea where Sheridan got it. Her father had a passable voice but had never played an instrument. Sheridan seemed to know how to play a variety of instruments almost instinctively. She'd started with a flute in grade school, then clarinet and viola later. In high school, she'd taken piano lessons. And she'd always sung. I think she sang her first words. I was in awe of her musical abilities and more than a little proud I'd produced such a talented child. And I still thought of her as a child, which was probably wrong. She was a young woman. But she'd always be my baby.

"You have a class today, don't you?"

"Math." Sheridan made a face. "I hate math."

"If you're having a problem with it, we could get you a tutor."

"Mom, you don't have to micromanage my education. I'm grown now, remember?"

"Just a suggestion," I said. I didn't like her reminding me that she didn't need me any longer. Or maybe I just didn't want to believe it. I couldn't imagine what I'd do when she decided to move out and live on her own. Maybe I should keep Speedway, after all.

"Oh, my God! I forgot the dog!" I ran back down to the parking garage and scooped Speedway off the car seat. He'd fallen asleep on the way home, and I'd totally forgotten about him. I felt like a bad doggie mother. He woke up when I lifted him from the car, yawned, and licked my nose. I guessed he forgave me. I carried him up to the loft where Sheridan was standing outside the door.

"Who's this?" she asked, holding out her arms.

I placed the dog in her hands and followed her inside. "This is Speedway." I told her how I'd gotten him and that we'd be keeping him for a while.

"Just for a few days, until Peter gets the dogs moved to another kennel."

"He's so cute, Mom. How come we never had a dog when I was growing up?"

"We did. A little schnauzer, I believe. He ran away a month after we'd gotten him. You must have been about four and you cried for a week. I wasn't willing to go through that again, so we didn't get another one."

"Was it my fault he ran away?" Sheridan asked.

"Sweetie, you were only four. Nothing was your fault then. I'm going to drop this film off, then go see Bobbi Jo and run some errands. I should be home around four. Do you have any dinner plans?"

"No. Why?"

"I thought you might want to see your grandmother. I doubt she'll be here very much longer." Actually, I was hoping her visit would be short. Of course, I felt guilty about it. Mom and I had been like best friends when I was growing up, and I wondered when and why our relationship had changed.

"I've got more homework tonight, and I stopped by Bobbi Jo's yesterday to see her. Bobbi Jo is getting huge.

When is she going to have that baby?"

"Soon. I think her due date is only a couple of weeks away. It could be anytime now."

"Her moods are all over the place." Sheridan shook her head. "I can't imagine feeling like that for nine months."

"It's not that bad. At least I don't remember it being so bad. But maybe the people who were around me would feel differently."

Sheridan laughed. "I'll ask Dad next time I see him. He'll probably have a different opinion."

"Should I take Speedway with me?" The little dog had curled up next to Sheridan and looked too comfortable to move.

"No, leave him here. I'll take him out for a walk in a little bit." She scratched his head, and he blinked at her.

"Don't forget to take a plastic bag to pick up his little presents." I gathered the film rolls I wanted to drop off, gave Sheridan a motherly kiss on the forehead, and left her to her math studies. She'd always been an excellent student, and I was a little concerned that she might not have as easy a time in college as she'd had in high school. Sheridan was used to excelling in her studies, so I was sure that if she needed help she would recognize it and tell me.

Peter's car was parked in the driveway when I arrived at the arena building, and the door was standing open. I parked my car close to the door so I wouldn't have to carry the box very far. I didn't know how heavy it would be, and I didn't want to ask Peter to carry it for me. If I was going to be a photographer, I should be able to haul around my own equipment and props. Peter stood in the center of the building and appeared to be looking for something.

"Hi, Peter."

Peter turned around and smiled. "Hey, Skye. I was just taking a last look at the place."

"Will the new kennel have a training arena?"

"Yes, she's got a very nice arena, not as big as this one, but I'm sure it'll be fine."

"I imagine you spent a lot of time in here." I thought Peter looked a little sad.

"Oh, definitely. I trained a lot of dogs for the show ring here." He spread his arms and turned in a circle. "Not many trainers have the advantage of a place like this. It's as big as a lot of show rings. Without the seats for spectators, of course."

"Does that make it easier to train a dog?"

"Not easier, really. But it lets you train the dog in an environment that is very similar to what he'll encounter in a show."

"So, the dog is more comfortable with the situation?"

"Exactly." He waved a hand in dismissal. "But

enough reminiscing. I found the box you mentioned. At least I think it's the right box." He walked over to the box and peered inside. "There's some doggie toys, along with some felt mice and a bunch of bottles of pet shampoo and stuff."

"That would be the props. Thanks for finding them for me."

"No problem. I had to come here anyway to feed and water the dogs. I'll feel better when I get them moved. I can't be here all the time, and I think they miss the companionship."

"Did Frank spend time with them?"

"No, not really. They were pretty much only a business for him. But he had a couple of handlers that took care of them and played with them. And during the day, they all got to be in the enclosed yard together. Unless Frank was training an attack dog. Both of the handlers quit last month, so I've been filling in."

That sounded like a not-so-great life to me, but then maybe dogs like it that way. Not Speedway, though. In the little time I'd had him, I knew he preferred to be with a human. Maybe little dogs were different from big dogs in that way.

"Is that difficult for them? To be moved to another place?"

"In some ways. But I know they'll be happy there. Until I decide what to do with them. I've got an animal talent agency interested in buying some of them. Maybe all of them. The dogs are well trained and they've got good résumés."

I picked up the box and turned to see Scott standing in the doorway.

"Scott. I didn't expect to see you here." That much was probably obvious by the look of surprise on my face.

"I saw your car in the driveway and thought I'd stop by." Scott nodded to Peter without smiling, which I thought was rude.

"I had to pick up a box of props that Lionel left here." I was kind of torn between not wanting Scott to think I was flying in the face of his advice and not wanting him to think I would blindly do whatever he told me to do.

"I've got to get the dogs' food ready and refill their water bowls," Peter said. "Just close the door when you leave, Skye."

"Sure, Peter." I scowled at Scott although he didn't seem to notice.

"Would it be possible to have a word with you when you finish with the dogs?" Scott asked.

"Sure," Peter said. "I'll come back here when I'm finished, or you can walk right over to the kennel building."

"Why do you want to talk to Peter?" I asked Scott. "Oh, no. You aren't going to arrest him, are you?"

"Honey, if I was going to arrest him, he'd already

have handcuffs on. Actually, I came to interview Taylor Hudson and some of the other neighbors. Then I saw your car and thought I'd say hello. And I figured Peter would be here."

"Really, Scott. I don't think you need to worry about me being around Peter. He didn't kill Frank. I just know it."

"No, you think he didn't kill Frank. But I know it," Scott said.

"You know it? So, he's not a suspect now? What happened to change that?"

Scott's mouth twitched like he might start laughing at any moment, but I didn't see what was so funny. "No, Peter is no longer considered a suspect in Frank Johnson's murder."

I'm sure my grin had a certain amount of smirk, but I refrained from saying I told you so. "How did that happen?"

"Frank's time of death is estimated at between eleven and one. Peter was having dinner with a friend on the coast at ten. They drove back to Portland, arriving at midnight, and the friend assures me they were otherwise occupied until well after two."

"How long have you known this?" I asked.

"Oh, I spoke with his friend the next day, but I had to wait until I knew the time of death before I could take him off the suspect list."

"So, you're really here to give Peter the good news."

"No. I wouldn't drive all the way out here to tell him something like that. I was going to call him later. I'm here to interview the neighbors."

"So, you think there's something to what Taylor Hudson said?" I asked.

"That's what I'm here to find out."

I left Scott to give Peter the good news and to interview Taylor Hudson. I would have liked to have been present for both conversations, but I had to drop my film off to be processed and besides, I was pretty certain Scott would have said no. Maybe not to me being there when he told Peter, but I knew he wouldn't want me there when he interviewed Taylor Hudson and the other neighbors. I'd have to call him later and wheedle the information out of him.

The film processor promised me contact sheets and transparencies by tomorrow morning. I would have liked to think it was because of his respect for me as a professional photographer, but I knew it was really because of the amount of business Steinhart threw his way. In any case, I was done with the shoot. Tomorrow I'd review the contact sheets and transparencies, choose the ones I thought were best, and go over them with Connie if she ever decided to return to Portland. I was still concerned about her. I mean, really, what chance does a marriage made under those circumstances have?

Connie was very successful. She lived in a beautiful condo in downtown Portland. She wore designer clothes and ate at expensive and exclusive restaurants. She was known in Portland. And she'd married some beach bum from the Caribbean whose most prized possessions were probably a bong and a sarong. I figured he'd married her for her money and she'd end up paying a tidy sum to get rid of him. Not that she couldn't afford it, but her heart would be broken and I hated that. Connie was a sweetheart and she deserved better than some man who only saw dollar signs when he looked at her.

My phone buzzed and I pulled it from my bag and looked at the display screen. A text message.

I need you at the house.

The message was from Lily and I immediately thought of Bobbi Jo. But it hadn't been the special code of two-two-two-nine for baby. Still, if Lily needed me at the house, and I assumed she meant Bobbi Jo's house, something must be happening. I couldn't text her back without stopping the car, and if she'd texted me, then I assumed there was a reason she couldn't call me. That thought was even more confusing. Why would she text me when she could have called? Personally, I don't get texting. I mean, sure, there are times when a text message is better than a phone call. Say, if you need to get a message to someone in a meeting and they can't really answer the phone. Or if you need to send certain information to someone, like an address or someone's phone number. But I really didn't understand why anyone would choose to type in a message with their thumbs on a teeny keyboard when they could call the person and talk. I punched her speed dial number and then *talk* and listened to the phone ring a few times, then go to voice mail. Something was definitely going on. I turned at the next street and headed for Bobbi Jo's minimansion.

When I arrived, Bobbi Jo's Escalade wasn't in the driveway. I rang the doorbell and heard some quick footsteps from inside. Lily flung the door open.

"Skye, what a surprise. I'm so glad you stopped by. Chase is here and wants me to take a look at the apartment. I'd love for you to come with us. You know how important a second opinion can be. And besides, you have such a good eye for design, you know, what with being a photographer and all. Must have something to do with visual composition, I guess."

Lily pulled me into the foyer, making some really strange faces while she was talking. She dragged me to the kitchen, where Chase was perched on a stool at the breakfast table.

"Chase, look, Skye showed up. Isn't that great?"

"Sure, I guess. So, can you come and look at the apartment?"

"Oh, of course. I mean, Bobbie Jo is out with Skye's mother, so it's not like I have to be here. And Skye can come, too. Can't you, Skye?"

"I guess I can. What are we going to look at?"

"I've marked off the areas for the skylights," Chase said. "I thought Lily should have a look at them before I cut into the roof."

"Good idea," I said. By then, I'd figured this was another case of Lily not wanting to be alone with Chase. I had no idea how she thought she could manage to never be alone with him until the apartment was completed. Actually, I did have an idea and it involved her calling me every time she had to see him. Like my life wasn't full enough already.

"I figured I could drive us over in my pickup and then bring you ladies back," Chase said.

"Oh, no, that's too much trouble. Why don't Skye and I meet you over there," Lily suggested.

"Seems like a waste of gas to me," Chase said.

Lily was a staunch supporter of carpooling, turning off lights when they weren't necessary, and taking your own bags to the grocery store instead of using disposable plastic or paper bags. Using gas unnecessarily was completely against her nature, and I could see the pain of the dilemma on her face.

"I guess you're right." Lily frowned, then brightened. "But if you take us there, you'll have to bring us home and that would be a waste of gas, too."

"Not really. I have to come back this way anyway."

"Oh, well, then, it all works out. Let's go." Lily headed for the foyer, took a sweater from the coat closet, and pulled me out the door to wait for Chase. He sauntered out behind us and Lily closed the door. When we got to Chase's truck, he opened the passenger door and Lily pushed me inside, then sat beside me and closed the door. I guessed she didn't want to sit next to Chase in the crowded front seat. Chase got in, started the truck, and we took off for Lily's shop and apartment. After the short drive to Hawthorne Boulevard, he parked in back of the building and we made our way up the outside stairs to Lily's apartment.

Inside, Chase walked to the center of the living area and pointed to a two-inch hole he'd made in the roof. Lily and I both looked up at the hole and the light spilling from it.

"You put a hole in the ceiling?" Lily asked.

"That's where I think the skylight should be in here," Chase said. "You can see where the light would go from the light coming in the hole."

I nodded. We could kind of tell what direction the light would come in at this time of day. But what about the morning?

"The slope of the roof here faces south, so you'd get the most light. But if you want less light, we'd need to put it over here." Chase walked a few feet and pointed up.

"No, I'd like as much light as I can get. So this is perfect," Lily said. "What do you think, Skye?"

"I like it." I nodded. "But do you think it would be too hot in the summer with the afternoon light?"

"Not a problem," Chase said. "The skylights have a screen that you can close with a remote, so if it's too much light or too hot, you can block the sun."

"Really? That's a nice feature." I looked at the kitchen. "Will the other skylights have the same screen?"

"Absolutely. And the remote will work on all the windows. Although each room will have its own remote." Chase walked to the kitchen and pointed to another hole in the ceiling. "Now, this part of the room points east, so you'll get more light in the morning. Not that you really have any other options for this room."

"Oh, that's good. It'll be nice to have light in the kitchen in the morning."

"You want to go to the bedroom?" Chase asked.

"No, I don't think so." Lily shook her head.

"I think he wants to you see the position of the skylight in the bedroom." I put my hand on Lily's arm in an effort to calm her down.

"And the one in the bathroom, too," Chase said. "I want to be sure the skylights are what you want and where you want them."

"Of course," Lily agreed.

After we'd checked out the position of the skylights and Lily had assured Chase they were exactly what she wanted, we all piled into the truck for the ride back to Bobbi Jo's. Lily had pushed me in ahead of her again, and as soon as Chase stopped the truck in Bobbi Jo's driveway, she opened the door and flew out.

"I've got to go get dinner ready," she said. "Thank you so much for everything you've done, Chase. Bye." Lily almost ran to the front door.

"Is Lily all right?" Chase asked.

"Oh, sure, she's fine. Just stressed out, you know. It's not easy being a doula and taking care of Bobbi Jo." I wondered if I should tell Chase what was going on with Lily, but decided I needed to clear it with Lily first.

"Yeah. Seems like everyone's stressed out right now. I hope it'll be better after the baby comes."

"Oh, I'm sure it will be."

"When's the baby due?" Chase asked.

"Anytime now."

As if on cue, Bobbi Jo's Escalade pulled into the driveway next to Chase's truck. Chase hustled over to open Bobbi Jo's door and help her out.

"Oh, thank you," Bobbi Jo said. "You are such a sweetheart. I swear, it's hard to do anything in this condition." She laughed and rubbed her belly. "Oh, the baby's moving."

Chase stared at her rounded belly.

"You want to feel it?" Bobbi Jo asked, then without waiting for an answer, took Chase's hand and placed it on the top of her tummy. "Isn't that something?"

"Wow. It is." Chase grinned.

Mom had extricated herself from the vehicle and pulled a couple of shopping bags from the backseat. She glanced at Bobbi Jo and Chase and raised her eyebrows at me, then walked to the front door. I knew what Mom's raised eyebrows meant. They meant she thought something was going on.

"Where's Lily, Skye?" Bobbi Jo asked.

"She's getting dinner started," I said.

"Oh, good. I'm starving. Of course, I'm always starving these days." Bobbi Jo laughed and placed her hand over Chase's hand, which was still on her belly. "If I don't have this baby soon, they're going to need a hoist and crane to get me into the hospital."

"It's good you've gained weight. Means you'll have a healthy baby," Chase said.

"Oh, you are the sweetest thing," Bobbi Jo said. "Do you want to stay for dinner? I'm sure Lily is making something wonderful. She always does."

"Thanks, but I have to deliver some flooring to a job. Maybe some other time?"

I watched Bobbi Jo and Chase say good-bye and

wondered if there was something I was missing. It was almost like he was flirting with her, but not exactly. Maybe he was just a flirtatious man. It would be understandable, as gorgeous as he was. Probably came very easily to him. And it was so good to see Bobbi Jo being herself again. When Chase was around, she seemed not to mind that she was hugely pregnant, her hormones appeared to level out, and she was smiling and happy. Anything he did to make that happen was fine by me.

"See you around, Skye." Chase waved and backed his truck out of the driveway. Bobbi Jo and I went into the house and I followed Lily to the kitchen. She wasn't getting dinner ready. She was sitting on a stool at the breakfast table with her head in her hands.

"Are you all right?" I asked.

"No. No, I'm not all right. Skye, I can't take much more of this. I like Chase, I really do. He's a nice man, and he's so good at what he does. But I'm terrified to be alone with him. What if he says something or does something?"

"Lily, you need to talk to him. Tell him how you feel. He seems like a very sensitive man. He'll understand." It sounded good to me. Not that I have a sterling record of understanding men or their motives. But what else could I say?

"I can't. I know what will happen. I'll start talking, then he'll say something and that will throw me off, and

I'll end up in a relationship with him."

I put my hand on her back and patted it sympathetically.

"I don't want to be in a relationship right now. Especially not with Chase. He's too young. He's too good-looking. He's too nice. I can't do it."

I started to point out that a lot of women would love to have such a problem, but I realized it probably wasn't what she wanted to hear.

CHAPTER FOURTEEN

Mom insisted on making dinner, saying it was the least she could do after Bobbi Jo and Lily being so nice and taking such good care of her. I felt a tiny bit guilty about not spending more time with her. Bobbi Jo, Lily, and I sat in the living room and chatted. Bobbi Jo was still in a good mood and hardly even mentioned her pregnancy, but Lily was still distressed about Chase. Her thoughts seemed to wander and more than once she lost track of our conversation. Bobbi Jo kept sending me quizzical looks, then finally turned to Lily.

"Lily, what in gawd's name is wrong with you?"

"What?" Lily looked from me Bobbi Jo to me and back again. "What do you mean?"

"I've asked you three questions and each time you didn't even know what we were talking about. So, I'm guessing you're thinking about something else. What is it?"

"Oh." Lily fidgeted and plucked some nonexistent lint from her sleeve, then smoothed the front of her shirt. "I don't know. I guess I'm just distracted."

"Distracted?" Bobbi Jo asked. "The only time I've been that distracted, it's been because of a man."

Lily looked startled.

"Oh, it is a man!" Bobbi Jo leaned forward as much as her belly would allow. "Who is it? We want details."

Lily shot me a look and I shrugged. I wasn't going to bring it up to Bobbi Jo because I thought if Lily wanted her to know she'd tell her.

Lily sighed and her shoulders slumped. "It's Chase."

"Oh, darlin', do you have a crush on him? Well, you shouldn't feel bad about that. He's the most gorgeous man I've ever laid eyes on."

"He's pretty good-looking," I agreed.

"I bet every woman who meets him develops some kind of little crush on him. I mean, what's not to like? Aside from the looks, he's just so kind and gentle and down to earth. Why, I feel like I've known him for years and today was only the second time I've laid eyes on him."

"It's not that," Lily said.

"What, you don't have a crush on him?" Bobbi Jo looked disbelieving. "Then what is it? Isn't he doing a good job on the apartment?"

"Oh, his work is excellent. He's a perfectionist about everything, and he has a really good eye for design. I couldn't be happier with what he's doing on the apartment."

Lily looked like she was in pain, and I figured it was difficult for her to talk about it, so I stepped in.

"It's that Chase seems to have a crush on Lily and she's not ready for a relationship," I said.

"Have you lost your mind, Lily?" Bobbi Jo asked. "I tell you what. If a man like Chase wanted a relationship with me, he wouldn't have to ask twice."

"I know, Bobbi Jo. He's good-looking and nice and wonderful. But he's also a lot younger than me and that could cause problems later. Besides, I just don't want a relationship right now. I'm still kind of getting to know myself without a man."

"Well, you have had more than your share." Bobbi Jo laughed. "I'm only kidding, you know. So, why don't you simply tell him how you feel?"

"That's what I suggested," I said.

"But . . ." Lily sighed again.

"But, what, Lily?" Bobbi Jo asked.

I knew what. Lily had already told me she was afraid she couldn't say no. But I decided it wasn't my place to reveal her secrets to Bobbi Jo. Fortunately, Lily decided to confide in Bobbi Jo, because I know myself, and, eventually, I would have told her anyway.

"I have a difficult time saying no to a relationship," Lily said in a small voice.

"You have got to be kidding me," Bobbi Jo said. "I have never known you to be the least bit reluctant to tell anyone how you feel about something."

"I know. And that's true for almost anything but this. How do you think I ended up married to one man and lover to another? I don't mean I didn't love both of them, but I'm not sure it was really my idea to do it."

"Is that why you had sex so often with them? Because you couldn't say no?" Bobbi Jo asked.

"Oh, no. Not at all. I was happy with the frequency of sex I had with Grant and Kyle. In fact, I miss it. I can say no to sex. I just can't tell a man I don't want to be in a relationship. It seems like such a huge rejection."

"It is a rejection, but, Lily, you can't go around having a relationship with every man who wants one," I said. "You need to think about yourself. Put yourself first."

"I'm trying. I really am."

"Well," Bobbi Jo said, "I think I can help you out. See, if you reject Chase, then I could have him. You'd be happy, he'd be happy, and gawd knows I'd be happy."

When I got back to the loft after having dinner with Bobbi Jo, Lily, and Mom, I found Sheridan sitting on the sofa crying her eyes out. Speedway sat next to her, a paw extended to rest on her leg. My heart ached for her.

Mothers spend so much time protecting their children while they are growing up that it's hard to see them get hurt in a way you can't make better. Scrapes and bruises are easy to deal with. Blow on a scraped knee, buy the special bandages with cartoon characters on them, and provide treats to distract the child from the pain. But there's not much you can do about a broken heart. I dropped my bag at the door and walked over to sit next to her. Speedway crawled up onto her lap to give me room. I put an arm around her shoulder, and she leaned her head against me, still sobbing.

"Sweetie, what's wrong?" Of course, I knew what was wrong. That bastard Zack had broken her heart.

"I tried so hard. I really did, Mom."

"I know you did." I stroked her dark hair and made sympathetic noises.

"I did everything I could think of. Nothing worked. Nothing was enough."

The more Sheridan talked, the angrier I felt. Zack had used her and it pissed me off. I'd tell Connie, and she'd fire him. That didn't seem like enough punishment, though. Maybe I could find a way to humiliate him. Humiliation would be an excellent punishment. Especially for someone like Zack, who obviously had a huge ego.

"You must be so disappointed in me," Sheridan said.

"What? Why would you say that?" I hugged her fiercely. "This isn't your fault, sweetie. It's a horrible thing to go through, but it's a part of growing up."

"Growing up?" Sheridan plucked a couple of tissues from the box on the coffee table and blew her nose. "I don't think you understand."

"Of course I understand. He used you. He's one of those men who take what they want without any regard for anyone else. I know you probably don't want to hear this, but you're better off without him. You're too good for someone who would treat you like this."

"What are you talking about?" she asked.

Her confusion broke through my anger, and I started to think possibly we were talking about different things. Sheridan hadn't really told me why she was crying. I'd simply assumed Zack had broken her heart.

"I'm talking about Zack. What are you talking about?" I asked.

"Mom!" Sheridan rolled her eyes. "I flunked math."

"You flunked math? What about Zack?"

"What about him?"

"I thought this was about Zack," I said. "When Zack came to the shoot to art direct the Christmas shot, he told me he thought of you as a friend, but he wasn't romantically interested in you."

"Yeah, I know that," Sheridan said. "Oh."

"Oh, what?"

"Well, I guess I kind of led you to believe there was something between Zack and me." Sheridan scratched Speedway's head and rubbed his ears. The little dog rolled over to give her access to his belly.

"Well, yes, you did. In fact you were pretty insistent that you two were dating and it was none of my business."

"Well, it wasn't," she said. "Okay. Really I told you that because I didn't want you to know Zack was tutoring me in math."

"Why not?"

"Because I've never needed a tutor before. I didn't want you to think I couldn't learn it on my own."

I was stunned. That's what all this had been about? I'd been worried about my little girl getting her heart broken, and it was only that she was having trouble with math? I didn't know whether to laugh or cry.

"I'm not interested in Zack, either. Well, just as a friend. He's a really great singer, and we have a good time together, but he's a single dad with two kids. Not that there's anything wrong with that, but we live entirely different lives."

"Sweetie, it's just math. Did you really think I'd be upset?" It was a horrifying thought. What had I done to make her think I'd be angry if she flunked math?

"It's just that I didn't want to disappoint you." Sheridan rubbed Speedway's little belly, then picked him

299

up and cuddled him to her chest.

My heart dropped. Did Sheridan really think I'd be disappointed in her? I felt terrible. Like I'd been a bad mother. What had I done to make her think that way?

"Oh, sweetie, you could never disappoint me. Why would you think that?"

Sheridan shrugged. "I don't know. I've always done really well in school, and I know you've always been proud of me for that, so I figured if I flunked a class you'd be disappointed."

I'd always thought my mother expected perfection from me, and now it seemed I'd passed it on to Sheridan. It was an awful feeling because Sheridan would always be perfect to me, no matter what she failed at. Then I wondered if I'd misjudged my mother all those years. Was I the one assuming she was disappointed in me? That I wasn't perfect in her eyes? Maybe I needed to reevaluate my relationship with my own mother. But first I needed to reassure Sheridan.

"Sheridan, I will always think you're perfect. I can't imagine what you could do that would ever disappoint me." I wrapped my arms around her and squeezed. "I feel terrible that you thought that."

Sheridan returned the hug. "It's okay, Mom. I think it was just a shock to me that there was a class I totally sucked at." She laughed. "Even Zack couldn't help me that much, and he's really good at math."

"Math." I waved a hand in dismissal. "Who needs it?"

"Well, I do in order to graduate," Sheridan said.

"We'll get you a better tutor. Or you can take an easier math class."

After the math discussion, Sheridan and I watched a movie on television with Speedway tucked between us on the sofa. It was good to spend a few hours with her. We hadn't done that in a long time. When we went to bed, Sheridan carried him into her room. So much for the doggie bed I'd bought him.

The next morning she went off to class, and I drank coffee and thought about the day ahead. I was relieved to have the photography finished, but I still needed to look at the contact sheets and transparencies. The processor had said the last of them would be ready today, so I'd probably spend the next day or so selecting the ones I thought were best, so Connie could make the final decision on which ones to use. Before I could summon the energy to get into the shower, however, my phone rang.

"Hello?"

"Hi, gorgeous," Scott said.

"Well, hello yourself, handsome."

"I was thinking we could do something this weekend. Maybe get away from everything."

"I'd love to," I said. Then I remembered Bobbi Jo. "But I can't. Bobbi Jo is going to have that baby any minute, and I promised her I'd be there."

"Right. I forgot about that. Well, with any luck, she'll have the baby before the weekend, and then we could go to the coast for a couple of days."

"That sounds great, but we probably shouldn't count on it." I didn't want to tell him Bobbi Jo might want me at her side after the baby arrived. I could wait and see how she reacted to being a new mom. Hopefully, having my mother and Lily around would be enough for her, because the idea for a weekend with Scott was extremely appealing.

"I understand. How about dinner tonight, then?"

"Sounds great. Somewhere casual? Maybe Fatz?" I wasn't in the mood to get all dressed up and I knew Scott loved the burgers and beer at Fatz.

"Fatz is perfect. And it's close to my apartment." His voice had dropped to a low tone I found very sexy, but I knew we couldn't get into one of those conversations while Scott was at the station.

"How did your interviews with Taylor Hudson and the neighbors go?"

"About what I'd expected. Most of the neighbors were open about how much the dogs had bothered them, and they weren't unhappy they'd been moved. But none of them seemed upset enough to take Frank's life over it. Hudson said he'd been home with his wife, and she said she'd know if he'd left the bed because she always woke up when his snoring stopped."

"Pretty much a dead end, huh?" I was a little disappointed. Not that I wanted one of them to be guilty, but Lionel was still considered a suspect, and I wanted something that would clear him or at least knock him off the top of the list. Scott hadn't told me if he had any suspects other than Lionel.

"So, Lionel is still a suspect?"

"Yes, I'm afraid so. But I have to admit I don't think he had a very strong motive. There's nothing to indicate he has an unstable personality, and it would be extreme for someone to kill over not being able to buy a dog."

I decided not to pass along what Lily had said about how some show dog owners can be. Besides, Lionel wasn't getting the dog to show; he wanted a dog to be a companion. I only wished Scott had a better suspect than Lionel. I still thought Irene was probably capable of murder, but Scott insisted it had to be a man because of the bruise pattern, and he didn't see that she had a motive to kill him. I wasn't sure Irene would need a very strong motive. I thought the woman was a little off center.

Scott and I agreed to meet at Fatz at seven, then he got another call and had to hang up. Sheridan had taken Speedway out for a walk before she left for school, and he was curled up on the sofa sleeping. I had to admit he wasn't nearly as much trouble as I'd thought he would be, and I enjoyed having him around. Sheridan was getting attached to him, and I knew I'd have a hard time giving him back to Peter. After a quick shower, I pulled on a pair of jeans and a sweater, tucked Speedway under my arm, and took the elevator down to the parking garage. I stopped by Steinhart's Studio to check my schedule, hoping I still had a few days before my next photo shoot.

"What the hell is that thing?" Steinhart stood in the doorway of his office pointing at me. Well, pointing to Speedway, actually.

"It's a dog, Benjamin," I said helpfully.

"I know that, Donovan. What the hell is it doing in my studio?"

"Nothing. I came in to check my schedule. I'm not going to let him down or anything."

"I should hope not." Benjamin gave the dog a look that conveyed distaste. Speedway rumbled a tiny growl, then blinked and wagged his tail.

"Sorry," I said.

"Don't let it happen again." Benjamin stepped into his office and picked up the photo schedule, then came back out. "You're scheduled for a fashion shoot next week. Should be three days, but there's some outdoor shots downtown, so I'm leaving the fourth day open for you in case we have bad weather."

"Great. Nothing for this week?"

"No. Are you desperate for work?" he asked.

"No. In fact, it'll be nice to have some free time. My mother is visiting, and my best friend is due to have a baby any minute."

Benjamin held his hand up. "I really don't want to know." He wasn't the warm-fuzzies kind of boss.

I said good-bye and scooted out of the studio before Speedway could do something to annoy him. Since I had the day free, I drove to Bobbi Jo's, hoping she'd have something I could eat for breakfast. I was in luck.

"Lily just got some fresh croissants from that bakery downtown," Bobbi Jo said. "And your mother made a fruit salad. I think we have some bagels and cream cheese, or you can make yourself some eggs, if you want."

"Fruit salad and a croissant sound perfect." I pulled the container of fruit salad from Bobbi Jo's enormous subzero refrigerator and spooned a healthy serving into a bowl, then plucked a croissant from the plastic bag Lily had stored them in and sat at the breakfast table. Bobbi Jo poured a cup of coffee for me and herself and sat down with me.

"Chase is coming by to see Lily today," she confided.

"About the apartment?"

"That's the story. I guess he has some samples to show her." Bobbi Jo grinned. "I wouldn't mind if he showed me his samples."

"Bobbi Jo, what has gotten into you?" I laughed because it was good to see my friend being her normal self again.

"I don't know what it is, but I'm feeling more like myself now. Maybe that means I'm going to have this baby soon."

"The last few weeks are hard. I remember that from my pregnancy. But soon you'll have the baby, then it'll be hard, but in a different way."

"The whole damn pregnancy has been hard," Bobbi Jo said. "Probably because of losing Edward." She shook her head. "That was a lot to go through. I still miss him."

"Of course you do. But it's getting easier, isn't it?"

"In some ways. Actually, I feel a little guilty about finding Chase so attractive. Does that make sense?"

"Sure. But don't feel guilty. Edward would want you to go on with your life. He'd be thrilled if you found someone to share it with. Besides, I think finding Chase attractive is a normal reaction. I mean, the man is really something to look at."

"He is that." Bobbi Jo laughed. "And it doesn't hurt that he's so kind and nice, either. I guess I've always had a thing for men who are attentive." Bobbi Jo yawned and stretched. "I think I'm going to go upstairs for a little catnap. I get so tired these days, and the doctor told me to rest anytime I want."

"Good idea." I didn't tell her she probably wouldn't be getting much rest for a few months after she had the baby. Some things are better left unsaid. Lily came in as

Bobbi Jo waddled toward the doorway.

"I'm going to take a little nap, Lily," Bobbi Jo said.

"Might as well get the rest while you can," Lily said. "Once the baby comes—"

I shook my head behind Bobbi Jo's back and made some frantic gestures to get Lily to shut up. "You'll be so excited, you won't want to sleep."

Lily watched Bobbi Jo leave, then turned to me. "So excited she won't want to sleep? Where did you get that from?"

"She was happy and calm. I didn't want to say anything that might upset her," I said.

"Good thinking. Did she tell you Chase is coming over?"

"Yes. What does he want?"

"Goddess, I don't know. He said something about carpet samples." Lily poured herself a cup of coffee and sat next to me at the table. "This whole situation is draining. I'm so terrified he's going to want something I don't want to give. It's gotten to the point it might be easier to simply tell him up front I can't be in a relationship right now."

"That would take care of the situation," I said.

"I really don't want to hurt his feelings."

"It's not like you're breaking off a long-term relationship. You're just letting him know what you are and aren't interested in from him."

"You think he'll be all right with it?" Lily asked.

"I'm sure he will."

The doorbell rang, and Lily looked at me. It was that deer-frozen-in-the-headlights look. I patted her hand and found it ice cold. "You want me to answer the door?"

"No. I need to face this head-on. I need to take control of my life." Lily rose and strode to the doorway, then turned back. "You'll be here in case I need you, right?"

"Absolutely," I assured her. I got another cup of coffee and settled down to eavesdrop on Lily's conversation with Chase. After the barest of greetings, she got right down to business.

"I need to talk to you about something, Chase."

"Sure, what is it?"

"I think of you as a very good friend. I know we haven't known each other a long time, but we've worked together very well on my apartment remodel."

"I think of you as a friend, too, Lily," Chase said.

"Good. That's good. But, Chase, I need to let you know I don't want anything else from you." Lily's voice was tight and a little squeaky, but I was proud she was able to say what she needed to say.

"Oh. I see. I'm sorry you feel that way." Chase sounded like his heart was broken. I wasn't sure what that really sounded like, but that was my take on it.

"I hate having to say it," Lily said.

"No. You should feel free to say anything to me. I mean I really care about you and about what you think of me. I'm just sorry it came to this."

"I'm sorry, too, Chase. Maybe if things were different . . ."

"Different how?" Chase asked. "If there's anything I can change or do differently that would make you happy, I'd be more than willing to try."

"That's so nice of you, Chase, but it's not that. It's just that we aren't compatible on a lot of levels. There's the age difference for one thing."

"Age difference?" Chase asked. "You think I'm too young? I have a lot of experience, and I have good references. If there's something you aren't happy with, just tell me and I'll fix it."

Suddenly I had the feeling that Lily and Chase were talking about two different things. I hoped Lily would realize it soon, too. Before she totally embarrassed herself.

CHAPTER
FIFTEEN

I inched my way into the dining room and squeezed into a corner behind an enormous potted plant. I was pretty sure Lily and Chase couldn't see me. Normally, I don't eavesdrop on my friends' conversations, but this was important. I needed to hear what Lily was saying to Chase, and I wanted to be close by in case an intervention was necessary. Lily stood in front of Chase, who was seated on the sofa. Chase had pulled out some carpet samples from the worn shopping bag.

"Oh," Lily said. "I see. Well, you know, I think it's because I'm second-guessing everything I'm doing."

"Don't worry about it, Lily. Everyone does it. Remodeling is a huge commitment. Exactly. You're bound to doubt your decisions along the way. But don't worry. Part of my job is to make sure you don't make any expensive mistakes. Now, are we good?"

"Oh, yes, we are. We are very good, indeed. So,

show me those samples you brought over," Lily said.

I decided I'd involve myself in the sample selection, so I placed some cups and the coffee carafe on a tray and strolled into the living room.

"Does anyone want some coffee?" I asked. Lily looked relieved at my interruption. "Oh, you've got carpet samples." I set the tray down on the coffee table and picked up a square of carpet.

"It's for the bedroom," Chase said. "The rest of the apartment is hardwood flooring, but carpet is usually more comfortable in the bedroom."

"Oh, I agree," Lily said. "Definitely carpet in the bedroom."

Lily looked like she might bolt from the room any second. I showed her one of the samples. "Do you like this one? It's got a little pink tone in the beige. That would look nice, don't you think?"

"I guess so. Let's go with that one," Lily said.

"You don't want to rush this decision," Chase said. "Take your time and look at all of them."

Lily seemed to calm down a bit and picked up the ring that held the carpet samples. She flipped past several. "I don't care for green, so I can eliminate them. Blue isn't good, either." That pretty much left the beige ones. She held a couple of them up to compare, selected one, and handed it to Chase. It was the pinky beige one I'd chosen. I wasn't sure she'd taken enough time to look at all of them, but I thought she'd be happy with it, and she looked like she really wanted to leave.

"I have to run. Lots to do. I'll see you later." Lily hustled out of the room and took the stairs up to the second floor. I figured she was going to hide in her bedroom until Chase left.

"It sounds like Lily's apartment is almost ready," I said to Chase.

"I figure a couple more weeks to finish everything up, then she's ready to move in." Chase picked up the carpet samples and stuffed them into a shopping bag. "Can I ask you something, Skye?"

"Of course."

"That conversation I just had with Lily. Did she think I wanted more than friendship with her?"

"Well, yes. I mean, I think she got the impression you might be interested in a relationship."

Chase chuckled. "Don't get me wrong. I like Lily a lot. But I'm not romantically interested in her. I didn't want to hurt her feelings, though."

"So, you knew what she was talking about and pretended she meant your business relationship?"

"Yeah. I probably should have been up front with her, but it seemed like she was nervous about the whole thing, and I thought she might be embarrassed if I knew she thought I was romantically interested when I wasn't. Does that make any sense?"

"Of course. And it was really nice of you to spare her feelings. I think Lily thought you were romantically interested because it appeared you were looking for opportunities to see her." I wanted to give Chase an opportunity to tell me what was really going on. I could dismiss some behavior that appeared to be flirtatious but might have just been friendly, but I believed Chase had been looking for opportunities to come over, and I thought I knew why.

"Oh. That." Chase shuffled his feet and ducked his head, looking like a seven-year-old. "That was because of your other friend."

"Bobbi Jo?" I asked.

Chase nodded. I chuckled.

"I can't help it," he said.

"What? Being attracted to her?"

"Yes. I mean, I know it's probably wrong with her being pregnant and her husband passing less than a year ago."

"Nonsense. You can't control what you feel based on circumstances."

"You're probably right about that," Chase said. "But I should be able to control my reactions."

"I don't know." I shrugged. "There's something to be said for reactions you have no control over."

Chase stared at me for a moment and seemed to be considering what I said. I considered what I'd said, as well. Should I be encouraging him? Should I tell him to back off? Bobbi Jo was obviously infatuated with him.

True, her husband had passed less than a year earlier, and she was about to give birth to that husband's son. But whoever decided mourning should take place during a certain time period was stupid. Bobbi Jo had mourned Edward's death. She had loved him completely, and she missed him madly. But did that mean she should ignore a chance at loving another man because the chance came along less than a year later? I didn't think so. I believed we should take love wherever and whenever we stumbled across it. And as Bobbi Jo's best friend, I felt it was my duty to encourage her.

"I really don't think I have any control over what I'm feeling," Chase said. "I mean, she's so damn beautiful. And charming. And . . . enticing."

"Do you have a thing for pregnant women?" I asked him.

"What?" He seemed to consider the question for a moment, then shook his head. "Not until now. But what do I do? I mean it seems a little weird to ask a woman out when she might go into labor in the middle of the date."

He had a point.

"You don't have to go out on a date. Just be there for her." I figured that was really the acid test. Any man who could *be there* for a woman in the emotional throes of the final days of a pregnancy got high points in my book. I didn't know if Chase was really up to the challenge, but if he was, it was to Bobbi Jo's advantage.

"You can date after the baby arrives. Not immediately, of course, but you'll know when it's right."

"That would be cool," Chase said.

"Yes, it would be. Now, go finish Lily's apartment because she needs to get out of here, and Bobbi Jo needs to stand on her own two feet when she has this baby." I felt immensely wise with those words. Chase must have thought so, too, because he happily packed up his samples, trotted out to his beat-up old pickup truck, and headed out to finish Lily's apartment.

I flopped back onto the sofa and enjoyed a couple of minutes of feeling superior until my cell phone chirped. I pulled it out of my pants pocket praying it wasn't some emergency that required my attention.

"Hello?"

"Hey, babe. I have to cancel our dinner plans," Scott said.

"Work?" I guessed.

"I'm afraid so. Irene needs to meet with me to get an update on the Frank Johnson case."

Irene again. That woman was swiftly becoming the bane of my existence. Why did she have to meet with Scott now? I asked him as much.

"I don't know. She's busy being the mayor and running for some state office or something. Anyway, the only time she has is over dinner."

"Of course it is." All right, my tone might have been

a bit sarcastic.

"Skye, it's only business."

"No, it's not only business. I can't believe you can't see it. The woman has made it obvious she's interested in you. She even tracked you to your apartment when we—well, you know—had a date. I think she wants a lot more than an update."

"You're wrong, Skye. You're reading something into it. Besides, this isn't a one-way street. Even if you don't trust her motives, you can trust me."

"Whatever. I'll talk to you later." I flipped my cell phone closed, ending the conversation. Of course, Scott was right that I could trust him. But still, I was pissed off at how incredibly stupid men could be when it came to women. Well, some women.

"You look fit to be tied," Lily said.

"What?" I jerked around to see Lily standing on the bottom step of the stairs. "I guess I am. I swear, men can be so freaking stupid."

"Honey," Lily said holding up a hand. "You're preaching to the choir. Did Chase leave?"

"Yes, he ran off to finish up your apartment."

"Skye, I totally misjudged him and the situation. Holy Goddess, I'm so embarrassed."

"You shouldn't be. For one thing, I thought he was flirting with you, too. And for another," I lowered my voice, "he's got a crush on Bobbi Jo."

"Oh, that's wonderful!"

"I know," I said. "That's why he's been making excuses to come over here all the time."

"How did you find that out?" Lily asked.

"Just a little conversation and it spilled right out of him." I wasn't about to tell her that he had figured out what was going on with her. "But, listen, I am so proud of you! You took matters into your own hands and set healthy boundaries for your relationship with him."

"But I was wrong. He never wanted a relationship with me. He thought I was talking about the work he's doing on my apartment."

"That isn't the point, Lily." I took her hands in mine and pulled her down to sit on the sofa. "You saw a situation and took control. You told him exactly what you could and could not deal with. It doesn't matter that it was a different situation. You crossed a bridge. The next time a man wants a relationship you aren't ready for, you'll be able to say no."

"Really? I did that?" Lily asked.

"Yes, you did that."

"Good." Lily straightened her shoulders. "I feel good about doing that. And I'm so relieved Chase never figured out what I really thought he wanted from me. Goddess, that would have been embarrassing."

"You have nothing to be embarrassed about," I assured her. Well, nothing she knew about, anyway. "I've got to run out to pick up some contact sheets and transparencies from the shoot."

"Of course," Lily said. "Goddess, I feel so much better about this whole thing with Chase. Isn't it wonderful he has a crush on Bobbi Jo? If you ask me, it's exactly what she needs. I just hope Chase isn't too impatient with her. I mean, she's about to give birth, and all her attention will be on the baby for a while."

"I had a little conversation with him about it. I think he'll be fine," I said. I gathered my bag and sweater, kissed Lily good-bye, and scooted out the door. I really did have to pick up the contact sheets and transparencies, and I thought it was better I get away from Lily. Less chance of me saying something that would make her question her judgment of the situation. I was halfway to the processor's when my cell phone chirped again. I pulled the phone from my pocket thinking it was probably Scott making more excuses.

"What?"

"Skye? It's Connie."

Evidently my patience had been completely used up by the situation with Lily, Chase, and Bobbi Jo, because I kind of snapped at her.

"Where are you?"

"Actually, I'm in a plane somewhere over the Midwest, and I should arrive in Portland in a few hours."

I wanted to tell her it was about freaking time she returned to reality. But maybe that was because I'd had a little too much reality myself. I heard something in the background about champagne. Must be nice.

"Are you flying first class?" I asked, trying to keep the envy out of my voice.

"Better than that, Skye. But listen, I'll be there soon. I wanted to let you know that and I wanted to ask if Bobbi Jo had her baby yet."

Oh, nice that she actually remembered a friend was about to go into labor. Perhaps this was an indication she'd ditched the Rastafarian dude and had come to her senses. I could only hope.

"No baby yet, but it could be any minute," I said.

"That's great. I really want to be there for the delivery."

Funny, at this point, I wasn't sure *I* even wanted to be there for the delivery. Then I heard some muffled giggling, a couple of sounds that had to be sighs, and a sound I interpreted as the clinking of glassware.

"So, I'm almost there. If she goes into labor, leave a message on my cell, and I'll pick it up as soon as we land," Connie said.

"We?" I asked.

"Me and Ty, of course. You didn't think I'd leave my husband behind, did you?"

I heard another muffled giggle, and the line went dead. Great. Connie was bringing her beach bum husband home. I didn't want to think about it. In fact, I didn't want to think about anything. I especially didn't want to think about Scott seeing Irene for dinner. I needed something fun to do that would take my mind off everything. Somehow looking at contact sheets and transparencies didn't sound like a lot of fun.

I considered taking Mom to the coast, but I knew Bobbi Jo would have a fit if she knew I might be over an hour away in case she went into labor. Still, I hadn't really spent any one-on-one time with my mother, and after my last conversation with Sheridan, I wondered if the problem with my relationship with Mom was based on my perceptions. It was something I wanted to look at, and the best way would be to spend some time with her without any other interactions. I turned the car around and headed back to Bobbi Jo's. Mom was in the living room winding a skein of yarn into a ball.

"Morning, Skye."

"Hi, Mom. I was just thinking that we haven't had any time alone. How about we go shopping and have lunch today?"

Mom practically glowed with pleasure. Which made me feel a little guilty about how little time I'd spent with her.

"I think it's a wonderful idea," she said. "I'll go change clothes."

I couldn't imagine why she needed to change clothes. She had on an emerald green velour jog suit, and I figured she was just going to change to another color. I looked down at my own clothes. Jeans and a sweater and sneakers. Good enough. Portland wasn't the kind of city where you needed to dress up to shop. I walked to the kitchen where Lily was kneading dough for bread.

"Lily, I'm taking Mom shopping and to lunch. We should be back before dinner."

"All right," Lily said. "I'm making a meat loaf, potatoes, and a salad to go with this bread. And you know you're welcome to join us."

"Thanks. I think I will." I might as well, since Scott had cancelled our dinner date in order to see Irene. That still annoyed me, but I pushed it out of my mind, determined to have fun with my mother.

"I need to stop by the processor's and pick up some contact sheets and transparencies first," I said as we got into the Escape.

"Oh, good. I can see some of your photography," Mom said.

"You want to see my work?"

"Of course, I do. You were always a talented photographer. I remember all the photos you sent me of Sheridan. They were beautiful, and you really captured her personality in them."

I'd never known she thought I was talented. I didn't know if she'd never mentioned it, or if I'd simply assumed she didn't think I was talented. But it made me feel good to hear her say it. When I got the contact sheets and transparencies, we sat in the truck for half an hour while

Mom looked at all the pictures. She complimented each of them and pointed out her favorites. I felt like a kindergartner who was proud of her finger painting.

After Mom had made a fuss over my photography, we headed to the Hawthorne District. She wanted to pick up some more yarn from the Stitch Witch. After that, we wandered around the streets, popping into whatever little shops caught our eye. Mom decided she wanted to try sushi, so we stopped at a small Asian restaurant for lunch. I ordered a combination plate with chow mein and broccoli beef and received enough food for four people.

"So this is sushi." Mom sniffed at the little rounds on her plate. She picked one up and took a bite, then made a face. She chewed a couple of times, then swallowed.

"You don't have to eat it if you don't like it," I said.

"I know. But I want to try it." She picked up another round and took another bite. Her expression was about the same, but she chewed and swallowed, then picked up her teacup. It was obvious she didn't care for the sushi, and I wondered how much she was going to force herself to eat. She picked up a third little round, held it for a moment, then shook her head and put it back on her plate.

"I can't eat another bite of this stuff. It's horrible."

"You can share mine. I have plenty." I signaled the waiter and requested another plate. "I'm not surprised you didn't like it. You hardly ever eat fish."

"I know, but the older I get, the more I like to try

different stuff. Silly, probably."

"No, it's not silly," I said. "I think it's important to do different things. It keeps you young."

We talked over the rest of our lunch, then went out to see more shops. The Baghdad Theater was showing one of her favorite movies, so we bought tickets and went inside. The Baghdad plays movies that have been out for a while. They also serve pizza and beer and the seats have tables between the rows.

"I'll have a beer," Mom said when we got to the concession stand. Her eyes twinkled when she looked at me. "Like you said, trying different things keeps you young."

"In that case, I'll have a beer, too." We laughed like girlfriends, and it felt really good. Kind of like we were when I was a teenager.

The theater was mostly empty, and we whispered to each other about the movie while we drank our beer. After the movie, we stopped in a few more shops, then drove back to Bobbi Jo's. It was one of the most pleasant times I'd had with my mother in years.

"I had a really good time today, Mom. We should do this more often."

"I'm all for that," she agreed. "You know, Skye, I've always thought our relationship changed somehow when you grew up."

"I know. I've thought that, too."

"I think it was probably my fault."

"No, Mom, it wasn't your fault."

"When you became an adult, I just didn't know how to deal with it. I guess I wanted to keep you my little girl forever."

"Oh, I understand. I'm going through some of that with Sheridan right now."

"Well, don't do it. Let her grow up, because she's going to grow up anyway. You'll enjoy having her as a friend." She patted my hand. "Trust me on that."

Lily was finishing up dinner when we arrived, and Bobbi Jo was fussing around the living room. She rearranged a few flowers in a vase, fluffed up a cushion on the sofa, and ran a finger across a book, then looked at it to check for dust.

Mom leaned over to me and whispered, "She's nesting. A sure sign she'll have the baby soon."

"Did you have fun?" Bobbi Jo asked.

Mom launched into a recital of everything we'd done that day. She seemed really happy, and it made me happy. Somehow we'd turned a corner in our relationship, and it felt good. Lily called us to dinner, and we all sat down and enjoyed her delicious food, chattering away about everything and nothing. It was one of those wonderful evenings where nothing special really happened, but just being with the people you loved made it special.

Unfortunately, I needed to go over the contact sheets and transparencies, and mark the ones I thought Connie should look at.

CHAPTER SIXTEEN

I laid the envelope of contact sheets on my light table, set my bag on the floor, and headed for the kitchen. What I really wanted was a glass of wine, but I had work to do so I started a pot of coffee and rummaged in the fridge for a snack. Then I realized I was still full from dinner. Wanting a snack was just emotional eating. Not that there's anything wrong with that.

My cell phone rang, and I pulled it out. Bobbi Jo. She'd been in an extremely good mood when I left her place. She hadn't shown any signs of being in labor. I needed to get this work done. Besides, if she was in labor, she'd text me the two-two-two-nine emergency code. I dropped the phone into my pocket and went to my light board.

I pulled the contact sheets and transparencies out of the envelope and went back to the kitchen to pour myself a cup of coffee. I laid the contact sheets out, telling myself that after I chose some shots for Connie to look at, I could console myself with a glass of wine and some mindless television. Then I remembered the grip-and-grin shots I'd taken of Scott and Irene. Scott had mentioned that the chief needed the shots tomorrow.

I was still a bit annoyed with Scott, so I wasn't really looking forward to looking at the shots. Still, it was a job. And there was the possibility of also selling the shot to some of the local newspapers. I spread the contact sheets out and sorted through them until I found the one of Scott and Irene, then I picked up my loupe and angled the lamp for the best light. A lot of commercial photographers had started using electronic contact sheets, but I still preferred seeing the actual black-and-white photos first, then I would review them on the computer. I routinely requested sheets with sixteen shots per page. They were a little more expensive, but I thought it was well worth the price for the quality. Most of the shots on the sheet were totally unusable, which was normal. I placed the loupe over each shot, then circled with an orange grease pencil the ones I thought might be suitable for the chief's news-letter and for selling to the local newspapers.

I had a shot of Scott alone before Irene had crawled all over him. It was a good shot, but I knew what the paper would probably want would be the standard grip-and-grin shot of Scott and Irene. I plowed through the contact sheets until I came to those shots. Some were blurry; some cut off part of Scott or part of Irene.

I finally had five I thought were usable. I scribbled the numbers on a sticky note and opened my laptop. After I hooked my camera to the laptop with the USB connector, I drank the rest of the coffee while the laptop booted up and brought up the photo program. I punched in the photo numbers I wanted to view and waited for them to appear. The first one was a little too blurry, so I pressed the *delete* key. The next one was good. Scott held the frame in his left hand and his right reached out for Irene's hand. But it wasn't a true grip-and-grin because their hands were barely touching. I scrolled to the next shot. That was it. Everything was in focus. Scott was smiling, and it looked almost genuine. Irene didn't have anything in her teeth, no unfortunate rolls of fat were apparent. Well, you can't have everything. Their hands were firmly clasped, hers almost engulfing his, and Scott didn't have dainty hands.

Wait a minute.

I enlarged the photograph and looked at it closely. How could I have not seen that before? Irene's hand was at least as big as Scott's. That explained everything.

Scott had been telling me Irene couldn't be the killer because a man had strangled Frank. But they'd only assumed it was a man because of the size of the hands. Irene's hands were easily large enough. How had Scott not noticed that?

Of course he hadn't noticed. He was too busy notic-
ing her heaving bosom and her long legs. I could hardly
wait to tell him how wrong he was about her. Not that I
was going to forgive him. Well, not right away. I punched
the speed dial number on my cell phone and listened to
his phone ring. I almost giggled with the anticipation of
explaining exactly how wrong he was about Irene.

The phone rang and rang, then I got his voice mail.
I wasn't about to deny myself the pleasure of at least hearing his voice when I told him. It was a few minutes after
nine. They had to be finished with dinner and Scott was
probably at home watching some kind of sports. Refusing to answer my call because of our last conversation.

That pissed me off. Now even a phone call wasn't
enough. I wanted to see his face when I told him how
wrong he was. I grabbed my bag and keys and headed
for the door. Wait. I needed my proof. I went back and
picked up my laptop. Probably I could just take the camera and USB cord, but I wasn't sure his computer had
an image program. It might have nothing but baseball
scores and pictures of big blond women with huge hands.
Murdering hands.

I lugged the laptop down to the garage and drove to
Scott's apartment building. I pressed the buzzer for his
apartment and waited. Nothing. I pressed again. Still
nothing. It really pissed me off that he was avoiding me
because of an argument. What did this foretell for our

relationship? Nothing good. I mean, communication is the cornerstone of a good relationship. If he was going to sulk every time I disagreed with him—well, I didn't really want to think about that. I pulled the key to his apartment building out and pushed it into the lock.

Pressing him right now might mean the end of our relationship, but if it did, then we didn't have a future anyway. I wanted a man who would talk to me. A man who would listen to me. I slipped the key into my pocket, took the elevator up to his floor, and marched to his door before I had time to reconsider rash actions.

He didn't answer my knock. Maybe he was sleeping. Snoozing in front of the television because the ball game was boring. I pressed my ear to the door, but I didn't hear any television-like sounds.

I heard voices.

Specifically, I heard Scott's voice and a woman's voice. I pressed my ear closer but only succeeded in blocking all the sounds. Who was he with? More importantly, why did he have a woman in his apartment? Oh, my God. He was with Irene. I shook my head. He'd never shown any interest in Irene, so maybe he was with some other woman. Somehow, that seemed even worse. Anger and hurt waged a short war until I decided I had a right to know. Scott wanted a committed relationship, and as far as I was concerned that didn't include having another woman in his apartment while he refused to answer my phone calls.

I pulled out my key chain and fumbled for the key to his apartment. Then I hesitated. Did I really want to know what was going on in there? Well, yes, but did I want to actually see it?

I swallowed hard, pushed the key into the lock, and turned the knob. Scott was pacing back and forth in front of his coffee table. I didn't see a woman anywhere. Maybe I'd just heard the television. Wrong. The television wasn't on.

"Hey," I said from the doorway.

"Skye. What are you doing here?" Scott's eyes jerked to the bathroom door, then back to my face.

"I found something I wanted to show you."

"Can it wait?"

"Why? Are you busy?" I pulled my laptop from my bag and set it on the coffee table.

"Actually, I am. Let's get together later, okay?"

"This will only take a minute. Unless there's some reason you don't want me here right now." I tried not to smirk when I delivered my clever challenge. I opened the laptop and pulled up the photos I wanted to show him. Anger flooded through me. He had a woman in his apartment. In the bathroom, from the way he'd looked at the door. Or maybe in the bedroom.

"You told me Irene couldn't be the murderer because the bruises had been caused by a hand too large for a woman, right? Well, look at this." I angled the laptop so he could see the screen.

"Skye, I really don't have time—" Scott stopped and looked at the screen closer. "What am I looking at?"

"That's a blowup of you and Irene shaking hands when I took the grip-and-grin shot at Steinhart's." I pointed to the hands. "See. Her hand is as big as yours. And Arnie said he thought she was having an affair with Frank. Even if they weren't, she's the mayor and Frank was on the city council. So, it stands to reason she might have had a motive to kill him. It could have been the affair, or some kind of political . . . something." I was at a loss for words, but I thought Scott would get my message.

He waved his hands, then put a finger to his lips and pointed to the bathroom. But I wasn't about to be shushed. His girlfriend could just stay in the bathroom until I was finished.

"Well, you have to admit that your theory is wrong. Evidently some women have hands big enough to leave those bruises."

"It's not my fault my hands are large. I'm big-boned."

I turned toward the voice I recognized as Irene's. Her weirdly large hands held a pistol.

"Irene." Scott put his hands up in front of him. Like that was going to stop Irene or a bullet. "Put the gun away."

"Oh, I don't think so." Irene shot me a glance, then looked back at Scott. "I heard what she was saying."

"She didn't mean anything by it, Irene. There's no need to get upset."

"I'm not upset, Scott. I'm disappointed." She waved the gun toward the sofa. "Why don't you two have a seat while I decide how I'm going to do this?"

Do this? That didn't sound good. It sounded final.

"Irene, don't jump to conclusions. There's no proof you killed Frank. You aren't even a suspect."

"Really, Scott, do you think I'm stupid? You're just saying that to get me to hand over my gun. That isn't going to happen. You know I killed Frank. You were just looking for proof, and now you have it." Tears filled her eyes. "I didn't want to kill him. God knows, I tried everything else first. He promised to back me for the state senate, but after I slept with him, he changed his mind. He owed me."

Scott and I hadn't sat on the sofa as she'd directed and that was making me nervous. Not that sitting on the sofa was going to make the situation any better. But I was hoping Scott has some really good idea about getting the gun away from her. I slid a glance at him. He didn't look like he had any great ideas.

My pocket vibrated and chirped.

I jumped and shoved my hand in my pants to pull out my cell phone. Scott jerked and turned toward me.

Irene gasped and waved the gun around.

"Turn it off!" she yelled.

"I have to take it."

Irene shook her head.

"It's my friend. She's pregnant, and she's probably calling to tell me she's in labor." The phone stopped chirping. Damn.

"She hung up," Irene said. "I guess it wasn't an emergency after all." Irene laughed a little, and it sounded weird. And evil.

Then my phone chirped and vibrated again. I looked at it and saw the special text message.

"It's her again. She said she'd text me this message when she went into labor. See." I held the phone up so she could see the text message. "It's two-two-two-nine. For *baby*."

Irene leaned closer to see the message.

"If I don't call her back, she'll know something's wrong." Actually, Bobbi Jo would probably just be pissed off and a little too busy with her own situation to wonder if something was wrong. But I was hoping that Irene would believe me.

She looked uncertain. "No. Even if she thinks something's wrong, she won't know what. Or where."

"Of course she will. Bobbi Jo and Lily are my best friends. I tell them everything. They know I'm at Scott's and they know why." I didn't know how good a liar I was, but Irene seemed to be considering my story. The text message disappeared and the phone chirped and vibrated again. "She's calling back."

"Okay. Answer it, but be brief. Tell her . . . I don't know. Tell her whatever you have to."

I nodded and fumbled the phone open.

"Skye! I'm having the baby! Now!"

"Calm down, Bobbi Jo. Mom's there with you, right? And Lily?"

"Yes, but they aren't you. I need you to be here. And you promised me."

"You're on your way to the hospital?"

"Well, where the hell do you think I'm going, Skye? We're in the car and Lily's driving like an eighty-year-old woman on the way to church. Faster, Lily!"

I heard my mother's muffled voice trying to calm Bobbi Jo.

"Bobbi Jo, how far apart are the contractions?"

"Less than two minutes."

"Bobbi Jo, you should already be at the hospital. Why didn't you leave when they were five minutes apart?"

Irene waved the gun around again. "Scott, you'd better tell her to get off the phone."

"Why? So you can kill us? Really, Irene, are you willing to kill two more people? Do you think you'll get away with it? You know how cops are. When one of us is murdered, the others stop at nothing to find the killer. You'll get the death penalty."

Irene's eyebrows drew into a frown, her mouth widened into a grimace, and tears pooled in her eyes.

"If you turn yourself in now, you'll probably get off light. I'm sure a good lawyer could make a case for self-defense," Scott said.

Irene looked skeptical but hopeful.

"Or maybe temporary insanity," he added

Why is it that men never know when to shut up?

"I'm *not* crazy. Is that what you think, Scott? That I'm a lunatic?"

I felt like I had when Sheridan had thrown a temper tantrum at the age of five over what to wear to a birthday party. I'd spent two hours trying to placate her. I'd tried to cajole her into wearing the party dress instead of just the bouffant petticoat and ruffled panties. I'd bribed her with cookies and ice cream. I'd promised her a doll that she'd been asking for. Finally, I'd had enough. I picked her up and deposited her in her bedroom, closed the door, and turned the television up loud enough to drown out her screams. I was at the same point now. I'd had enough. My best friend was in labor and expected me to be there for the birth of her child.

I'd promised her I would be there. Besides that, Sheridan expected me to live long enough to become a burden to her, and my mother expected me to live long enough to put her in a nursing home. I was not going to let this overblown, imbecilic woman dictate whether I would live to fulfill those expectations. I'd had enough.

"Irene!" I used my best mom voice. The one that had usually stopped Sheridan in her tracks.

Irene whirled toward me, her grip on the gun loosened by the surprise reflected on her tear-streaked face. I snatched the gun from her hand and pointed to the sofa.

"Sit!"

Irene stumbled to the sofa and sank down, then started to get up.

"Stay!" I commanded.

She sat down again and buried her face in her hands, sobbing like a two-year-old.

"Scott, I have to go. Bobbi Jo's about to have the baby. Here." I thrust the gun in his hand and ran out of the apartment. He'd have to deal with Irene by himself. I was fairly certain he could handle her now that he had the gun.

Bobbi Jo was sitting up in bed glaring at Lily when I got to the hospital.

"Oh, Skye, I'm so glad you're here." Bobbi Jo held her arms out for a hug, and I enveloped her in my arms. She rested her head on my shoulder for a moment, then began screaming. I thought she was going to choke the breath out of me before the contraction stopped.

"What took you so long?" Lily asked. "I called

Sheridan when you didn't answer your cell phone, but she didn't know where you were."

"It's a long story," I said. Lily didn't ask any more because her attention was drawn back to Bobbi Jo who was grinding her teeth and grimacing.

"If you'd just do the breathing, you'd feel better, Bobbi Jo," Lily said.

"I'm doing just fine," Bobbi Jo growled. "And I don't need any of your drugs."

I shot Lily a questioning glance. Lily shrugged.

"Bobbi Jo," I said in as gentle a tone as I could manage. "I thought you'd decided to have an epidural."

Bobbi Jo waved a perfectly manicured hand. "I had, but that was before I realized that I'm having a baby. A *baby*. I can't put drugs in a baby. What kind of mother would I be to do that? And now, this one"—she waved at Lily—"wants me to get a shot or something."

"She's been completely out of control," Lily said. "The doctor said she's only three centimeters dilated, and she's having ninety-second contractions every thirty seconds. I thought maybe she should take a little something to calm . . . let her relax a bit. At this rate she's going to wear herself out before the delivery."

Bobbi Jo screamed again. A long, piercing wail that made me worry about her. I could understand why Lily had suggested some pain relief that would allow Bobbi Jo to rest for a bit. Lily could probably use the rest, too.

"I don't know how much more of this she can take," Lily said. "She was two centimeters dilated when we got here and that was a couple of hours ago. If she's only going to dilate one centimeter every two hours, this could take a long time."

I didn't think the doctors would let her continue the way she was for very long. At least I hoped they wouldn't. Lily seemed to read my thoughts.

"The doctor suggested they might have to do a caesarian section, but she refused," Lily said.

I realized I hadn't seen my mother since I'd arrived and glanced around the room. She sat in a rocking chair in the corner knitting a pile of blue and green yarn into a blanket. "The doctors are letting her try for a couple more hours. They have a monitor on the baby and it's fine."

"Oh, honey, it's going to be all right." I placed my hand over the one Bobbi Jo had clenched on the bed railing. She screamed some more, then the contraction ended and she gasped for breath.

"I'm not taking drugs, and I'm not having this baby in an operating room. It's *my* baby and I'll have it my way."

"Of course you will." I smoothed damp, unruly curls off her forehead. I knew the doctors would decide when and if they really needed to do a caesarian section, and they wouldn't give Bobbi Jo much of a choice about it. In the meantime, she might as well believe she was in charge.

"I gotta push," Bobbi Jo announced. She crunched

forward and put her hands under her knees, pulling them up.

"No!" Lily yelled. "You can't push until the baby has dropped into position and you're fully dilated."

"Bet me!" Bobbi Jo's face contorted and turned bright red.

"I suppose she's through transition now," Mom said, setting her knitting aside. "Lily, ring for the nurse."

Bobbi Jo took a deep breath and grunted as she pushed. I remembered the urgency of that feeling when I delivered Sheridan. And I knew there was no way to stop Bobbi Jo. Where was the damn nurse? Bobbi Jo stopped pushing and collapsed back against the pillows just as the nurse strolled in.

"I'm having the baby," Bobbi Jo told the nurse.

The woman in faded green scrubs smiled indulgently and shook her head. "Not yet, dear. I just checked you half an hour ago and you were only three centimeters dilated and we really don't want to push too early, now do we? Maybe she should consider a little something to help with that."

"No drugs!" Bobbi Jo shook her head. "I'm having the baby. Right now."

"Let me check you again." The nurse moved to the foot of the bed. She propped Bobbi Jo's feet in the stirrups, dropped the end portion of the bed, and lifted the sheet to Bobbi Jo's knees. She snapped on a surgical glove and her hands moved beneath the sheet. Her mouth dropped open and her eyes widened.

"Oh, my God. You're having the baby. The head is right there. I'll get the doctor." She turned and ran from the room. "Don't push," she instructed as the door closed behind her.

"I gotta push," Bobbi Jo said and sucked in a lungful of air.

Mom stood and walked over to look beneath the sheets wadded around Bobbi Jo's knees. "Somebody better get ready to catch that baby. The head's almost out. Lots of curly dark hair, too."

I looked at Lily, fully expecting her to take charge until the doctor arrived, which surely should be within seconds. Bobbi Jo collapsed back against the bed again. Her face was dotted with tiny blood blisters from pushing so hard.

Lily rolled her eyes and moved toward the foot of the bed.

"No!" Bobbi Jo screamed. "I want Skye." She gave me a pleading look and took another deep breath. Lily put her hands on my shoulders and pushed me to the end of the bed.

"I'll see what's holding up the doctor." Lily strode from the room without a backward glance.

I looked down to see the baby's head had fully emerged. Dear God. One more push and the baby would be out. I didn't want to deliver the baby. I only wanted to be there to comfort Bobbi Jo.

"I gotta push again," Bobbi Jo said.

I looked at Mom, who had returned to the chair and taken up her knitting again. She looked up at me and smiled. "You can do it, Skye. You can do anything. Go ahead and catch the baby."

Bobbi Jo grunted and the baby slipped into my hands. All I could think was that I wasn't sterile. Wasn't I supposed to be sterile? I should have had gloves and a gown. I should have had a doctor!

The baby squalled and I leaned forward, clutching it to my chest. The warmth and dampness of the baby seeped through my blouse, the tiny cry reverberating through my chest. It was the most beautiful sound in the world. The nurse rushed in, followed by the doctor.

"Looks like I'm a little late," the doctor said. She held her hands out for the baby. "May I?"

"Oh, please." I placed the baby in her hands and stepped up to the head of the bed. Bobbi Jo grasped my hand.

"It's a little boy, Bobbi Jo," the doctor said.

"Oh, I bet Edward is so happy right now," Bobbi Jo said.

The doctor placed the infant on Bobbi Jo's deflated stomach and clipped the umbilical cord. "He looks strong and healthy. We're going to clean him up and check him out, then we'll bring him right over." She handed the baby to the nurse, who turned and placed him on a table she'd wheeled over. Bobbi Jo struggled to sit up so she could keep her eyes on the baby.

"It's only going to take a minute for them to do all the tests." I pushed her against the pillows. Bobbi Jo laid back but kept her eyes on the back of the nurse who hovered over the baby. The doctor pushed a stool over and caught the afterbirth in a steel basin, then handed it to a nurse and examined Bobbi Jo. That activity helped distract Bobbi Jo until the nurse brought the baby to her.

"The nurse said it was okay to come in." Chase stood in the doorway looking uncertain.

"Oh, Chase. Come on in. How did you know I was having the baby?"

"I was going to your house and saw you three leave in a big hurry. I had a hunch it was the baby. I've been down in the waiting room, but the nurse said I could come in if it was okay with you."

"Come look at him," Bobbi Jo said. Chase walked over to the bed, and Bobbi Jo pulled the blanket back from little Edward's face.

"Wow. Look at what you did," Chase said.

"I know." Bobbi Jo grinned. "Isn't it something?"

"You need to nurse him now," Lily said. Bobbi Jo fumbled around trying to hold the baby in one arm and pull her gown down with the other hand.

"Should I leave?" Chase asked.

"No. Here, hold the baby for a minute."

Chase took the baby from her, cuddling him to his chest and looking at him in awe. Bobbi Jo got her breast exposed and held her arms out for the baby. It looked like the most natural thing for her and Chase to be sharing the moment.

"Not too long," Mom advised. "You'll end up with sore nipples."

Lily nodded her agreement. "I made that mistake with Bo. Took forever for them to heal. Five minutes on each breast, maximum." Mom and Lily watched from the foot of the bed while she nursed little Edward. Chase maintained his vigil at Bobbi Jo's side. The nurses cleaned up the room and were removing all the equipment when Scott poked his head in the door.

"You up to visitors yet?" he asked.

Bobbi Jo nodded and waved him in with her free hand. Scott came over to wrap an arm around my shoulders and drop a kiss on my forehead.

"You want to see him?" Bobbi Jo asked.

Scott looked a little panicked. "You're busy. I'll take a closer look later."

I had to smother a laugh at his reluctance to view Bobbi Jo's bare breast.

"He's done for a while," Bobbi Jo said tucking her breast back into the bra and pulling her gown over it. "He's so beautiful. I think he looks just like Edward."

Scott and I walked to the edge of the bed and

admired the baby. Of course he didn't look anything like Bobbi Jo's late husband. He looked like any other newborn. A little red and slightly puckered with a cone-shaped head covered in dark hair.

"He's really something," Scott agreed.

Mom and Lily resumed their hovering and clucking over Bobbi Jo, pushing Scott and me away from the bed. Chase looked like he was rooted in place, and I didn't think they'd have an easy time of making him move. Scott looked like he was ready to leave, so I guided him toward the door.

"That is an incredibly ugly baby," Scott said when we closed the door behind us.

"Scott! All babies look like that when they're born."

"If you say so."

"Skye!"

I turned to see Connie walking down the hallway toward us, a tall, handsome, dark-skinned man behind her. They both wore brightly colored, tropical print shirts with jeans. He looked vaguely familiar, but I couldn't think why.

"I heard Bobbi Jo had her baby," Connie said. She gave me a hug, then turned to hug Scott.

"How did you hear?" I asked.

"I called your house and Sheridan told me." Connie turned and wrapped her arm around the man's. "This is

Tyreese Halloran. My husband."

He held a hand out and I took it.

"Everyone calls me Ty. I'm happy to meet you."

"Ty, this is Skye Donovan, my good friend and a great photographer, and this is Scott Madison, Skye's boyfriend."

Ty and Scott shook hands. I kept staring at Ty wondering why he looked so familiar, then it hit me. I'd seen him numerous times on the news. Ty Halloran was a multimillionaire—possibly a billionaire—businessman. He owned about a thousand hotels along with a couple of casinos.

"Do you think Bobbi Jo would mind if we go in to see the baby?"

"She'd love it," I said. I watched Connie and her incredibly rich husband walk down the hall. And all that time I'd thought she was marrying some Rastafarian beach bum she'd be supporting the rest of her life. A slightly hysterical giggle escaped me.

"You look exhausted," Scott said.

"I am. It's been a long day with a lot of emotional ups and downs. I take it Irene is in jail?"

"Oh, yeah. Arnie showed up almost immediately. When I left he was blubbering like a baby about losing Irene."

"I'm just glad it's over."

"You were pretty awesome taking that gun from Irene."

That was supposed to sound like a compliment, I'm sure, but Scott was frowning. I laughed a little hysterically.

"I'd almost forgotten that. Bobbi Jo needed me and I started thinking about how much Sheridan still needs me and even my mother." I shook my head. "Hearing that Bobbi Jo was really, finally in labor put me over the edge. I wasn't about to let Irene kill me when so many people are depending on me."

"I need you, too." Scott leaned down and placed a soft kiss on my lips.

"You do?" I kissed him back with a little tongue. "But we still need to talk about our relationship."

"No, we don't."

"Scott, we have to talk. I know you want to move in together and consider marriage, but I don't know that I'm ready for it, and it's not fair of me to ask you to wait until I am."

"I'll wait," Scott said.

"You'll wait?"

"Until you're ready. However long it takes."

I just stared at him, my heart swelling with happiness.

"You're worth waiting for."

That was exactly what I wanted to hear. He pulled me close and nibbled my neck.

"But you have *got* to stay out of my investigations."

twitter

Sign up now at www.twitter.com/MedallionPress
to stay on top of all the happenings in and
around Medallion Press.

For more information
about other great titles from
Medallion Press, visit

medallionpress.com